GW01229498

On Anvil

by

Jim Herity

To Geoff - all the best & Merry Christmas

[signature]

West Cornwall Publishing Company

West Cornwall Publishing Company, N.A.

340 River Road

West Cornwall, CT 06796

This book is a work of fiction. Names, characters, places, and incidents are products of the author's imagination and are used fictitiously. Any resemblance to actual events, locales, or persons living or dead, is most likely coincidental.

Copyright © 2013 Jim Herity

Cover Photos Copyright © 2013 Jim Herity

All rights reserved, including the right of reproduction in whole or in part, in any form.

Manufactured and printed in the United States of America by Sheridan Books, Inc.
Shipped to our readers by the United States Postal Service

ISBN: 978-0-9884503-1-8

On Anvil

an-vil (an'vil). noun.
   1. a heavy steel or iron block with a flat top, upon which metal can be hammered or shaped
   2. anything upon which blows are repeatedly struck
     [ME *anvelt, anfelt* <OHG *anafalz*] pertaining to an article or material formed under great pressure

On Anvil

–New Mexico–

✧

Cal stands beneath a strobing florescent bulb in a coffee shop, six back in the line of customers at the counter, a vague parade of morning ghosts one day deeper in the valley of habit, hoping for coffee's sweet deliverance from the blur.

The man behind the counter has the look of someone who tried smiling years ago. "What'll it be now?" he says, and his words fall into the canyon of time carved there. His countenance the stamp of a question mark, but his eyes could not have said less.

Cal steps into the vacancies, stands as blank at the counter.

"What'll it be now?" the man says.

Cal orders a coffee, black, searches his pockets for the feel of a dollar.

One day again, like the last or the next. The minute hand on the clock notches forward, the hum of engines outside like hearts burning things deep-hidden inside, wheels within wheels turned by the magic of belief, dust rising in pools at the bite of souls crossing the dirt-dry earth, coffee served up hot in a cup and all of it to go.

That alone is fuel and direction enough.

All of it, to go.

✧

Departure.

1.

Cal drove up the interstate ramp heading south, matched his speed with the flush of morning traffic. He saw the night mists hanging low over Santa Fe light up red with the first angle of sun, watched the town shrink behind him in the rear-view mirror.

Morning radio voices choked with speed-talk, chopping out machine-gun babble in locked step with the buzz of the highway, the click of miles. Reports of urgency mattering somewhere, to someone. The silence of seconds ticking past like the highway markers at seventy, each one separate, together a blur. Cal spun the dial in search of a single lonely tune to wrap his head in. There were none he could find.

The race of chemicals through the caverns of mute memory, the lone stark images jumping bolt upright and insistent like a sudden freeze in the machinery of his mind. An image of Gayle trying to talk around the toothbrush in her mouth, her hair wrapped up wet in a towel turban, her jeans half-on, beads of water sparkling the sunlight from the window across her neck and back.

The wandering tag of phone calls, her voice on the other end like velvet, or sugar, and the words "Hi, it's me."

Me. The abbreviation for an entire world. Who can ever call themselves that, save the one closest to heart?

A snapshot of Gayle caught in mid-smile, like the birth of a thought. Her long dancer's legs and the strength she held there, her poise and fragility bound together in a tenuous balance.

Her scatter of paints and brushes, her canvases stacked in disorder against any wall that would hold them. Her poems and favorite sayings, all penned like magical incantations in her flowing hand and crowded by mythic creatures she'd sketch to the borders of each page like curious onlookers trapped by the spell of her words.

Her tabletop collections of artifacts, of the stones and bones and endless things of nature, wrested from the "there" of the day to the "here" of home.

"To connect the dots," she said. "To rope in the wildness and hold it all tamed, in small measure, like a captured prize. Like an altar to the Deity of Adventure." Her arms spread wide.

A Zuni basket woven by ancient hands, bought at a reservation roadside stand and filled to the brim with the gathered essence of two scorched days and a frozen night camped out in the Painted Desert: stones tumbled and worn smooth from long ago, or knife-like and jagged as lightning, branches of skeletal cactus twisted like the arms of a frantic dancer escaping the heat, mineral rocks flashing with opalescent windows, the wire-thin bones of a humming bird she'd found laid out perfectly in the sand, "Like a tiny soul's calling card, left behind," she had said. "*I was here.*"

All of it like an open phone line back to Creation. "Back to the original state of things," is how she put it.

Her *borrow* from the bank of nature.

"Doesn't the word borrow imply some kind of payback, or interest?" Cal asked. He stood in the middle of her living room, crowded by a healthy sampling of nearly the entire planet. "Because somehow I can't see you returning all this stuff."

"Oh, there's lots of interest," Gayle nodded, pure enthusiasm. "And as for payback . . ." she pulled her t-shirt back tight, tucked it in all around and struck an exaggerated pose, like a body builder at the edge of a stage, "I'm a part of nature too, right? So the payback's built in. Am I right?" The way she could hang that question in the air, her head cocked one way and her hips the other. "Am I . . . right?"

Cal stared out the windshield as the highway washed past. He pulled off his sunglasses, rubbed his face, tried to erase the glaze of time and no sleep from his eyes, the miles of memory from his mind.

Six weeks gone now. Or was it seven? He wasn't sure. He'd lost track.

Six weeks of hours, of minutes, the clamor of their seconds spilling over, crowding out the remnants of any coherent thought he might have had left him. An eviction of major sorts, each night a liquid darkness he waded through reluctant, each day claimed anew by some reincarnation of hope but then unclaimed by the sameness of those seconds and sunken to the chattering depths, woven to the single endless cloth of time he faced down, the world indecipherable from that view, shorn of all purpose save the reckoning of more time.

Time. Like a life sentence.

Gayle was gone.

Then she was gone again.

"All I need," he said, and the words fell flat, like he'd said them a hundred times over, or thought them so in silence. The simplicity of what was left to him.

He pulled his sunglasses up. He set his jaw rigid.

"All I need," he said again. Like an amen to some unspoken prayer. Or the answer to an extinct question.

The speed and the miles. In that part of the country, there was never enough of the one and more than could ever be swallowed of the other. Rusted wire fences holding back the empty space against itself, rags of dust-colored plastic snagged on the barbs and pocketing in the wind. Tufts of parched grass scattered like stragglers under the sun, orphans of some greater prairie long gone past. The web of wires cordoning the crystal sky, pumping power to places more important over the blue rim of distance.

At the base of the mountains to the east, hidden and then not in the pockets of morning light downcast from the peaks, an ore train as long and straight as the highway itself, matched in speed to the traffic, trailing soundlessly along like a shadow to Cal's thoughts . . . pulling up to the house that night, stumbling in through the darkness, the wall of silence rising, the tumble of questions crowding him, roaring up to cacophony, the sentinel of guilt or its mirror-image, blame, standing guard over every thought.

"All I need," he said. Like a stone would say it.

Sleep. He could barely remember the feel of it, the soft release, that silken crossing to another world, liquid and elastic of its rules, the unsunned sky of dreams, of shadow plays reconstructed from the noise of the day, unfolding across that silent stage.

The noise of the day.

That was all he had left.

Inside him turned the incessant chatter of a thousand thoughts, and the wind dragged at his face from the open window at eighty-five miles an hour. His eyes felt sunburnt. Scraps of paper danced up from the floor of the truck and were sucked outside to play behind him in the traffic.

He reached to the seat for his cigarettes, tapped one free from its pack. He saw that he held one already in his other hand, freshly lit. No memory of how it got there.

He reached over to turn the radio off, nothing but static and noise leaking out, disembodied voices crowding the airwaves, sawing at his ears. Ghosting anonymously through his brain.

The knob wouldn't turn that way. The radio was already off.

2.

Seven years ago, like a half-recalled dream, Gayle wrote on the back of their first photo together:

"Two threads to weave a cloth."

They met, they loved, they laughed. They dreamed. They had a season of good times, then another one even better.

They found a small house to rent. There were some dry-rotted planks on the deck off the back side of the kitchen, so Cal arranged a fair trade with the landlord, the first month's rent for the repairs. They sent out a raft of invitations:

"A Moving Party, with Construction."

Their friends showed up in numbers. The guys let loose with their power tools and the pop of nail-guns echoed like a backyard war while the deck grew solid again beneath a small army of work boots. Gayle and her girlfriends hovered close by like a ring of summer angels, mixing frozen Margaritas, icing beers, pushing waves of snacks and running a comparative commentary about bare-chested hunks in shorts and "How sexy are those tool belts, huh?" The garden hose fired off in grinning repartee, wet t-shirts spiked and blessed the view. Moving boxes unpacked all day long like some up-beat off-season Christmas.

The hanging things are hung, the house becomes a home.

The day cooled off as the sun lowered down and the work party's notion of work faded to play. A full round of toasts ensued, the happy wander of good wishes. In near silence they watched the last of the sun go flame-red as it burrowed into the mountains to the west and blinked out. Spontaneous applause sounded for that, then for the new deck, then for all the good folks standing upon it.

The tools and power cords were packed away, the deck swept clean. Chairs and benches and a picnic table appeared, the coals were fired up and flared hot against the cool of the desert twilight. Gayle's Oklahoma-style barbequed chicken vanished in fast waves beneath its tide of fragrant smoke. That and the drifts of party music drew the new neighbors in from blocks away, and the earlier question of whether they'd stocked too much beer had its happy answer.

Later that night after all of it, the house a scatter of empty boxes and plastic cups, paper plates everywhere, the last of the best wishes and see-you-soon's out the driveway, Cal fell asleep in Gayle's arms, exhausted on their mattress on the floor. The closest thing he'd ever felt to home.

He awoke in the thin hours just before dawn. He stood and walked through the darkened house. He stood alone in the front room, looking out the window to the street, up at the inky night sky. The thinnest slice of a crescent moon hung low in the east, above the black cutout of the mountain range. He saw clouds unrolling there in silent procession, watched them cut to ribbons on the moon's horns, shred downwind to a silvery haze that soon enough became the first glow of dawn.

He made his way back down the hall, stood at the bedroom door in the quiet, wishing for time itself to halt in its tracks.

Gayle lay asleep beneath the open window, the curtains above her lifting and sighing in the breeze. She lay so still, so silent in that half-light, like an angel fallen to earth and draped, outlined and translucent beneath the sheets.

3.

His speed eighty-five miles an hour now, four hours south of Santa Fe, his hands wrapped knuckle-white to the steering wheel. The replay of that life thinning away, the roadway flooding back into view before him, his planned exit rolling past like a mirage in the desert heat, off into the rear view mirror.

"Dammit."

He punched the pedal to the floor.

Another twenty miles at one hundred, exactly the length of a cigarette, the next exit showed. He flicked the spent butt out the window, pulled off the exit ramp, turned a wide left onto the state road, rolled up onto the shoulder. Braked hard into the gravel.

He stared straight ahead, his truck idling, the road dust circled up and drifted away. He dropped his hands from the wheel, flexed his fingers open and closed. He reached for the key and shut the engine off.

He watched his hands shaking in his lap. For weeks now, beyond any control he could manage, they shook like that, like tremors at a fault line. He pulled his sunglasses off.

Silence again, pressing in like a fat tide. His vision blurred. He shut his eyes, like extinguishing two hot coals. Fatigue like a lead blanket draped his limbs, his brain an urban blackout viewed from a great distance, a few nerve cells left firing raw on the fringes in scattered rebellion. He opened his eyes again to a day already extinct and endless.

Steering wheel . . . dashboard . . . gauges . . . all lying before him without weight or importance, neutral elements of vision vying for attention by their shape or color alone. Round. Or red. Or numbers. Red numbers, curling up like dogs into their rote shapes. A six. A two. An eight.

He felt himself being dragged backwards against the grain of something much larger, something so great as to be invisible, lying face downward to an ocean of sand flowing around him, past him, over him. Cal, one of the infinity of sand grains, as shadowless under the sun.

He stared ahead though the windshield. Nothing out there moved, the terrain completely ownerless, every detail of it welded hard into place, anchored motionless into the mix. Still there . . . still there . . . still there, as if by some mordant decree. An abortive creation frozen at birth. A world beyond sense, endlessly recited.

This was nowhere. Nowhere with a capital 'N.' A nowhere completely at home with itself and lacking for nothing. He sat square in the middle of it now, its latest acquisition.

To his left the highway stretched out flat and black to the ground like a shadow cast from somewhere else. Cars shot past like angry thoughts aimed at one horizon by the other.

He looked into the rear-view mirror. A buffalo shimmered in the heat currents two hundred yards behind him, a cartoon buffalo standing up on its hind legs, waving an arm.

The billboard clipped an insistent hold from the vacant sky. A small building like a concrete shoebox sat on the ground beside it. Blue-gray smoke slanted up from the rear of the building towards the sun. A chef's hat flopped down between the buffalo's horns, a red apron covered its massive gut. Across the apron in tall letters it read, "Bill's Wild Buffalo Burgers." The buffalo held up a dinner plate piled high with French fries and a huge hamburger roll off to one side. Poking its head out from one end of the roll and its feet out from the other was a smaller buffalo lying on its back, lathered over with ketchup and smiling away like a born-again, with a pickle in its hand.

Cal shut his eyes to it. He listened in that closer dark to the punctured rush of cars passing on the highway, heard them as waves breaking against a crumbling shore, each wave sliding over the next and draining away . . . rising up again . . . draining away. His breathing had stopped.

He opened his eyes from that.

He saw the shapes and numbers lying before him, the sun directly above and hot through the windshield. He reached for the ignition and gave the key a half-twist, the lights and gauges jumped back to life. He stared at the clock. Watched its red digital numbers morphing one to the next, one to the next. Each minute that passed, a measure less of something left in the world.

He looked again to the rear-view mirror. A State Trooper's car was idling behind him, the road dust circling away.

"Damn."

He had no driver's license on him, no ID at all. Proofless of who he was in a world that demanded proof.

He watched the trooper stand from the squad car. He reached back inside the car, placed his hat on his head. He closed the door. He checked his hat in the window's reflection and adjusted his belt. He walked toward Cal's truck.

Cal opened the door and stepped to the ground.

The trooper froze in his tracks.

"You're supposed to remain inside the vehicle." He stood right and rigid. He readjusted the lay of his belt.

Cal watched him in silence and blinked in the hard noon light. He glanced past him to the buffalo billboard waving in the distance, then further off to the empty miles beyond that. Nowhere had just vanished.

"Well," he said. "I thought you were just being neighborly, is all. Alright then . . ." He edged himself back toward the door. "You want me to get back inside the truck?" He pointed to the open door.

The trooper looked around in a slow half-circle. He took a few steps forward. He nodded toward Cal's pickup. "Trouble with your truck?"

Cal looked over at his truck, gave a half-shrug. "Not yet."

The trooper nodded. He looked around again. "Lost your way?"

Cal thought about that. "One exit too far, is all." He nodded toward the highway. "Taking a break here. From the highway." He raised his hand. "Having a smoke." His hand was empty of any cigarette. It shook noticeably.

The trooper glanced toward the highway.

"Where you traveling from?"

"Santa Fe."

The trooper nodded. "Early start, huh?"

Cal nodded back. "Early enough." He looked off in no direction in particular. Time like a thick glue, hardening. "Pretty damned flat out here," he said. "The land, that is."

The trooper took a few steps forward, looked into the bed of Cal's truck. He looked back at Cal. He nodded. "We got us plenty of flat out here, if we got anything. What's inside the tarp there?"

Cal looked at the bundled tarp lying in the bed of his truck. He shrugged. "Nothing much."

The trooper gave him a close look.

"A backpack," Cal said. "Some camping gear, is all."

That drew another long look from the trooper. "Why'd you say nothing then?"

Cal thought more about it. "It'd be nothing to most people."

The trooper took a closer look at the tarp, another look at Cal. "I'm not most people. Can I see?"

Cal nodded back. "Sure."

They both stood a minute in the heat, not moving, one staring at the other.

Cal stepped onto the rear tire, reached into the bed of the truck. He rolled the backpack free of the tarp, pulled it closer to one side. He stepped down to the ground.

The trooper took some time looking over the gear. He nodded, he backed off a notch. "We get us a lot of drugs running up through here." He tipped his head toward the highway.

Cal dusted his hands against his pants. He looked out at the terrain. He nodded vaguely. "If I were a drug out here, I think I'd be running too."

The trooper gave him a long silent look. Half a smile showed. He glanced at Cal's trembling hands. "Are you Cal?"

Cal hesitated. "Yeah. Do I know you?"

The trooper shook his head. "I called in your plate numbers, that's what." He walked toward the front of the truck. Cal stepped out of the way. The trooper took a look inside the cab. He turned around and faced Cal. They stared awhile.

Cal nodded over toward the buffalo billboard and the building smoking alongside it. "That a good place to eat over there?"

The trooper stared off in that direction. "Depends. You see any other place to eat in the last sixty miles?"

Cal shook his head no.

"Probably a good place to eat then." He walked around to the other side of the truck, took a look inside the cab from there. "You say you're just down from Santa Fe this morning?"

"Yep."

The trooper finished his walk around the truck. He looked again at Cal's shaking hands. "You worked for a telecom outfit up there? A company named Angel Fire? For a long dry fellow named Hank?"

Cal stiffened. "How'd you know that?"

The trooper nodded. "Hank's my brother." He smiled and relaxed a bit. "And there's a pay stub down there on the floor of your truck that says so. That's a real coincidence then." He gave Cal an appraising look. Cal looked at the trooper's badge for his name.

"Hank was just telling me, last week or so, telling me about a guy he had working for him, and how he had to let him go, because of . . . well, because of . . ." He paused. He glanced again at Cal's hands.

"Because of what?" Cal said.

The trooper's smile faded a notch. "Hank's a good man. He wasn't talking you down, if that's what you're thinking. He was just saying that his man, well, that's you, that you sort of, well, that you sort of hit a rough patch, a while back."

Cal glanced at the trooper's face. "A rough patch?" He cocked his head. "He said I hit a rough patch?"

"Yeah. That's what he said."

Cal nodded. "A rough patch." He laughed. He turned and looked off into the desert. Dust devils were rising to the south, spinning away across the flatlands like a sign of industry where there was none. "A rough patch," he said again. "That's what he said it was?"

The trooper stood awkward. "Yeah. Hank told me it was a good man he was losing too. Told me straight out, that he was hard pressed to fill your shoes. He was asking me if I knew anyone up that way, someone looking for that kind of work. That's why it all came up in the first place." The trooper watched Cal. "You were with him a good while, right?"

Cal half-nodded. "Good enough to be here right now."

The trooper adjusted the tilt of his hat. "Well. So how about that. Sure is a small world, huh?"

Cal fixed his stare further off down the desert. "I don't see it that way, just now," he said. "Sometimes it is."

Six feet of distance stood between them.

The trooper looked over the hazy spread of the highway. He looked back at Cal. He touched the brim of his hat lightly with two fingers. "Well. Good luck to you, alright? And, ah, well . . . I'm sorry." He nodded those last two words across, direct and business-like.

He turned and walked back to the squad car. He stood by the door a while like he was trying to think of something more to say. He opened the door, took his hat off, slid in onto the seat. He closed the door. He backed the car up and turned around. He drove off down the highway.

Sunlight sifted through the dust he left behind.

Cal stood in silence beside his truck. He watched the trooper's car grow smaller into the distance, vaporized eventually where the horizon was lost to the heat.

"A rough patch," he said. He turned the words over in his mind. Rough. Then patch.

The cartoon buffalo waved to him from the billboard, a blue twist of smoke rising beside it like a lazy thought released to the sky.

Nowhere descended again around him, this time with a small hole in the middle of it into which he well fit.

Cal exhaled. He up glanced at the high-noon sun. He climbed inside his truck, started the engine, turned the truck around.

4.

A few cars were parked alongside the building, a small silver trailer tethered in back by a clothesline hung through the smoky air and a power cord snaking along the ground below it. Clothing hung there stiff on the line like cardboard pennants, huge pairs of pants staggered with smoke-colored t-shirts and a dozen pairs of socks strung up and down like musical notes over dirt. Just miles and miles of yellow dirt, pressed flat by the sky in every direction.

Cal pulled up to the storefront and braked in the gravel. Yellow dust bloomed from his tires and withered away.

The glass front door was propped wide with a wedge of wood, hopeful for any breeze. Floor to ceiling plate glass windows stood all in a row to either side. Posters and notices taped up everywhere, competing for attention.

The place was an auto parts store once. Cal read the ghost of its last name from a series of holes punched in the cinder block above the windows where the plastic letters once hung. Half Tank's Auto Parts.

He shut the truck off. Looked in through the plate glass, saw a few people sitting inside at the tables.

He opened the glove box, pulled out a ten dollar bill from a tattered envelope. He pulled his sunglasses up and opened his door, stepped to the ground and walked inside.

A dozen or more tables were scattered there, unarranged, three of them busy already with customers. The kitchen was out in back behind a pegboard wall painted white once. Paper plates were tacked up on the wall with the specials of the day. Country music lolled from a 1950's pea-green plastic radio shaped like a toaster with a bulls-eye dial glowing yellow, half-bright.

The cook shuffled out through a swinging door like a man set on autopilot. He was a big man, as big and wide around as a refrigerator, industrial-sized, with a red apron covering his massive gut, all of it faded and greased. The same two buffalos were on the apron as outside on the sign.

"What d'ya have?" the cook huffed, out of breath. He dropped a ham of a hand down on the relish-green counter and leaned a bit of his weight there, the counter creaked.

Cal looked down at the man's hand. He looked up at the cartoon buffalos on the apron. Further up to the big man's face. He nodded hello. "You must be Bill."

The big man stared back like a whole wall of slow. "Well I must be a lot of things by now," he said, his voice as flat as an anvil. "But I ain't that. Name's Jimmie. What d'ya have?"

Cal looked down again at the man's apron, saw the word "Bill" stitched in yellow thread across the top.

"Says Bill, right there."

Jimmie tried for a look at his own chest but came up a little short. "Got another apron out back that says Ed, but I ain't him neither. What d'ya have?"

Cal couldn't tell if that was a smile on the man's face or something less. "Didn't have anything yet."

The big man angled his face a notch lower. He was a full head and a half taller than Cal. "I know you ain't had nothing. That's why I'm here asking ya what d'ya have."

Cal stared back. "I, ah . . ."

The big man straightened himself up. "Did you come in here to eat, or you just looking?"

"To eat."

"To eat, then." A slight smile showed on his face. "Well that's real good, because we serve food. So, what d'ya have then . . . to eat?"

Cal nodded back. "Alright. Well . . ." He looked around for any menu. Up at all the paper plate specials hovering that he couldn't read a single one of. "I'll just have what's up there on the sign outside . . . burger, fries, a coke, will do it."

Jimmie nodded to the order. "How you done for it?"

Cal stared back at the question.

"The burger . . ." Jimmie said. He was looking down at Cal's shaking hands. "How . . . do . . . you . . . want . . . er . . . done?"

Cal nodded back. "Medium done, I guess. Medium rare." He shrugged.

The big man backed away a step. "You guess?" He took another look down at Cal's shaking hands. "You ain't too sure about it?"

Cal slid his hands down into his pockets. "Yeah, I'm sure."

Jimmie looked back at him a good long while, right in the eye, right in past the sunglasses. He leaned in, spoke so quiet that it was just Cal that could hear him. "You got the money to pay for it?"

Cal blinked. "Yeah." He felt around for the ten in his pocket, pulled it out, showed it to the man. He took his sunglasses off, hooked them in his back pocket. He stared back at Jimmie a while.

Jimmie looked down at the ten in his hand, then back up at Cal's bloodshot eyes. He nodded slowly. "We get some in here every day who can't pay, or who don't want to. I thought you might be one of them, is all." He bent down, leaned in closer. "Shit blows in off the highway. Every day. Gets to being tedious."

Cal backed away a step.

Music scratched out from the radio on the shelf, a sawed-off baseball bat was propped against the wall below it, dark and greasy at the handle end.

"Well. I'm not that," he said.

Jimmie nodded back. "That'd be a good thing, for both of us." He gave Cal another long look. He rocked himself sideways, wedged himself back in through the swinging door and was gone.

Cal watched that door until it stopped swinging.

A large wall clock hung on the wall above it, its bowed glass face gone hazy and yellow with smoke and time. The minute hand notched itself forward. A shoal of dead flies lay trapped behind the glass beneath the number six. The ceiling fans moved the smoky air all about in no direction at once.

There were two wooden stools standing at a counter long enough to seat twelve. Cal sat down onto one of them and turned his back to the kitchen, his elbows propped up to the counter. Another car pulled in. He watched the two people get out and shuffle inside. They settled themselves at a table, chairs squeaking across the tile floor. There was no sign of a waitress anywhere. Cal sat back to wait for his order.

5.

Out on a first date with Gayle, a Saturday morning.
They met up for coffees at eleven.
"Not just any coffee," Gayle had said. She directed him by cell to a small grind shop called Red Molly's on a side alley off Galisteo. "The kind of place you won't find on your own," she had said. She was right.

Gayle was sitting up at the counter when Cal walked in. There was only one other stool in the place. Barrels and sacks of coffee crowded the aisle everywhere, a few antique grind machines for sale, hand-made coffee mugs, and for some reason, maybe just color, a rack of imported Indian scarves. Gayle was chatting it up with a hot-wired, roundish woman with flame red hair. Red Molly, Cal guessed. Gayle turned to Cal as he came in and gave him a broad smile. She waved him over and introduced him to Molly like he was an old friend. He pulled up on the other stool, settled in beside her.

She gave him an appraising look, that first, close-up-in-the-daylight kind of look. She shoulder-bumped him and said, "Hey." She turned to Molly and ordered a triple-shot cappuccino concoction for herself, something called a "Mo-Fro-Rocket," spelled out in flaming blue letters across the chalkboard with the other fare.

"Mostly hand-picked, high-altitude Bolivian beans," Gayle nodded to Cal. "The caffeine closest to God," she whispered. "That's the Rocket part." Like letting him in on the secret. "Then there's a small scoop of Moroccan French-roast thrown in for its penchant mystery. French roast is Fro. Moroccan is Mo."

Cal laughed out loud. "A Mo-Fro-Rocket, huh?"
Gayle smiled. "I came up with the name."
"You did?"
Gayle and Molly nodded in unison.
"Make it two Mo-Fros then."
"Two Mo-Fro-Rockets," Gayle said to Molly. "To go."

"Two-go Mo-Fro-Rockets," Molly nodded. She turned, her machines clanked and wheezed and spat and there was no talking above the racket.

Two tall frothing cups were delivered.

Gayle topped hers off with a light rain of cinnamon, another of cocoa, then held a plastic honey bear over it upside down and squeezed. She seemed to be counting.

"Honey?" Cal had never connected the thought of honey with coffee before.

"Kiss of a thousand bees," Gayle said. "Eleven seconds worth. Depending on the bear, of course. Shhh, you'll make me loose my count."

"Oh, sorry." Cal watched the honey streaming down. Gayle finished her count, she put the bear down, she stirred it all in.

"Eleven seconds worth?" Cal asked.

Gayle nodded back. "That's what it takes, mostly. From that bear, anyway."

"I take it you know that bear well."

"Yep. He's an eleven second bear for sure. My treat." She paid for the coffees and they stepped outside.

They walked a good part of downtown Santa Fe that day, up into the Old Town, along the mission markets and the plaza, drifting in through the odd shops and galleries there, threading their way through the curious crowd. No plan as yet between them.

"A walky-talk," Gayle called it at one point. "You gather your clues."

"Clues?" Cal asked. "Clues . . . for what?"

Gayle nodded her head to the question but offered no answer. She watched him a long moment, smiling, walking along beside him like a stealthy cat with a secret. She made a quick left turn up a few steps into an ice cream shop that happened by just then. Cal was looking the other way and he stopped short when she went missing. He backtracked a few steps, saw her waving through the glass. He followed her inside the shop.

She was standing at the counter waiting for him. "You order first," she said. She nodded at the long list of flavors on the board.

"Don't you want to grab some lunch first?" Cal asked.

"Me neither," Gayle smiled back.

Cal laughed. He shrugged, turned and scanned the list of flavors above him. He said, "Vanilla."

The girl at the counter said, "Okay." She looked next at Gayle.

Gayle shook her head no. "I'm good here."

"You don't want any?" Cal asked.

"Nope. I'm good."

She was smiling slyly, nodding her head to some personal rhythm. Or maybe she was counting something again. Mysterious girl, this one. Definitely. And playful.

"I don't get it," Cal said. "Why did we come in here then?"

"So you could order . . . vanilla."

"Yeah. And so?"

"And . . . so." She leaned in a bit closer. Her shoulder brushed against his. "You didn't even read the other flavors, did you?"

Cal laughed. He scanned the board again. "There are way too many."

She looked him in the eye. "There are some really good flavors up there."

He looked over the list again. Shrugged. "I always get vanilla."

Gayle nodded. "I figured you for a vanilla guy."

Cal half-smiled. "Is that a bad thing?"

She laughed at his expression. "It's not, if you like vanilla."

The girl handed Cal his cone. He took a bite off one side. He paid the girl, left some change in the tip jar. They stepped outside and walked down the street.

"So, do you?" Gayle asked him. "Really like vanilla?"

Cal nodded his head. "Oh yeah." He took another bite.

"Mmm-hmm. It's not what you might just call, a default choice? Something easier not to think about?"

"No," Cal said. "I don't do default. Never have. I like vanilla just fine."

"And why's that?"

"Why?" Cal had never really given it much thought. He offered Gayle a bite, she shook her head no thanks. They walked on. He took a good look at the ice cream cone, turned the question over in his head.

"Well. It's an honest flavor, for one." He took a bite.

She nodded back. "Straightforward, right?"

"Absolutely. No nonsense."

"You don't think chocolate is honest?"

Cal gave that some thought. "No. Chocolate lies to you."

Gayle laughed out loud. She had a sweet laugh. "How does it lie?"

"It tells you that you have room for more when you really don't."

Gayle laughed again. "Ah. The man speaks from experience." She gave him a curious look. He offered her another bite. She shook her head no. "So, back to vanilla. No nonsense, huh?"

"None. It's a completely businesslike ice cream. What you see is what you get."

She gave him a small smile. "Some might think, plain."

Cal shook his head slowly to that. "I don't eat what others think." He popped the remains of the cone in his mouth.

Gayle hovered close by at Cal's side the whole day like that, glowing fresh as a flower. Had it been rainy or cloudy that day, Cal still would have said from memory that it was sun bright.

"So, Cal. Do you dream much?" She peeked over at him past a sweep of wheat-blonde hair that hid half her face at that angle. It swung forward and back as she walked like a curtain to a view in a breeze.

"You mean, like at night? When I'm sleeping?" he asked. He was enjoying the view.

She gave him a small nod. "Well, yeah, that too."

He smiled. "Right. Well, I'd have to say I'm a big dreamer. Crazy dreamer, even."

Gayle raised an eyebrow. "Crazy? As in, raging insane? Or just plain . . . much?"

Cal laughed. "Not insane. More like . . . cinematic. Epic movie quality, full-length feature crazy."

Gayle nodded to that. "I knew it."

"How'd you know it?"

She pointed to her forehead, to that small spot where women from India wear a red dot. "I have a built-in dreamer detector, right here." She nodded. "I can spot a prolific dreamer a mile away."

Cal thought about that. "So why'd you need to ask?"

She shrugged. "Confirmation."

They walked on.

"So. Do you dream in color, or in black and white?"

"Black and white? Like those old gangster movies?"

"I was thinking more, 1950's French art films. The choice is yours though."

"Well. It's color, either way. Most definitely color. Yep." He looked over at her. "How about you, Gayle? Big dreamer?"

She nodded. "Takes one to know one."

"Mmm. True. So is it color, or black and white, with you?"

"Right now?" She looked all around at the day. "Oh, it's definitely color." She skipped a few steps, like a small dance, until she synced up with Cal's longer gait. She took him by the arm. She hummed a little tune.

"So you mentioned before that you're an artist," Cal said.

Gayle smiled back. "Sort of. What I said was, I sold painted canvases."

"Well, yeah. But you said you painted them too, didn't you?"

"True. I do get paint on most of them." She smiled. "A true artist would never tell you she's an artist. 'Bad form,' the British would say. It might insult the muses, or something like that. So, I won't say I'm an artist."

Cal thought it over. "Like a true con man would never tell you he's a con man."

She laughed at the comparison. "So, are you a con man, Cal?"

He thought that one all the way through. Talking with her was like playing chess. "Yes," he said, shaking his head no at the same time.

She grinned. "Excellent response. So I have nothing to fear from you."

"Nothing at all," Cal said. "Over time, you'll grow to be genuinely fearless of my . . . non-conesty. And I, on the other hand, will grow to be increasingly enthralled by your . . . unspecific non-production of art."

She gave his arm a little squeeze. "What a nice thing to say!"

"That settles it," Cal said. And then a few seconds later, "Well, almost. If not an artist, what would you call yourself? Or, more precisely, what should I call you, if I were ever called upon to call you something? For future reference, that is. By some third party."

Gayle grinned widely. "I like that *future reference* thing. It sounds so promising, doesn't it? As for the third party . . . let's see how the first two parties go, alright?" She smiled and looked up at the big blue New Mexico sky. "You could call me . . . an ambassador," she said. "No, wait. An interpreter." Her eyes were sparkling. "Yep. That's it. I work as an interpreter, for the Embassy of What Is."

"An interpreter for the Embassy of What Is. That's an excellent position," Cal said. "So that makes you . . . a What Is-ian?"

"Exactly."

"You should be proud of yourself."

"I will be. I just got the position. Actually, you're the first to know."

They walked on.

Half a block later, Gayle said, "The name Cal. Is that short for Calvin?"

"Nope."

"Short for Caleb?"

"No."

"Hmm. Short for, ah . . . Calaboose?"

Cal laughed. "Calaboose? Isn't that a slang word for jail?"

Gayle smiled back. "Exactly. As in, *I'm going to throw your bad ass in the calaboose, hombre.*"

Cal cracked up. "There might be some merit to that. Depends on what you catch me doing. Or not doing, maybe. Sorry, though, it's not my name."

"Hmm. Short for, ah . . . Calamanco?"

Cal looked aside at her. "Calamanco? Sounds like some sort of lizard."

"Nope. It's a dusty haze in Spain. Up on the plain. Just in the summertime, in August mostly, I think, when it's been dry for too long, then the wind comes along and kicks up all the dust. They have other dusty seasons too, mostly in the fall, sometimes in the spring, but they call those something else."

Cal laughed. "Did you just make that up?"

She smiled. "Sometimes. And not all of it."

He nodded. "Well, that's not my name. I never get that dry. Not in August, anyway."

"I see," she said. "So. Your name then. Is it short for, ah . . . Calawishus?"

"Calawishus?"

"Sure. Why not Calawishus? I've always liked the name."

"Have you ever known a Calawishus?"

She shook her head. "No. But there's always hope."

"Well, I'm afraid there's no hope here, honey bear. With me, the name's just Cal. That's all of it." A few seconds passed. "Ah, my pardon. May I call you honey bear?"

"Mmm-hmm."

They walked on.

"So. You've always liked the name Calawishus."

"Mmm. Not always. But I'm liking it more now. So, yeah, pretty soon, you could say that."

They sat in the shady corner of a small park, on a sandstone bench, beneath a tree filled with a thousand birds, more or less, all of them chattering at once.

"The feathered bickering congress," Gayle called them.

They watched the show in progress above them, the birds pushed from one branch to another in some endless comic quest for order.

"Your eyes," Cal said at one point, having had a closer look. "They're a slightly different color, right? One is bluer than the other?"

Gayle half-nodded. "Or greener. Depends on which one you noticed first."

A few minutes drifted past.

Gayle clapped her hands sharply then, like an urgent thought had exploded inside her. All the birds were silenced, waiting.

She stood. "We should find us a soothsayer!"

Earlier in the day, Cal would have had pause, he would have asked why, or what for, to a statement like that. Just now he watched her face all lit up like it was, and he stood beside her and said, "Sounds like a plan."

She nodded back.

"So where do we find one?" he asked.

Gayle shrugged. She looked around the park, up at the blue sky hovering. "Actually, I think they find you first."

They started walking. The birds rose up en masse and circled the park once in a peppery cloud. They resettled then, and recommenced their bickering.

"What exactly is *sooth* anyway?" Cal said, crossing over to the next street. He threw Gayle a look. "I mean, okay, so there's some guy and he's going around calling himself a soothsayer, right? So by definition he must be saying *sooth*. So what is *sooth*?"

Gayle smiled. "Sooth is the truth."

"The truth?"

"Yep. The truth."

"You know this for real?"

"Yep. The word is from the Old English. Medieval stuff. Sooth is what is held to be true, whatever is taken to be real. As in, *Forsooth, young Calawishus, do you not walk beside a comely maiden?*"

Cal grinned back. "Comely as they go."

She gave him a sweet look.

He gave her a handsome one back.

"So soothsayers are truth sayers?"

"One and the same," she said. "That's why it's so soothing when they have something to tell you."

"What's soothing?"

"Having sooth told to you. Hearing sooth is soothing."

"That's what *soothing* means?"

"To a seeker of truth, sure. If sooth is the truth, then the act of hearing sooth is soothing. Like the act of being a sleuth is sleuthing."

Cal laughed at the word tangle. "Really? Because that's, like totally confusing."

She agreed. "It is at first. After a while you get over it. It's like seeing airplanes in the sky. You got over that, right? I mean, they weigh more than a fully loaded semi. They shouldn't be up there, right?"

"Well, yeah. No, I mean."

"See. You're already on your way."

What Cal remembered most by day's end was the feeling that he was finally home, with Gayle at his side. She was a stranger to him still, less so by the minute, but the feeling was there from the start, as unexplained as it was undeniable. He just felt like he was home. Not much else mattered.

Near seven o'clock the sun was fading, dropping into a bright orange haze.

"Like a maraschino cherry sinking into a mango margarita," Gayle said.

Cal nodded back. "Great idea."

They headed south on Guadalupe, out to a small club named Camino de Estrellas. It was a thin slip of a space half a block deep, with an Old West-style bar running its full length with a brass foot rail anchored below, a copper spittoon sprouting a big painted cactus in the corner and clouds of sawdust scuffled across the floor. A few thin tables were angled across the aisle from the bar and a scatter of tables farther back where the room opened up. Strings of tiny lights hung everywhere from the ceiling like candy-colored stars beneath a velvet-black sky.

They pulled up a couple of seats at the bar. A handful of customers sat at the far end watching baseball from a TV mounted above the mirrored back bar. A few seats to the left of Cal's was a half-finished drink and a cigar in an ashtray, with a handful of change and a few singles laid out alongside it.

Nouveau flamenco music peppered the air.

The bartender greeted them like two old friends come over for a backyard barbeque. "Hey, what can I get you folks?"

"Frozen mango margarita," Gayle said, to a drum-roll of her hands on the bar top.

Cal said, "Make it two."

"You bet," the bartender said, and left to tend to his work.

Gayle mostly kept her eyes on Cal. She sat sideways to the bar with her feet propped up on a rung, one of his hands captive in hers and resting in her lap.

Halfway through their drinks, something else caught her eye. She leaned into the aisle, looking past Cal toward the back room, a half-smile balanced on her lips.

"Whoa, I think that guy is really drunk."

Cal almost turned around for a look, but he'd seen enough drunks before. He waved it off.

"Sometimes that's just what a bar does to you," he said. He picked up his glass and took a long sip to make his point.

Gayle furrowed her brow a little. "No. I mean this guy is really drunk. Way off his balance. The poor thing."

Cal glanced around into the mirrored back bar. Through the rows of bottles and glasses there he watched the dark reflection of a man distorting its way down the aisle toward them. The man was huge, and round, six-and-a-half feet tall and nearly as wide, dressed in a crumpled black suit, a white shirt and a black string tie.

"Mr. Moon," the bartender called out. Like announcing the man's return from a long journey. "How we doing there now, Mr. Moon?"

Mr. Moon mumbled back something unknowable to most, but the bartender caught his meaning. "I'm afraid I can't do that, sir." More mumbles from Mr. Moon, a nod or two from the bartender.

Moon wandered past his own stool and came to a tentative halt. He eyed the seat next to Cal's, more by default than conscious choice. He bumped Cal off to the right a few inches when he sat down. He reached out, slid his half-drink, the cigar and ashtray, and the pile of change along the bar with a wide sweep of his arm. He settled into place then like a dark lump of clay.

He rattled off some more words in the bartender's direction.

The bartender stood before him and nodded back. "Yes. I know you can pay for another one. Yes, I do know that, sir. But you haven't finished this one yet." He pointed to the half-finished drink between them.

Moon spied it there with one eye cocked. He slanted forward, scooped it up with his enormous hand. He sipped at it, once, twice, genteelly, like he was checking it for its quality.

He turned halfway around and stared one-eyed at Cal, then other-eyed at Gayle, surprised to see them both there all at once like that. They each nodded a tentative hello. He lifted his glass toward them, he nodded hello back, then tipped the glass up and drained the remains down. He held it at eye level a moment, rattled the ice cubes around for their empty sound. Checked their sparkle against the light. He positioned the glass closer to one eye, watching the bartender through the cubes. He laughed and put the glass down.

"Well done, sir," the bartender said.

Moon's empty hands fished the air all about him with a flourish. More word-shaped sounds tumbled from his mouth.

"No . . . you already paid for that one, Mr. Moon," the bartender said.

"Gumpeezer mumbersum," Moon aimed back.

"No, you cannot have another one, sir. That one was your last, do you remember? We agreed on it earlier . . . that this one would be your last one."

The bartender glanced at Cal and Gayle with a worn smile and moved on down the bar to tend his other customers. He kept an eye on Moon from a distance.

Moon fumbled out more words and gestured at random to the space around him. Cal and Gayle turned away.

Moments passed.

The man's words were gathering more focus. Gayle nudged Cal on the shoulder at one point, she leaned in and quietly said, "I think he's talking to you."

Cal smiled back. "What's that?"

"I believe he's speaking to you," she said. She pointed over his shoulder toward Moon.

Cal turned around on his barstool and Moon's face was right there, inches away and as big as day. Moon's features seemed all disconnected; they traveled around on his face like a handful of swarming bees. Cal slid his stool back to a safer distance.

Moon mumbled away and Cal tried his best to catch the man's meaning but for all his efforts, came up empty. He turned back to Gayle. "Do you understand what he's saying?" he whispered.

Gayle looked down at her margarita with a short laugh and a wave of her hand. "He's all yours, sweet pea."

Cal listened harder but he was clueless as to what the man was trying to say. He guessed there was some other kind of accent at work besides that of bourbon on the rocks. He shrugged it off. He apologized to the man and turned away.

Moon poked at the back of Cal's head with a finger.

Cal turned around again to face him. "What is it?"

"Pah . . . umdembed . . . tahay," Moon said carefully. One of his hands fluttered up alongside his face like a fat bird. His eyes winked alternately.

Whenever Gayle tried to stifle a laugh, she ended up with a giggle. "He wants to know about your day," she giggled into Cal's ear.

Cal laughed and turned halfway around to face Gayle. "My day?"

Moon's fingers were short and fat like sausages, or a handful of big toes. He poked at Cal's head again with one of them.

Cal sighed and turned back to face the man. "Jeez man. What is it now?"

"Tez yomain."

Cal listened hard, looked even harder into the man's face. "What's that again?"

"Yomain. Tez yomain."

Cal shook his head. "I don't know what it is you're saying."

"Wah mtayn es . . . tez yomainmm," Moon said, more distinctly.

Gayle leaned in closer, like an interpreter, and whisper-laughed into Cal's ear, "Tell us your name."

"Really?" Cal said, turning back around to Gayle.

"Reedee?" Moon said to Cal. He poked at him again with another finger. He inched his face closer, one eye opened. "Yomainm es Reedee?" He winked his other eye at Gayle. "Ndyoors?"

"Gayle," she said. "My name is Gayle. Hiya."

"Welly. Mnainms Moon, eer."

"Well a fine hello back to you, Mr. Moon," Gayle said.

Cal looked back at Gayle. "How do you know what he's saying?"

She said quietly, "Listen sideways."

"Pookenz," Moon said.

He seemed to be regarding them, making some kind of assessment. He held a hand up in the air, his palm vertical. He held his other hand up the same way, then moved them slowly together, closer, like he was squeezing something invisible between them. "Pookenz."

"Bookends?" Gayle asked.

"Jess. Zackly dat. Pookenz," Moon said, and he nodded his head, bulldog-like.

"Bookends," Cal repeated. "Got it." He nodded and took a sip of his drink.

"Zactly dat," Gayle repeated. She grinned and took a sip of her drink. "So what is it about bookends, Mr. Moon?"

Moon nodded back sagely, more or less. He straightened up, held his head a little higher, and focused one of his eyes on both of Gayle's. "Wen tengz . . . tart . . . and wen tengz end . . . is da pookendz."

Cal looked back at Gayle.

She nodded tentatively. "When things start, and when things end, is the bookends?"

Moon gave a knowing smile in her direction. "Pookenz, iz what mtayn. Da same teng twyzz, ride now, end ride eer, you two arh da pookendz. Yah zee?"

"*We're* the bookends?" Gayle asked, pointing to herself and Cal. "You think we're the same thing, twice?"

Moon put his two hands down on the bar top with a fat slap. "Jess dat. Zackly . . . dat." He picked up his empty glass. He sipped at the melted water. He put the glass down. He leaned in closer. "En da wayyit iz, wit pookendz, iz dis . . . how it iz inda beginim . . . iz aways howit enz." He nodded his words out, one eyebrow up, and looked them both over, sort of.

Cal turned around to Gayle. "What was that last part?"

"Mr. Moon," the bartender called out. Moon's focus went there immediately. "I called your brother. He's coming down to take you home. Your brother. Did you hear what I said?"

Moon nodded. He shrugged. He pushed his glass and the cigar off to one side, he slid the pile of change toward the bartender, he looked around for anything else he might need to attend to, then folded his arms on the bar and slowly put his head down on top of them.

They all watched him a moment in silence.

"We should move," Gayle said quietly. She nodded to a small table near the front door. Cal motioned to the bartender for two more drinks. "We'll be over there." The bartender nodded back.

They settled themselves at the table, Gayle in the half booth against the wall, Cal facing her in the chair in the aisle. She leaned across the table and took hold of one of his hands. She looked over toward Moon.

"In some other lifetime, or maybe some other culture," she said, "I think that man would've been a sage." She nodded over toward Moon.

"Moon?" Cal said. "You think so? Why's that?"

She glanced back in the man's direction. "I think he sees things, you know? I think he sees things how they really are. And he sees it all so clearly sometimes, that it causes him pain." She nodded. "And he can't deal so well with that pain." She thought more about it. Cal watched her face. "He can't turn his vision off. He can only dull it down. And so that's his only option this time around."

Cal looked back at the man. "You don't think he just drinks too much?"

Gayle frowned. It was the first one he'd seen from her.

"That word *just*," she said, looking across at Cal. "It sure takes care of lots of things, doesn't it?" She leaned in closer, aimed a fake smile toward him and batted her eyes. "So you and I, we're *just* out on a date, right?"

Cal conceded her point.

She nodded back. "There's always a deeper reason beyond the *just*." She glanced back at Moon. "I'm guessing, with someone like him, it's how intensely he sees things. It's how he sees the world, or sees beneath the surface of it, maybe. So it's hard for him to deal with it. Hard to have the kind of leverage he would really need to deal with it." She thought for a moment. "Maybe that's what makes him so round as well."

Cal assessed that. "Yeah. Moon is rather roundish."

Gayle nodded back. "Planetary even, don't you think? In a good way, I mean."

"Mmm, yeah, maybe. I'd say, he's approaching planethood."

Gayle smiled. "Oh, I like the sound of that much better. Approaching planethood. It sounds so deliberate. Heroic even, like he's on some kind of mission."

Cal laughed. "He definitely is." He glanced back in the big man's direction. He tried to see him differently.

"So. With the extra weight and all. You're saying that's somehow connected to the vision thing?"

Gayle thought about that.

"Well. Let's break it down. Suppose a man was born with a huge spirit, a spirit way bigger than normal. Almost like a sort of cosmic birth defect, right? Who really knows? So being born with a oversized spirit like that, he would tend to experience the world more intensely than the average guy, because of it. So he might need more gravity to pull him down than the average guy too, just to keep that big spirit from flying off the grid, blowing right out his ears and leaving him dry." She watched Cal's face for any reaction. "It's like if you tried fitting the ocean inside a jam jar, right? You would need a bigger jar."

Cal blinked at the idea. "A huge spirit, huh?" He thought it over. "And all this time, I thought spirits only came in one size."

He glanced over at Moon. "So you don't think he just eats and drinks too much?"

He saw that slight frown again at Gayle's face.

"Whoops. It's hard not to use that word *just*, right?"

She smiled. "Actually, it's pretty easy. You just stop using it." She waved her hand aside. "Just pretend it doesn't exist."

She refocused her thoughts on Moon.

"I think it goes deeper than that, with him. Like tree roots go deeper. I think he sees the real rawness of life, or the immediacy of it all, and he can't hide from it like most people do."

"Like most people do?"

"Yeah, like most people do," she nodded. "We all hide in some way from the rawness of life, from its immediacy. From being one hundred percent in the present, in the right here and now."

Cal glanced around the room. He shrugged. "I'm not seeing much rawness here. Not much I'd consider hiding from, anyway." He gave the room another good look. "Everything looks pretty well-cooked to me. Over-cooked, even."

Gayle let out a long laugh.

Cal frowned. "Uh oh. Does that mean I'm one of the most?"

Gayle leaned back and gave him an appraising sort of look. She shook her head slightly and smiled. "No. I'd say you're definitely less than most. You're just not aware of it yet." She smiled more.

Cal stared back. "Okay. I'm confused here."

She nodded. "It's temporary, my dove." She gave him a playful look. She reached out and petted one of his hands with hers. "You'll be fine."

Cal took a sip of his drink. "Okay. I'm feeling a little better now." He looked back towards Moon. "So what was that last thing he said? I didn't quite catch it."

Gayle studied Cal's face at close range. "It sounded like he said, *The way it is with bookends, is this: How it is in the beginning, is always how it ends.*"

Cal nodded tentatively. "What do you think that means?"

Gayle shrugged. "I don't know, but it has its hooks in me." She gave him a long look, then a smile. "We best make sure it has a very good beginning, don't you think?"

"I've been thinking that all day."

They both looked over at Moon, sitting there face down at the bar. Cal raised a glass in his direction. "Looks like the Moon has set."

Gayle grinned. "What a lovely image." She raised her glass. "Salut." She hooked her arm into Cal's and pulled him closer, their glasses hovering. She was looking into his eyes like she would find an answer there. An answer to some long held question, maybe.

"What is it?" Cal said.

She smiled back. "I don't really know. It's all so . . familiar."

They drank their toast to Moon. They put their glasses down. Cal nodded over towards the man. "So, do you think Moon was saying some *sooth* back there?"

Gayle leaned back and laughed out loud. She was still smiling broadly when she took hold of Cal's face in both her hands. "You're very cute," she said, and gave him a first kiss.

Cal looked surprised.

Gayle nodded to that look. "The world is full of sooth."

They ordered another round.

Cal slid into the booth beside her. They ordered a staggered helping of appetizers that grew steadily into a greater feast. The crowd picked up around them three and four at a time until the place was jammed and the music shifted into a loud Saturday night. They both looked through the crowd at one point and saw that Moon was gone, as if by magic.

"Wow," Gayle said, popping her eyes wide and checking the room over. "How did that happen? Someone so large, so immeasurable even, by most standards, and he just . . . vanished?"

"Just?" Cal asked.

She smiled and shook her head. "Just never vanishes."

Their night spun on. They joked and laughed about everything, about nothing. More drinks crossed their table with no effort on their part.

Gayle had a smoky laugh, rich and deep-textured like velvet. Sexy without effort. A sound so perfectly suited to his ear, Cal found himself doing whatever he could to hear more of it.

And he found he couldn't get enough of her face. He felt he could look there forever and not get tired of the view. Another gesture, another glance, another turn of phrase or tilt of her head. She reminded him of those boxes of chocolates, the ones with all the pieces in their pleated wrappers and when the top layer's gone, the cardboard tray lifts out and there's a whole new layer waiting below. Only with Gayle, this went on forever.

"What ya thinking, Calawishus?" Her tone as sexy.

"Oh. Just . . ." He shrugged. "Delicious."

She folded both his hands in hers. "What's delicious, my dishus Calawishus?"

Cal laughed at her playfulness. "Jeez, woman." He shook his head. He looked deeper into her eyes. "I don't know. Just, all of it. All of it is delicious."

Not the kind of girl to blush at a compliment, Gayle rewarded him handsomely with another one of her smoky laughs, and then a second kiss, one lip bite longer than the first.

6.

"You want that to go, or you gonna set it down some?"

Jimmie's face filled the service window from the kitchen.

"Oh. I guess . . ." Cal started to say. He turned around to scan the room for a table.

"To go then," Jimmie huffed back. "You got it." His face exited the service window.

Cal nodded back to the empty frame. He turned again to face the room.

A wave of exhaustion, just pure fatigue, hit him broadside, slammed down against him like a fast tide. He held onto the counter for balance, he saw the color of the world drained away to ghost white. That thin metallic sound in his ears that he would follow, that he was following down, following down to . . .

The wave faded.

He was standing.

Still standing.

Always that. Still standing. Six weeks gone now, and he was still standing. He stared out from his private vacancy to a view of a world apart.

Two people were seating themselves at a table. A man and a woman so old and weathered, so worn together like two river rocks rolled downstream in the same current, that they no longer needed to speak, their actions were tethered in a telepathic dance.

A little girl sat the next table over with her mom, her legs dangled from the chair. She swung them back and forth. She wore a pair of mismatched sneakers. The left one was blue; the other one was black and yellow striped, with a smiley bumblebee's face on the toe. She took a first bite of her burger and looked over the rim of the huge bun like she was peeking over a mountaintop. Her eyes connected with Cal's. He could see her smile there before it showed on the rest of her face. Ketchup squeezed out the sides all around the burger and the whole thing fell apart and slipped from her grip and flopped upside down onto her plate.

"What did I tell you?" her mother told her again, about putting ketchup on both sides of the burger. The little girl looked up at Cal all ketchup-faced and smiley. Cal gave her a little wink.

A faded-looking man sat off by himself at the next table over, his back turned to the rest, his face drawn to the wall plastered with posters and flyers for singers, for rodeo stars, for workers for hire and trucks for sale, equipment to rent. He looked like a faded black and white photograph of a man taken fifty years back, having lunch at the same table. Misfiled in time somehow. He held silent conversations with someone or something unseen. Long white hair twisted back in a loose braid, tied off with a strip of flannel cloth. A scruff of white beard rounded his chin.

Cal scanned the rest of the restaurant without focus. Chairs circling tables, spoons circling coffee cups, ceiling fans spinning in the cooked and smoky air. Outside through the wall of hazy glass, the desert's endless flatness, and the glare.

"You know a three legged tortoise?"

The faded-looking man was turned halfway around in his chair, looking directly at Cal, his voice more distant sounding than the space between them would account for.

"You talking to me?" Cal said. No one else in the room paid him any mind.

The old man rose slowly from his chair. He walked over and stood before Cal.

"A three legged tortoise," the man said again. He pointed outside.

Cal looked outside.

"He's trying to get himself across the road one day, up early in the morning before the asphalt gets too hot. Except he's missing one of his front legs, so he doesn't get to move too well in a straight line. More like a wide circle he gets to travel in."

The man drew a wide circle in the air between them. Cal blinked.

"The longer it takes him to get across the road, the hotter the asphalt gets, so the faster he starts running, so the tighter the circle gets, so the longer it takes him all over again to get to where he's trying to go. He can see it alright the whole time, his eyes are working just fine, it's just his missing front leg that won't take him there directly, so around he goes, over and over."

The old man gave Cal a close look, eyebrows up, his eyes wide. They would have stood eye to eye once, but the collusion of time and gravity had drawn the old man's visage a foot or so closer to earth.

A withered ghost, Cal thought. Withering.

"It takes that old fella a good long time to clear the road, because of that missing leg. People coming by in their cars slow down for a better look. Some of them pull off the side of the road so as not to run him over. Some of them stop altogether just to see it, because it is a sight to see, him going round and round like that, faster and faster." He shook his head. "If tortoises could sweat, he'd be the first of his kind to do it."

The man reached out past Cal and grabbed a handful of napkins from the counter.

"You know tortoises don't sweat, right?"

"Yeah," Cal said, tentatively. "I know that."

"Sure you do. So now here's something else you can know. Crossing paths with a three-legged tortoise changes your life. You see him going round and round like that, and you stop what you're doing to watch, then you start it up again, but now you're in a whole different place you'd be in if you didn't do the stopping in the first place." He nodded that to Cal, then stood silent.

Cal stepped back half a step. He looked down at the full weathered length of the old man, then back up. "How did he loose his leg?" he heard himself ask.

"We can't ever know that," the old man answered, shaking his head. "What's gone is gone. The one thing we can know is that there's no more straight lines left for him to travel. Circles are all he's got coming. The best we can do is leave him to it." He stood motionless and stared at Cal, or past him. Or through him.

Cal blinked. Time slipped a joint. It felt like an enormous déjà vu had jumped up in front of him, or he had just fallen through a wall to the past. The old man and the diner surrounding him, the tinny music sifting the air, the ceiling fans spun in lazy circles out of sync, it all felt like a memory not exactly his.

"I . . . know this," Cal said, looking past the old man. "All of it."

"Of course you know it," the old man laughed. "You told it to me first. I'm standing here now to tell it back to you." He nodded his head at that, then turned away. He walked back to his table. He sat down, slid his chair in tight, took his burger up in his hands and took a bite, put the burger down, looked up again at the wall cover with posters and faded to gray.

Jimmie rustled up behind Cal and caught him off guard. "Six-fifty," he barked to the back of Cal's head.

"Jesus!" Cal said, spinning around.

"Well, hey," Jimmie said. He edged himself back a bit. "That ain't so much for a burger, fries and a coke, is it?"

Cal gave the big man a long look. "That's not what I Jesus'd about."

Jimmie gave him a longer look while those words worked their way around in his head. "Well, that's between you and Him then. Napkins?" He nodded toward the dispenser on the counter.

"Sure, napkins."

Jimmie folded a handful of napkins and wedged them down onto the tray.

Cal laid a ten-dollar bill down on the counter.

The burger was paper-wrapped and taped, the fries were boxed, and both were laid out on a gray cardboard tray. His soda sat off to one side in a plastic cup on the counter. Cal put the soda onto the tray and picked it all up to go.

Jimmie held his change out in the air. "Hey, whoa, whoa. Three-fifty back to you."

Cal put the tray down and pocketed the change. He picked up the tray again and turned to leave.

"Ketchup?" Jimmie asked. He held up a clutch of small plastic bags in his huge fist.

Cal stopped again. He turned around. "Yeah, ketchup."

Jimmie didn't move. Cal put the tray down and reached his hand out. Jimmie watched his hand shaking. He dropped the near-dozen ketchup bags into it.

"Thanks."

"Well, thanks back."

Cal picked up the tray to go.

"Straw?" Jimmie said.

Cal looked down at the tray, then back up at the man. "Yeah, sure. Straw."

Jimmie picked up a straw and held it out in front of him. Cal didn't move. Jimmie leaned forward and laid the straw down alongside the soda.

"Salt and pepper?" Jimmie said. He grabbed a handful of little black and white envelopes and held them up over the tray. He waited.

"I'm good here," Cal said.

Jimmie held the bags up a little higher. "I didn't put no salt on it."

Cal shook his head no. "I'm . . . good."

Jimmie watched the tray shaking in Cal's hands, the soda nearly spilling, the fries chattering in their box. "You don't look so good. What's wrong with you anyway, your hands shaking like that?"

They stared at one another a while.

Cal would have turned, he would have walked away from that question but there was nothing inside him calling him to leave or stay. There was no difference. He set the tray down on the counter. "I don't sleep," he said.

Jimmie watched him a moment, computing what he'd just heard. "You mean, like at all?"

"Yeah. Like at all."

Jimmie gave him a different kind of look. "That damn war do that to you?" He waited.

Cal shook his head. "Life," he said.

"Life?" The big man's forehead tightened. "What kind of life does that?"

Cal thought it over. "The kind of life I'm having."

Jimmie scratched at the side of his head. "Well I sure don't know about that." He stared back. He shook his head after a while. "What's that like then?"

"Like?"

"Never having no sleep. I can't even think on that. What's it like?"

Cal looked off at the room, once around at all the tables and all the people and he wondered why he was still standing there taking questions, but there he was still, and right now one place was about as good as any other or just as bad, so what the hell difference did it make.

He turned a tired look up toward Jimmie's greater face.

"It's like being inside one of those stores that sells nothing but TVs, and they're all turned on, and there's no leaving it."

Jimmie thought that over. One eyebrow went up. "If it's all sports, that ain't so bad."

"It's not sports."

The eyebrow went down. Jimmie felt tired just looking at him. He glanced away toward the front door.

"Well," he sighed. "I got some work coming in. You have yourself a day." He turned and rocked his way back inside the kitchen.

Cal stood there and glanced down at the food on the tray. There was nothing he saw there that moved him one way or the other in respect to hunger. He picked the tray up anyway and turned to leave.

A Trailways bus had just rolled to a stop outside. The big chrome door hissed open wide and a bucketful of people staggered out blinking like possums in the noonday glare. They stumbled en masse for the front door.

Cal quickened his pace to make it to the door before they all did. He passed the table with the little girl and her mom said, "Chin," and pointed and the little girl wiped away another spot of ketchup with her napkin. Cal gave her another wink and she gave him one back.

On either side of the front door were the plate glass windows all in a row.

Cal stepped behind the faded-looking man who dropped his fork just then and it clattered away across the floor and he slid his chair back in the aisle to fetch it. Cal spun around sideways to avoid tripping over him and his tray just missed the guy's head.

The old couple at the next table over turned their faces up in unison as he passed. Cal felt he was looking down into the roots of two old oak trees felled by a storm. The old woman spoke a slow something to him and she pointed ahead with a boney finger, her voice like gravel in a wooden barrel. The bus group was almost to the glass door. Two quick steps more and he'd be out.

Cal with his tray hit one of the plate glass windows at nearly a full run. He bounced from it like a trampoline and landed flat on his back. The soda shot straight from the cup and the fries scattered in a wide circle. The paper-wrapped burger rolled away across the floor. The sound of it was enough to grab everyone's attention; the whole of the room arrested now in a silent gawk. Outside the door the possum-people all froze still. Jimmie's face appeared at the service window and filled it out to its very edges.

Cal sat forward, his legs stretched out flat before him.

"Let me get you another soda, son," Jimmie called out from his window frame.

"That one over there's the door," the old root woman purred, pointing to it again with her boney finger. "I did that once myself," she said. She looked up at the plate glass window like it held a genuine threat. She cowered slightly, shook her head slowly and made a clucking sound. "My, my."

Her partner was on his hands and knees beneath the next table over, corralling the runaway burger.

Cal scraped up the mess of coke-soaked fries with the box they'd come in. He flattened out the fold in the tray and placed them all there. He got to his feet and set the tray down on a vacant table. He was dripping wet with soda.

"Looks alright from here." The old root-man stood before him with the still-wrapped burger in his hand, holding it up to the light, inspecting it all around like a nearsighted country doctor. Cal watched the old man's forehead crease, de-crease, re-crease. Like a skin accordion.

Jimmie appeared beside him like a sudden wall of flesh with a fresh soda in hand. "You want some new fries?" He was staring down at the dirty old ones.

"Thanks, ahh . . . no, thanks. I'm . . . good here," Cal managed. Everyone watched him.

Jimmie elbowed Cal in the shoulder and nearly knocked him off balance. "You ain't good now at all. Set yourself down some, and I'll get you some new fries."

"No, I, ah . . ."

Jimmie was already rocking himself sideways and heading back toward the kitchen. The radio went silent. The big man's shoes were busted open at the back seams and nearly hanging sideways off his feet. They scuffled across the floor as he went. Shhh-shhh, shhh-shhh . . . the only sound in the room.

Cal felt the weight of all those blanked faces staring at him. There was a density to it, the way a flat tire must feel to the road, or the road to it. His mind was glazing over.

The little girl caught his eye. She raised two ketchuppy fingers and gave him a little wave of goodbye.

"Right," Cal said.

He straightened himself up. He reached to his back pocket for his sunglasses and pulled them out. They were torqued to one side and flattened out, like a pair of small plastic spatulas. He slid them back in his pocket.

He picked up his tray and stepped out through the door into the middle of the Trailways crowd. They parted for him in two solemn lines like the Red Sea opening for Moses. He sported a coke stain in the shape of Texas down the front of his shirt. Cold and sticky.

The bus driver stood at the end of that line, shepherd of that traveling flock, in charge of moving them through time and space and they were doing neither right now and he wasn't happy. His eyes on Cal, his face bent to a scowl and his hands on his hips, "You walked right into the damn glass."

"No shit," Cal snapped. He gave the driver a hard look.

The driver gave him a hard one back.

Cal walked on past and dropped the tray with the food on it into a steel drum at the side of the parking lot. He turned and walked back to his truck and climbed inside. He slammed the door shut. He fumbled again with his broken glasses and gave up, and tossed them aside onto the seat. He turned the ignition key and the engine started. He looked out the windshield at all those faces staring back at him like he was some sort of exotic creature in a zoo.

"You all got nothing better to look at?" he yelled out through the side window.

Not a one of them moved or blinked.

On his windshield was a flyer wedged beneath the wiper blade, its corners lifting in the breeze. He turned the wipers on, reached around and caught it off the blade as it came up. He turned the wipers off.

It was an announcement for a country singer named Star Rose. She was smiling out from the photograph, her long cowgirl hair flowing down onto her cowgirl shirt. Singing her hit song, "I'm Not Your Daydream," the flyer said. He looked back at her face to see why not. The date at the bottom of the page was for a week ago.

He crumpled the flyer and tossed it aside on the seat. He turned the ignition key again and the starter motor squealed like a choked pig. His teeth clenched at the sound. The bus driver winced and shook his head like he just witnessed a grave sin. The bus crowd stood transfixed and motionless. The faded-looking man slipped through the door, then through the crowd, and stood like his own shadow in the noonday sun.

Cal shifted his truck into reverse and looked out through the rear window. He would just clear the back end of the bus. He floored the gas, spun his tires backwards off the gravel and out onto the asphalt.

A double-load semi roared by just then, Cal blindsided by the bus, the truck's horn blaring, its tires locked up and smoking blue and squealing towards the diner. Cal slammed on his brakes, the big truck just missed his tailgate. It fishtailed off across the road and onto the far shoulder where it raised a huge cloud of dust, then swung back onto the road with its engine revved and its clutch grinding, and it dragged that cloud of dust and its blasting horn with it down into the distance as it worked its way back up through the gears. It receded into the desert haze like a bad dream half-awoken from.

Cal leaned forward and dropped his head heavy against the steering wheel. He closed his eyes. He felt the hum of the engine against his skull, his heart pounding down inside his chest.

"Dammit," he said to no one. "Just . . . dammit."

He sat there like that.

He heard the passenger door click open. He felt his truck sink lower by a notch, tipping down to one side, then the sound of the door closing again, the latch clicking home.

He did nothing about it. His eyes shut tighter, his head turned sideways to the curve of the steering wheel and the engine vibrations humming up into his brain, filling it with white noise, his bottom teeth chattering up against his skull. Time like a pudding.

"Thanks."

A voice beside him in the cab, distant sounding, thin. The voice cleared itself with a small cough.

"Thanks . . . for the ride."

Alright, Cal thought. He could keep his eyes shut, he could wrap himself more in the shade of that small dark space, take a few measures of time aside and attend to their eventual passage, but the quiet of that inner world wouldn't last because it never did, and the chatter of its demise would evict him as always, then the questions would arise like they were rising right now, like a flood across a flood-hungry plain, and the . . .

Cal opened his eyes. He turned his head to his right.

The old man from the diner, the faded-looking man, was sitting in the passenger seat, quietly staring out through the windshield, nodding his head to some private rhythm.

Cal sat by and watched. Seconds drained away into minutes.

"What are you doing?" Cal finally said.

The old man turned his head. He said, "Patience," quietly. The word hung in the air a long time.

"Patience? What patience?"

"Whose patience," the old man said. He continued staring out the windshield.

Cal waited.

He dropped his hands from the steering wheel. "Look. Padre. I'm not giving out free rides here. That's not why I . . . I didn't stop here to give you a ride. Comprende?"

The old man took a long look at Cal.

"It's better this way."

He turned away and stared forward again.

Cal threw his hands up in the air. He looked away, not knowing where else to look. Out the windshield to the diner, to the crowd still clustered there and staring back. Out his side window to the dusty ass end of the bus and its diesel stink in his face and a ratty bumper sticker that read "Enjoy Life . . . Back Off!"

He reached in and pulled the key from the ignition and the truck fell silent, backed half out into a roadway that was just as silent.

"I'm not here to give you a ride," Cal said again. "Do you understand me? Hombre, do you understand?"

The old man pursed his lips. "What you're telling me, I understand."

"Well that's good then," Cal said. He waited. "That's real good," he said louder.

The old man nodded back. "Yeah. It is good." He settled back into his seat. "Understanding is a good thing."

The Trailways crowd settled itself in the front tables in twos and threes, turning their chairs around and staring out through the glass like so many fish in a tank.

"Jeez-us," Cal said to all of it. He turned again to face the old man. "You don't even know where I'm going here. You can't . . . you don't just jump up and get inside someone's truck like that, like there's some deal that's been made here, because I didn't make any deal. So you think you're all set for a ride, right now? I mean, dude, you're not all set for a ride right now. So what gives? What's up with you?"

The old man turned to face him again. He watched Cal, his eyes ancient and watery, but had nothing to say.

"So where is it you think you're going, huh?"

"Same way as you're going," the old man said.

Cal stared back. "You don't know where I'm going."

The old man nodded. He raised his hand and pointed a thin finger off to the left. "South," he said. "You're headed south. I'm headed south too. It's better this way."

"Better than what?"

No reaction from the old man. He just sat there.

"Hell, man. And goddammit too, you don't know it. You don't know where I'm going. And you're not going with me, either. And how the hell would you know it anyway, where I'm going?"

The old man watched him in silence, all the time in the world sitting beside him. He craned his neck and looked up the road to where the highway stretched south and the mountains rose up beyond. He twisted the other way and looked off into the desert. He settled his gaze on Cal.

"You look to be in a bit of a fix here. From what I'm seeing, I'd say you're running." He gave Cal a closer look. "Yeah, you're running from something."

Cal gave him a tight look and his words a few seconds of thought. "I got what I need right here with me. What the hell would I be running from?"

The old man laughed a little. "Doesn't much matter from what, does it? Running is running. Whatever it is, though, if you're out here, and you're running, south is the direction you'd be running. Yep. And right now, I'm sitting here with you. We might as well get going," He nodded over toward the highway. "South is that way." He pointed. "Right over there."

Cal tapped his key ring against the steering wheel.

He threw his arms up.

"Yeah, alright. I'm going south. South for a little ways. Then I'm heading off west."

The old man nodded back. "More south than west, I would say." He sat watching Cal a while, waiting for whatever might come next. Not much came. He turned away and stared out the front window.

"Fuck it anyway," Cal said, shaking his head. "You know that saying, old man? Fuck it anyway?"

"Yeah, I know it. It's a good saying. It has lots of uses. That's what makes it a good saying." He nodded his head wisely. "So fuck it anyway."

Cal looked away.

"Yeah. Fuck it anyway."

He put the key in the ignition. He started the truck. He backed into the roadway, shifted the truck into first, spun his tires and left a fat cloud of dust behind him.

He looked over at the old man as he shifted through his other gears. "I don't plan on talking much," he said. "Just so you know it." Wind buffeted his face from the open window.

The old man nodded back. "I didn't make plans to listen much."

Cal left the state road behind him. He rolled back onto the highway. He hit his speed, lit up a cigarette and smoked it down. The miles rolled past, rolled past.

When he looked aside again, the old man was dead asleep on the seat beside him.

7.

Eight years earlier.

Cal had his engineering degree behind him. Tucson was feeling empty and claustrophobic at the same time. He checked out the job markets in the region. He was leaning toward Santa Fe. He'd heard there were good times to be had in the Land of Enchantment. He watched the listings there for a place to live and answered an ad for a house to share:

> House to share, good street, 2 bedrooms,
> common living room, kitchen,
> big fridge, yard to party out back and garage.
> Call Billy.

He called and it was a good fit.

Billy was the kind of guy who felt familiar right from the handshake. Twenty-nine years old and working new home construction "for the right now."

"A good day's work for a good night's party," he answered to any question of what he did for a living. "Sun's out, guns out," he'd say. He was a big man all around, linebacker style, his personality blanket-like and warm in a linebacker sort of way. His was a complex mind, re-attired in Zen. Faded, comfortable Zen, like a worn-out denim jacket. He held a degree in physics and two others like it in math. He had the bud of a career once up in Los Alamos, but a year of days spent in the windowless labs and the god awful yawn of nightlife there found him rolling downhill from that holy mesa with barely a foot on the brake or a look back in the rear view mirror, unemployment be damned. He found solace in Santa Fe. He set aside a year to recalibrate his professional direction and took up a temporary job in construction to help him not think while he paid the bills. He was well into the second year of that recalibration when he placed the ad in the paper.

Cal moved in. Soon enough, he had landed an I.T. job with Angel Fire Communications, planning installations, troubleshooting, driving up and down the state in a company truck, with gas, motel, and all expenses paid. Room enough there for advancement.

Santa Fe felt like an open window to fortune and the big blue sky back then. As Billy put it, "The future has a presence here."

Cal could feel it in his bones.

He was home from work one Friday evening past seven, after a few days out on the road. He was primed for some partying. He showered, was half-dressed and still wet-headed with his face down inside the fridge searching for something remotely edible when Billy walked in through the kitchen door, singing.

Billy broke into a full-on grin when he saw Cal. He rattled a small paper bag he held up in his hand.

"Dude, I am so glad that you're here. I'll definitely be needing your help tonight." Billy had a whole range of looks that he could stage-manage, depending on the occasion. The one he staged just then was that of a devil mistakenly cast to play the part of an angel in a high school play. Cal had seen that look before. Here it was again.

"What's up?" Cal asked. He glanced down at the stiff slice of ham he'd just recovered from the bottom of the fridge. He put it back and closed the door.

Billy unrolled the paper sack and reached his hand in. He pulled out a wad of cash with a fat rubber band wrapped tight around it. He held it up in the air a moment, still and silent, then let it drop to the kitchen table for the dull wooden thump it made. "You hear that?" He picked it up and dropped it again. "What else makes a sound that sweet, huh? You try it."

Cal picked up the cash. He snapped the rubber band off, thumbed his way down through the bills. They were all twenties in the middle, a handful of fifties at one end, a few tens at the other. The bills all pretty weathered, nothing too crisp. Two inches thick, more or less. He held it to his nose and sniffed it.

Billy grinned wide. "I did the same damn thing. Must be some kind of animal reaction, huh? Smells just like money, right?"

"You look a little crazy right now, you know that?" Cal glanced back at the cash. "How much is here anyway? Where the hell did you get it?"

Billy smiled. "That's one dollar, Cal. Sure as I'm standing here in front of you, that's what you're holding right there."

Cal wondered about that in any direction it might wonder. "How so?" he finally said.

Billy took a half-step back. He put on his story telling face, a laconic, all-the-time-in-the-world kind of face.

"So. I walked into this convenience store on the other side of town, to buy myself a can of beer and a bag of nuts for the ride home. I had a buck something left over in change, all nickels and dimes and pennies and I don't want to be carrying it around. I don't like the feel of change in my pocket. Never did. Maybe I've got some kind of allergic reaction to it. You think there might be such a thing?"

Cal gave it some thought. "Numismataphobia?"

Billy stared. "No. I'm pretty sure I don't have that. So anyway, I buy myself one of those scratch card games with the change. Now that's the first time ever for me doing something like that, Cal. The odds of winning are right up there with getting hit by a frog in a blizzard. So I'm sitting back in the truck, and I scratch off that gray rubber shit with the edge of my key. The thing says two thousand bucks, three times in a row. I don't know what that means, so I read the thing over, it says Match Three. I flip it over and read the rules on the back, I read what all the prizes are. I check out the front again. It still says two thousand bucks, three times in a row. So I go back inside, I show it to the guy at the counter and say, 'What's up with this?' He takes a look at it, right off the bat he says, 'Two thousand bucks,' like I'm stupid and I'm keeping him from his work or something. He opens a drawer, counts out the money, snaps a rubber band around it, hands it over and says 'Enjoy.' Enjoy, right? Like I need his advice.

Billy started gyrating around the table in a loopy circle. "Oh sweet Friday night in a hard-drinking town . . ." His singing off-key by the usual half-dozen notes.

"Two thousand bucks!" Cal said.

Billy stopped his dancing. He shook his head, his grin tempered. "That's just one dollar you're holding there, Cal. A dollar in change, no less." The look on his face like a ticking clock attached to a stick of dynamite.

"Meaning?"

"Meaning I'll exercise my usual care tonight when it comes to the spending of that dollar."

Cal eyed him. He eyed the money. "There's a lot more here than a dollar, Bill." He wagged the wad back and forth like a fan. "Just checking in with you here. You know, that little thing called reality? A lot more than a dollar?"

Billy gave the bundle a closer look. "Well, you know what the real deal here is, with this reality? The real deal is, I've spent a whole lot more time with this thing than you have. Whole minutes of time by now, big fat minutes, with smiley faces on each one of them. And so it looks a bit different to me now, from that more advanced perspective." His eyes narrowed. "You well know me, Cal, and so you well know that I have always had a healthy respect for the greater sums of money to be had out there in the world. I am the responsible party, as they say. I work hard, I pay my bills. But different realities run by different rules. Now that's a proven fact. And in this particular reality, the one that we're standing in right now," he pointed around the room, "no matter how it might appear at first to the casual eye, a dollar is a still a dollar. You just have to see it that way first, then the rest of the rules fall into place. And the rules are the only thing that protects us from making mistakes."

Cal saw the kind of night they had in store. His smile widened. He held the cash up high, bowed his head down low. "God help us."

Billy nodded in agreement. "I'm sure he will, Cal, I'm sure he will. Good old God likes a night out on the town as much as the next guy. Why else would he have created Friday, then created cash, and then put the both of them in our hands at the same time? What's a mortal to do?"

"Ah . . . practice restraint?" Cal said, hearing the hopelessness of that suggestion as he spoke it.

Billy eyed him like a cat to a bird. He straightened his posture, he pulled on a Sunday-morning preacher face.

"Cal? Will you help me worship a magnanimous God here, on one of his best nights ever?" He dropped that face for a smirk. "Or would you rather pay a visit to the stiffs down at the Savings and Loan?"

Cal laughed. "Amen then, and so be it." He offered the stack of bills back to Billy.

"No way," Billy said, pulling his hands back. "You hold onto it for now. I don't trust me at all. I might do something rash."

He pulled a cold can of beer from the bag and cracked it open with a smile.

A few hours later, a few beers later, a new pair of cowboy boots each later, a couple orders of spare ribs and a fat pair of steaks tucked away with a dozen ideas downstream by then about which bars they should hit and the order in which they should hit them, they drove south out on Rt. 14 past Los Cerillos, walked in through the door of their fifth bar, paid their fifth cover charge that night, and stood square in the teeth of an excellent Friday night.

"Let's get us some tequilas," Billy said right off, pulling for the bar.

"Whoa, Billy," Cal said, in a manner of speaking. "Maybe we should slow things down a bit."

Billy checked out the scene around him. He nodded his head at what he was seeing.

"Cal . . . the way things are going right now, I don't think we're going to have to hit the brakes."

They downed a pair of Don Patrons. They stepped off to the side of the crowd with a beer each in hand.

"Prospecting," Billy yelled out against the din.

"What for?" Cal yelled back.

Billy nodded his head like the wisest man in the room.

"What we're looking for here, Cal," and he chose his words carefully, "is no less than the very heart of the night, that ultimate, extremely rare and golden moment. But first . . ." he held a finger up in the air, "what you have to understand first is this: it's not the time or the place or even the people in the place, that makes the moment golden, that transforms all of it from the ordinary, into the living, breathing, heart of the night. El ultimo momento, hombre."

"What the hell are you talking about, Billy?"

Billy nodded wisely again. He held his hand up like he was balancing something precious in his palm. Something round and difficult to hold onto.

"The Magic Spot, Cal. That's what I'm talking about here." He pointed to his empty hand. "The Magic Spot."

Cal looked down at the empty hand. "The Magic Spot. What is it, some kind of make-believe dog?"

Billy shook his head solemnly. "Oh the fun you poke. They laughed at Einstein too, you know. So you've never heard of the Magic Spot?"

"Not this particular one."

"Well, it exists, alright. The Magic Spot is . . . it's . . . well, let's just say, it's this diaphanous . . . thing."

"Diaphanous?"

"Yep. Way diaphanous."

"What's that even mean?"

"What? Diaphanous? It means . . . it means something that's almost not there."

Cal nodded. "Like . . . my bank account?"

"No. More like a . . . more like a negligee. A negligee on a second date. Yeah. Only it's better, because it's the Magic Spot." Billy gave it some more thought. "You might even call it an invisible, self-creating, party vibe. No, wait. That doesn't do it enough justice." He was trying to wrap his head around it. Cal waited through the wrapping.

"Hell, Cal. You know what the problem is? It's the more words you use, the further you get from the truth of it. So it's just the Magic Spot, that's what. And it floats. It floats down to earth from God's navel itself, I'll bet."

Cal nodded. "Like holy lint."

"Exactly. And that's probably just what it is. A small leftover piece of creation, all on its own, and it's down here looking for a place to land. But the thing is, it can only land in one place at a time, and just for a short time at that, because . . . well, because it's the Magic Spot. It has to keep moving, always, or it loses all its magic."

"Then it's just a spot."

Billy looked at Cal. "You know I'm not making this shit up, right? I mean really. How many times have you seen something like that happening for yourself, right there before your own eyes?"

Cal waved his hand aside. "Oh, like, plenty."

"That's what I'm saying. You're out partying somewhere, and one minute everything's hot, the place is jumping, and then the very next minute, the energy's gone, just drained away to somewhere else, and the whole vibe goes flat. Bam! Right?"

"So true," Cal said. "And sad."

"Sad it definitely is. Indefinitely sad."

"Why do you think that happens?"

"That's exactly what I've been trying to tell you. It's the nature of the beast we're talking about here. But anyway, here's what I'm thinking for tonight. I'm thinking, first . . . we find us the Magic Spot, to start with."

"How do we find it?"

"That might be the tricky part, right there."

"Because of the diaphanous?"

Billy nodded. "Because of the diaphanous. It's hard to hold onto diaphanous. That's what they say, anyway."

Cal gave him a curious look. "Who exactly are the *they*, anyway?"

"The they?" Billy thought it over. "Well. I'd say, it would have to be two or more people, right? And they'd have to be standing someplace else, where we're not."

"Why?"

"Well . . . because if we were standing with them, we'd be them, right, so that would make them us. But they can't be us and be *they* at the same time. So they have to be somewhere else, where we're not."

Cal nodded. "Point."

"Right. So . . . where the hell were we?"

"The tricky part. Finding the Magic Spot."

"Right, right. The tricky part. We'll get back to that. For now, let's just say that we do find it. So, there it is now, hovering right in front of us. The Magic Spot. And we'd have to stay real focused on it too. I mean, real focused."

"Like we are now?"

"Exactly. So here's what I'm thinking, Cal. Just for tonight. You ready?"

"Yep."

"Alright, here it is. Tonight . . . because God has already smiled mightily in our direction, so it just could be . . . that we could hold onto that Magic Spot, and stay right there with it when it picks up and moves on, and this could be the first time in history that it happens, Cal, but it might just be possible that, tonight, we can ride that Magic Spot, ride it like a wild beast, ride it like it's some insane kind of flying horse or something. Ride that Magic Spot all night long, ride it right into the flaming jaws of the dawn. Ka-bam!" Billy popped his hand open like an explosion in mid air. He smiled wide. He took a long pull off his beer.

Cal laughed out loud. "Wow. That is some seriously weird thinking there, buddy. Seriously . . . and weird."

"You think so?"

"Not really."

"Me too."

Cal tipped his own bottle back.

"What happens after the flaming dawn jaws?"

Billy shook his head sadly. "Sunlight breaks the connection, Cal. Shatters it completely. We can't do a thing about that. The Magic Spot cannot hold its own against the Glare. The Glare is a daytime thing, it's meant to kill any buzz. That's why people go to work in the morning. But the Magic Spot, that reigns the night supreme. Just, supreme."

Cal grinned. "Makes a whole bag of sense, right there." He sipped at his beer again. "You think it's here right now, this Magic Spot thingy? You seeing it bouncing around out there anywhere?"

They both turned a closer look around the room.

"No yet, Cal, not yet," Billy said, the voice of authority itself. "But it's on its way. It is definitely on its way." He checked his watch. "Yes sir, it's definitely on its way. C'mon. We best prepare."

They shoveled their way back into the crowd, shouldered their way up to the bar. Billy yelled an order for a couple of beers and got them. They squeezed off into the back room for a better look at the band.

The music was a hi-octane mix of country and rock, sleek and spare like a polished piece of chrome reflecting a big blue sky. Billy boogied his way out onto the dance floor and held court with a comic sort of dignity. Cal held the fort and minded their beers at a side table as big around as a dinner plate. He steadied it from time to time and stood back-to-back with the jostling crowd. He ended up with a side order of jalapeno nachos that a passing waitress dropped off without notice and had nothing more to say about, one way or the other.

It was past midnight and the crowd had thinned out just enough for them to think. Billy got a look on his face like a lit firecracker. They eased their way through the dance hall, past the bar crowd and out through the front door for some fresh air, then turned around and walked back in, prospecting all over again like the first time. They scanned the room through the bar smoke and their beer haze.

"Bingo, dingo," Billy said, pointing to the bar with a short nod of his head. "The ever-loving, big as day, heart of the night."

Cal followed his glance. At the bar sat a couple of great looking girls, just really great looking girls, in their mid or late-twenties, deep into their own spin of Friday night fun.

Billy had his best grin going. "You checking your doubts, dog?"

"At the door," Cal said. Because there it was right before him, the unmistakable, impossibly sweet, can't-take-your-eyes-off-it, forever-beating, heart of the night, in waiting.

"See how that one dollar works now?" Billy said. "Oh sweet vindication!"

They put their heads together as best they could, considering.

"Never fail," Billy had always maintained. "It remains of paramount importance in matters of love and attraction to admit no defeat."

Billy claimed authorship to a wide range of strategies for picking up women. "From A to Z, my friend. For every lock there's a key, right? Otherwise it wouldn't be called a lock."

So far, Cal had pretty much witnessed only one strategy from the man. Strategy A: "If the girl seems enough like all the other girls you've gotten lucky with, you walk up to her and do what you've always done . . . let the body talk and the eyes listen." But as odds would have it, just a few weeks ago, over a ripping-hot plate of chicken wings and four ice-cold Coronas at the bar, Billy had explained in relative depth the more subtle nuances of strategy B.

Strategy B: "If the girl looks like way more than you've ever gotten lucky with, then you're going to have to use your mind to sow the seeds of desire. And for that you're going to need a plow, to prepare the ground for the seed." He nodded. "Humor is the plow, Cal. Humor, is the plow."

They checked out the two girls sitting at the bar.

"Strategy B," Billy said.

"Absolutely," Cal said back. "I'm thinking, the girl on the left."

Billy smiled. "Thinking's a beautiful thing."

They both stood a while, thinking their thoughts.

"So," Cal said. "The Abigail?"

Billy nodded back. "The Abigail it is. You remember how it goes?"

"I've heard you run it a few."

"Hearing it is different than running it. You sure now?"

"Absolutely."

Billy clapped his hands. "Showtime then. Let's make it real." He peeled off a few twenties from the shrinking wad and handed them to Cal. "See you in five."

They walked up to the bar, separated by a few minutes. Cal positioned himself first, wedged in alongside the blonde on the left. He ordered a beer. He tried out some small talk in her direction, offered to buy her a drink. She declined with a fair smile.

Billy showed up a few minutes later on the right. He ordered a beer. He looked all around. He offered both girls a drink and stood declined as well. He looked away and sighed, seemed about to settle into his lesser fate. He made a big show of noticing Cal then, all-of-a-sudden-like, two seats over at the bar.

"Cal? Damn, is that you?" he said over the two girls' heads. "Cal?"

Cal glanced over, squinted his eyes, looked surprised. "Billy? Whoa, dude! Billy! Hey, man!" He reached out and they shook hands in a big way behind the girls' backs.

"What's it been, something like nine years now?"

"Yeah, something like that. Nine or ten."

They ran down a short list of how you been's, what you been up to's, how'd you end up here's, no shit's and I can't believe it's. The two girls edged themselves closer to the bar to be clear of the line of fire.

"So hey, you get back to Wisconsin much?" Billy asked.

"Hell no but thanks for asking. How about you?"

"No desire there, son. None at all. I don't even eat cheese anymore. But good lord, the memories, huh?"

Cal nodded back. 'Oh yeah." They each took a few pulls off their beers.

"Hey, speaking of memories, I still owe your pop some money."

"You owe my pop money?"

"Yeah. Some money, for some milk."

Cal laughed. "You owe my pop some money for some milk?"

One of the girls gave an odd look up in his direction.

Billy nodded. "Not a whole lot, but yeah. You remember that motorcycle I had, back in senior year?

Cal nodded. "Kawasaki?"

"Suzuki."

"Suzuki. Right. I remember you were always working on that damn thing. Not all too successfully, I recall."

"Hey, I got her running once or twice, Cal. A few days here and there, once or twice. Anyway, this one day, it was up towards the end of summer, and I had her out for a test run, and I was riding up on that long loop road north of town, out alongside the lake, then I went west up over the hills on my way back in."

"Past my pop's farm then."

"Yep. Right past it."

"Was that bike ever registered?"

"Not that I knew of. Anyway, it started raining pretty hard when I was coming down off the hills. The road got pretty slick back in there, but what the hell, I was laying the bike down hard into the turns anyway, side-slipping through some of them. I kept pushing it, you know? I just wanted to see if that bike could crack a hundred, maybe even a buck ten."

Cal's eyes went a little wide. The girl nearest him registered a pinch of interest.

"A hundred and ten on that bike? C'mon Billy. And on those roads up there, in the rain?"

Billy nodded solemnly. "Teenage hormones, my friend. Oh, the day! And back then a hundred was still a big number."

"It's not now?"

"Not as big as it was then. Anyway . . . there I was, coming down off that long straightaway through your pop's pastures."

"The Upper End."

"Right, the Upper End. Then the road starts curving like a son-of-a-bitch, back and forth like a drunk's nightmare, just past that old grove of apple trees."

"Pear trees."

"Pear trees?"

"That's what they were back then. Probably still are."

Billy shrugged. "Well. Anyway, the road dives into that hard right turn just before your pop's big barn and all his garages and tractors and stuff."

"Yeah, it does dive."

"Right. Well damned if I didn't forget about that hard right turn. Heat of the moment, right? The rush of adrenalin. I came off that last stretch and slowed down a bit, probably still going about forty, forty-five, but then right smack in front of me, there's that right turn. Whoa, huh? So I leaned the bike over, like way the hell over, and the tires were skipping loose on the pavement some, but I was holding onto it, Cal, I was holding it, trying like hell not to go into a full out slide. Rain's smacking me in the face, big fat drops, whack, whack, whack, so I'm half blind . . ."

"No helmet on you?"

"Never found one for free."

The two girls, the bartender, a dozen others at the fringes, all of them were leaning in, half-listening.

Billy took a few sips off his beer and set it down on the bar.

"So there I am, Cal. I'm halfway through that hard right turn and I got the bike laid down nearly sideways to the ground, and I'm doing it, Cal, son-of-a-bitch, I'm doing it. I'm holding on.

And I'm thinking, I might just live through this thing yet, but then all of a sudden, like the next capital fuck-me, there's one of your pop's prize-winning milkers in all her enormous bovine glory, standing right broadside in middle of the road."

"Abigail?"

"That's her name?"

"If we're talking the same cow here, yeah. Was her name, though. She's passed on."

"Well God rest her cow soul. How long do cows live?"

"Eight or nine years."

"That's it?" Billy frowned. "Guess they don't need to know so much. Anyway, there she was, old Abigail, standing right smack in the middle of the road, a whole wall of steak if ever there was one."

Cal shook his head. "She wasn't an eater."

"Why not?"

"She was a milker."

"So what do you do with her afterwards? Like after all the milking is done?"

"Dog chow."

"Ouch. Really?" Billy took a hit off his beer. "Well, so there she was anyway, broadside in the middle of the road . . ."

"The road gets pretty narrow there, one side to the other."

"Yeah, it sure does . . ."

"Abigail was always getting out too. She could lift up the gate latch with her teeth. Might take her a few tries, but she'd . . ."

"I guess blue ribbons will do that to you, right? Anyway, this day she was definitely out. And you know how there's that low stone wall running up the left side of the road?"

"Not so low, actually, but yeah."

"And then there's that huge old oak tree on the other side, right at the elbow of the turn."

"Yep. Howard's oak."

"Howard's oak? Howard's . . . oh, right, right . . . Howard's oak. Damn nearly forgot. Dude really hanged himself there?"

"That's what they were saying."

"All because of his . . ."

"We'll never know for sure now."

"Oh that's sad. So . . . anyway, there's Abigail now, standing right sideways in the middle of the road, there's the stone wall to one side and the tree to the other, and I'm still going about thirty clicks or so in the pouring rain." Billy shook his head at the thought of it. He sipped slowly at his beer. Cal sipped at his. A twelve-foot circle of relative silence held around them.

Cal counted off a few seconds.

"So what did you do, Billy?"

Billy counted off a few seconds of his own.

"There was only one thing I could do, and I had to do it real fast, too. I laid the bike down on its side, I mean all the way down on its side, and me along with it, and still going thirty too, and I slid right beneath your pop's prized cow, popped out the other side, righted the bike, opened up the throttle and off I went down the road, no second thoughts about it. It was a miracle, Cal, sliding right between her legs like that. Nothing but a pure, honest-to-god, miracle."

Billy tipped his beer all the way back and drained it. The two girls looked on, they each lifted their drinks, nearly empty now, each looking at the other. Half entertained, half confused.

Cal finished his beer, he placed the bottle down on the bar. He stared at Billy.

"So how is it that you owe my pop money for some milk?"

Billy nodded back. "Oh, right, right. I almost forgot." He nodded to the bartender for a beer. "Two more of these, okay?" The bartender didn't move.

Billy turned to face Cal. He shook his head from side to side.

"That was one hell of a moment, Cal, I can tell you that much. A moment like that can make a grown man's mouth go bone dry, to say nothing of a kid's. That being the case and all, and me being beneath your pop's prize cow at the time, well, hell, I reached up, grabbed a hold of one of her teats and gave myself a few squirts in the mouth before I popped out the other side. So I still owe your dad some money for the milk."

The crowd around them burst into one huge guffaw, peals of laughter rising. Cal and Billy directed their gazes right on cue toward the two girls. Cal had one of his best grins going, the kind of grin a court jester would have lived another day by. The kind of grin that would cause world peace if you could package it as a weapon.

"How about those drinks now?" he said.

The two girls cracked up. Big smiles all around.

Strategy B.

The girl nearest Cal had a rich smoky laugh, deep and straight from the heart. A few seconds and she was laughing with the best of them, so hard she had tears from her eyes.

As Cal thought about it later, it was right there inside the sound of her laughter that he completely fell in love with her. He couldn't stop thinking about her all that next week. And about how he'd lost that damn napkin she'd written her phone number on.

Fate placed them together again at a different bar the following Friday night. Another golden moment hovered, visible to any with the right eyes to see it. Cal walked up to her with a sure smile and remembered her name right off as Grace. She eased his foot from his mouth with a smile and said, "It's Gayle, Cal."

They had their first date a week later.

Billy eventually had a few dates with the girl's friend. Her name was Grace. The word grace was a difficult word to connect in any way to someone like Billy, so their dates connected that way. Cal and Gayle hit it off though. They had a season of good times, and then another one even better.

A few more months later and there were no more questions about it. Cal and Billy exchanged some farewell bear hugs and went out on a few pub-crawls to commemorate all their previous pub-crawls.

Cal and Gayle rented a small house a dozen blocks down the street from Billy's. Billy became a regular dinner guest then, pleased as hell that Cal had finally found them both a damn good cook.

And about a year later, he stood as their best man.

8.

Back up on the highway, roaring out of nowhere, his memory tethered and dragging behind him like a shadow. Wind gushed in through the open windows at ninety. Cal's eyes twitched, the roadway jumped before him, left right left. He rubbed the twitch away, he steadied the steering wheel in his other hand and a car raced past him in the fast lane with its horn blaring, a hard look from the driver and that extended middle finger.

Seemed the world's choice of salute to him lately, that extended middle finger.

He hadn't the energy to return it.

The old man was slumped asleep on the seat beside him, his head slung down on his chest, his own private version of the world blowing past.

Good for him, Cal thought. And just as well.

He caught up to his missed exit, his turn signal going for the last two minutes like a metronome keeping time or reminding him to. He barely slowed for the stop sign at the end of the ramp. He turned a hard right, pulled west down onto Route 52, his tires protesting.

The terrain there looked about the same as it did at the last exit, a déjà vu of nowhere. The Route 52 sign was a dull comfort, rusted and bent at the side of the road. He had circled it earlier on his map, and there it was now in living color, proof of something. Of distance gained. Of time lost.

A few hours more and he'd make it to the back roads, wind his way into the sand hills below the Black Mountains and loosen the grip of this desert highway madness, the tyranny of its flatness, the tunnel-like compression of its endless straight lines.

Parched road kill pressed flat beneath the dust-colored sun punctured the vacant miles. Fence posts advanced, retreated, repeated.

Destination.

From the word destiny: A place to which we are meant to go.

Meant to go, since when? The beginning?

He wondered what difference it would make when he got there. If there even could be a difference.

What would change enough to make a difference?

What could ever change enough?

He stared down the sameness of the miles pouring past him through the windshield.

Just to be clear again, to remember who he was, who he had once been. That would make a difference.

Who had he once been?

Who was he now, to be asking that question?

A marked man, like the doctor had said.

No. The doctor hadn't said that. The doctor said it was a death sentence. That's what the doctor had said. He said it was a death sentence.

That's what makes you a marked man, then. A death sentence makes you a marked man.

A marked man.

Who came up with that one? Did it happen that way once, that a mark was put on you and you were doomed?

He shook his head to the buzz of his thoughts.

But if you have no future coming, why waste time making the mark? Just get it over with.

"A marked man," Cal said. "Marked man, driving south."

So long in coming, this final drive. Prelude to an ending. The end of something. An escape, maybe.

He looked into the rear view mirror. He saw his own eyes there, looking back.

Escape.

The word fell apart right there. What could ever be escaped? Gravity?

He said the word aloud.

He looked aside at the old man asleep beside him.

"Did you escape anything yet, old man? Or do you still need more time?"

Silence for his answer.

He shook his head at his questions. His endless questions.

"Gravity," he said again, louder.

Relentless Mother-hugger, Gayle had called it.

"Goddamn gravity!" he yelled out the window, picking up speed. The old man didn't budge.

9.

They sat at the edge of a sheer cliff in the Chiracahuas, their legs dangling over a thousand-foot drop.

Gayle rolled a round stone the size of a walnut in circles in the hollow of her palm. She hummed a little tune absently. She reached her hand over the edge of the cliff and tipped it to one side. The stone fell free. They watched as it sped through the air, diving silently for the deeper realms of earth, shrinking away to a speck.

"I accept," she whispered softly.

Cal looked up from the drop. "You accept what?"

"Not me," she said. "The stone. The earth has been calling to it for ages, pulling at it incessantly, and the stone just now said, 'I accept.'"

Cal looked over the edge again. "Gravity helped."

Gayle shook her head at that. "I've never liked the word gravity much. Way too serious for the job description, don't you think? I mean, c'mon. GRA-VI-TY." She pronounced each syllable like it was cast in iron.

She reached behind her, searching through some of the stones there, and found one that suited her.

"Watch closely, young Calawishus." A smile at play on her lips. She held up the stone.

"See its shape, its form. Its presence. From one moment to the next, it's here. Yep. Still here. Oh look, still here. See? It's an entity embedded in time. It's reinventing itself every second."

She let it roll away. "Uh oh, there it goes." They watched it tumble and disappear, swallowed by the measure of sky beneath it.

"Looks to me like it needed to get someplace else, and in a hurry, too. That was the dance of reunion between the stone and her mother. I removed my hand from between them and voilà! The race to embrace. Maybe old Mama Earth even rises up to meet the stone halfway but that's something we just can't see, because if we did it would totally freak us out. Either way, I'd say there's a major two-way attraction going on there, way too primal to be contained by the word gravity. That word just kills all the magic."

She thought for a minute. "The grave has gravity. That's a pretty final event. The gravity of the grave. It totally sucks. And it's permanent too, unless you're a vampire."

She held her arms out wide. "But not this." She patted at the ground beneath them. "This is playtime. This is a dance here. It's flirtation. It's just sweet Mother Earth holding her babies, being Mama, forever calling each and every one of us home. Hauling all of creation back to her immense burgeoning bosom."

"Burgeoning bosom," Cal said with a smile. He sat a while with the idea, staring into space.

He looked back at Gayle. "So what would you rename it if you could, this attraction formerly known as gravity?"

Gayle closed her eyes in thought, a smile at the corners of her mouth. She opened her eyes, reached out and grabbed Cal's head and pulled it in tight, hugging it close like a captured melon. She whispered her answer in his ear.

"Relentless Mother-hugger."

The spin of days with her, the memories as endless as time, all falling away.

Lunch by an oasis of mountain-caught rainwater tumbling down as cold as ice across heat-cracked rocks, to disappear as suddenly in the desert sand. Afternoon naps beneath the shade of an unlikely tree clutched beside a crystal stream in a hidden side canyon, a golden eagle wheeling above in the thermals, rising to a speck in the vast blue, then gone.

"All the beauty you can eat," Gayle would say.

A red rock canyon at sunset, a sudden desert flower in full bloom, the patterns that the wind would draw in the sand or a single cloud racing through an empty sky like a whisper against the blue.

"All the beauty you can eat," she would say.

A weeklong hike into the Superstitions, east of Phoenix, Peralta Canyon yawning wide, flashing its red hoodoo teeth and swallowing them whole. The high desert trails shimmering in the heat, the bandit-like saguaros up in arms. Silver-spiked cactus mobbed in frost green carpets across the bowls of hot brown mountains, mountains so old they might rise up each one of them and speak of creation first hand.

There was a sign at the trailhead parking lot bearing a long list of official precautions: warnings about snakes and scorpions and Gila monsters, about the sharpness of sawgrass, about magnetic anomalies and the need to drink plenty of water to avoid sunstroke. Warnings about leaving visible valuables behind in your car. Then a final line set off by itself and delivered in fine bureaucratic English:

> Encounters here with nude hikers common
> due to excessive heat not to be encouraged.

Cal read it over and let out a laugh. "Why the fuck not?"

Gayle came over and read it and she laughed out loud.

"Fuck the why not, and thanks for the suggestion."

They stripped off all but their hats, socks and shoes after the first mile, "due to excessive heat not to be encouraged." By day's end they'd forgotten their nakedness, like Adam and Eve in an oven.

Gayle was possessed of a sixth sense of sorts, a focus that sharpened whenever she was in the wilderness. She could find the secret places, the hidden things of beauty or utility. She claimed that there were invisible strings that connected her to the small treasures of creation.

"Rewards for those with the eyes to see them," she told Cal.

They cleared the rim of the first canyon and stood a while in the breeze at the high pass. They scrambled down into the bowl of the next. At a dusty trail junction they dropped their packs for a lunchtime break. They tucked their near-naked selves under the shade of an unlikely tree, out from under the glare of a sun grown madly hot. Their plan was to cover another five miles or so before sunset, find a campsite with a good view and call it a day.

Cal broke out a couple of sandwiches and an apple to slice that had stayed cool in the deep of the backpack. Gayle stopped him with her hand on his.

"Un momento, niño." She looked over the terrain, scanning it with her personal radar. "Over there."

Cal looked to where she pointed.

"See it? Right down there." She pointed out a thin passage through the thorny scrub and prickly pear.

"Where?" Cal said, tired enough of moving. He had his pack off and the slight coolness of the tree's shade had already claimed him.

"Just down there," Gayle said. And with that she had her pack half-slung again and was walking away down the faint path.

Cal sighed. He watched her as she went. Her legs, muscular as they were, tucked into her oversized hiking boots and big socks, and the rest of her naked as day and deep-tanned beneath her wide-brimmed hat, springing now like a deer down through the woods to her new secret spot.

The sexiest thing he'd ever laid eyes on.

He stowed the apple and the sandwiches away, refolded his knife and gathered up his gear. He wiped sweat from his brow with a bandana that was dry again in seconds. He stood and pulled his pack on.

She was nowhere to be seen.

"Gayle?"

"Here. " Her voice a good distance ahead.

He followed her tracks into a shallow ravine that was hidden just seconds ago in the flat expanse of the canyon bottom.

"Where?"

"Here."

He was getting closer.

Another few dips and ducks through the spiky brush and there she was, already out of her pack and boots. Her hat was still on. She stood in a small clearing. A single large boulder was nestled off to one side within an apron of bright green grass. A small stream flowed beside it. The water upstream bubbled out from a crack in the sandstone and down over the lip of a flat rock. It dropped about two feet to a small pool tucked beneath the shade of a dwarf cottonwood, all of it looking like a miniature Hollywood set built for an elf movie. Ten feet further downstream, the water vanished into the desert sand.

Cal dropped his pack on the spot. "Damn, woman."

Gayle edged her sweat-dusted body into the pool. It was deeper than it looked, so crystal clear, and colder than that cold version of hell. She made short puffing sounds for every inch of skin that sank beneath the surface. The water came up to her breasts. She tossed her hat aside and lay back to soak her head.

Cal held his arms out to the scene. "How on earth did you know this was here?"

Gayle laughed and cupped handfuls of water to her face. "It's an illusion, sugar cube. A desert mirage. I'm just more gullible than you are." She filled her mouth and squirted water toward him. "You should pretend to get your skinny ass in here, Bones."

Cal got his skinny ass in there and the same puffing sounds came from him now as he inched himself under the water's surface.

"Oh . . . God." Chanting away, the both of them, like celebrants at their altar of choice. The water was cold enough to give them a headache, the sun hot enough to make them not care.

Cal hugged her close. He gave the top of her head a kiss.

"We have to never stop doing this."

"We haven't even started yet," she said. Her hands spoke more.

They climbed from the pool skin-sharpened, and made taut love on the small lawn, halfway beneath the shade of the little tree, four feet dangling in the cold stream.

"Ohhh . . ." Gayle said when they had finished, her breath so short she could barely speak. "I nearly . . . saw God . . . that time."

Cal's face was inches from hers. "Well I sure caught sight of her. One of her eyes was bluer than the other."

Kisses delivered. Kisses received. They drifted off to sleep.

"There was a mountain, once."

Gayle was first to float back from their after-love nap. She yawned, she stretched her arms up over her head. "A mountain named for heaven."

Cal floated awake beside her. He yawned. He pulled Gayle tighter to his side. They lay naked on the grass, looking up through the branches of the little tree to the sky. He dropped one of his feet back into the cool pool.

"A mountain . . . named for heaven." He yawned again. "Sounds nice. Where is it?"

"Down near the border of Mexico somewhere," she said. "No one knows for sure anymore. It's been lost."

"A mountain's been lost?"

"Mmm . . . more like forgotten. Misfiled in time. It was first named by the Spanish, back in the 1500's . . . El Punto del Cielo."

"The point of . . . the ceiling?" Cal asked.

Gayle laughed. "Close, Blankito. Bigger ceiling, maybe. Cielo is heaven. El Punto del Cielo means the Point of Heaven."

Cal nodded. "Did you just call me Blankito?"

"Si."

"And that would be, what? A small blanket?"

She shook her head. "I'm thinking more, a blank canvas. An absolutely virgin canvas upon which I'd just love to paint." She gave him a little squeeze. "My little Blankito."

"Hmm."

"Figuratively speaking, that is. Is that okay?"

"I'm defenseless."

"Mmm. But you still like it, right?""

"Absolutely. So. This lost mountain. How did it get lost?"

"When the area became U.S. territory back in the 1850's, a lot of the Spanish place names were dropped. It's called something else now."

Cal reached over and cupped one of Gayle's breasts. It fit perfectly in his hand. "The Breast of Heaven."

She smiled. "I doubt the U.S. government would name a mountain that."

"I wasn't referring to the government. Or to the mountain."

"Sweet man."

"Oh, and look! There are two of them."

"Purr." Gayle arched her back and stretched out beside him like a kitten.

Cal sat up and pulled their boots closer. He propped them together and folded some t-shirts over the them, made them into a pair of headrests. They settled back.

"Why'd the Spanish name it that?" he asked. "The Point of Heaven. It's a strong image."

Gayle nodded. "Maybe they thought they'd find heaven when they got up there. Or thought they could make it into one, if it wasn't already that way. You know, with a little bit of work."

Cal laughed at that. "Sounds more like you than them."

"What does?"

"Thinking they could make it into heaven with a little bit of work. Is that what all artists do when they get somewhere? Start rearranging things?"

Gayle smiled. "Well, I can't speak for all of them, but . . . yeah, probably. Tidy things up a bit, you know? Customize it. One man's heaven is another man's . . . blank canvas."

Cal nodded. "Sounds about right. So this lost mountain, this Point of Heaven . . . how did you find out about it, if it was lost all that time?"

"Oh, we heard about it back in grade school. Like fifth or sixth grade. There were just bits and pieces of different stories floating around, like some kind of legend we started talking about and all got hooked on. The main story went that the Conquistadors came riding up from Mexico, overrunning the whole place, looking for gold everywhere, all the standard rape and pillage scenes, history as usual, right? So the natives in this one area pointed them up to this mountain and told them that there was a ton of gold up there; so much gold that it was just sifting in the wind, all the gold they would ever need. So the Conquistadors got all jacked up and ran up there and scoured the whole mountaintop, looking everywhere, but they didn't find any gold. Uh-oh, right? So they came back down and they were pissed. They grabbed some of the natives and dragged them up to the mountaintop and said, "Where's the goddamn gold?" and the natives smiled and pointed all around them and said, "The gold is everywhere here. It is everywhere you look." The Conquistadors didn't think that was too funny, so they shoved the natives over the edge. Then they went back down to the village and lined everyone up and asked that question again, "Where's the goddamn gold?" but they just got the same answer, that the gold was everywhere on the mountain, so much of it that it was blowing in the wind. So they rubbed the natives out. A little anger management problem? Never piss off a guy with a sword.

"Then the Spanish learned later that the natives' word for gold, and their word for wisdom, was the same word, the same word for both things, so it could be used either way. All that time, the natives thought the Spanish were asking them for wisdom, and that's why they kept pointing them up to their sacred mountain."

"Ouch."

"Yeah, big ouch, huh? So that's how the story went. And then there were some other stories about old time prospectors disappearing up there, getting lost for years and then returning like it was a few days later, like a real Land of the Lost kind of place. And few stories about the ghosts of those poor Indians still wandering around up there, looking for their lost families.

"We all talked about finding that mountain, about rediscovering it by figuring out what it was renamed. We searched through all the maps in the library. We tried hunting down some of the older maps, the Spanish ones that might show us where it used to be. Anything for a clue. It was like a quest for a while. A magical quest."

She wiggled herself a closer fit to Cal's body. "For a few years, anyway. I outgrew it. I started chasing boys instead. Boys that mostly ran away."

Cal smiled. "You caught one."

"Yeah. I sure did." She gave him a little tug.

"So what did you all think you'd find up there, if you ever found it?"

Gayle smiled. "Oh, gold for sure, right? Just tons of gold. The boys mostly thought that, though. They figured the Spaniards must have just missed it somehow, and it was all still up there, just waiting to be found."

"What was the draw for you? I can't see a twelve-year-old you lusting for gold."

"No." She thought a minute. "I guess I thought there'd be more to it than that. More than just the gold. I liked the wisdom angle a lot. And if there was a place on earth that actually *was* the Point of Heaven, it would have to be a place of magic too, right? A place where you could think of something, or dream up something, anything at all, and it would just be that way, instantly. Oh, the blind faith of youth, huh? The simplicity of it all, back then. Like a magic carpet ride, wasn't it?"

Cal nodded. "Then the Easter Bunny dies, and we all grow old."

Gayle laughed. "Speak for yourself. My bunny never died."

She thought for a while.

"It *would* be amazing though, wouldn't it? If there was really a place like that on earth, an actual piece of heaven."

Cal shrugged. "There's always Las Vegas."

Gayle gave him a short poke in the ribs. "Fools rush in . . ."

He gave her idea more thought. "So how do you think that would actually work, then?"

"How would what work?"

"Having a heaven on earth like that, an actual place, up on a mountaintop somewhere. So it's a heaven that you didn't have to die first to get into. It would be a heaven that you could just hike up into with all your stuff, you know, the pack on your back, your feet hurting, all the rest of you sweaty and tired and thirsty. Warts and all, right? Then suddenly you walk in through this nice big gate and there you are. Heaven."

Gayle watched him a moment. She shook her head. "There's not going to be a gate."

"No gate?"

"No way. Why would there be a gate? If there's a gate, then there has to be a fence too, right, because that's what gates are attached to. You think heaven needs a fence, like it's some kind of prison or something, keeping everyone locked in?"

"Not locked in. Locked out. A fence to keep all the others guys out. The losers."

Gayle blinked. "A fence to keep the losers out? Cal, what are you talking about? I thought we were talking about heaven. How can it be heaven if it keeps anyone out?"

"But what about the guys that usually go to hell?"

Gayle laughed and shook her head. "That's their choice. But if we're talking about heaven here, heaven has to be all-inclusive. That's what makes it heaven in the first place. Why would it need a gate? Think it all the way through." She waited.

Cal looked unsure. "I've always had this image of heaven with the big pearly gates right out in front. The great big pearly gates."

"Hmm. You have to ask yourself where an image like that came from in the first place. From some country song you heard once, maybe?"

Cal shrugged. "Maybe."

"Jeez, Cal." She sat halfway up. "You just can't believe everything you hear in a country song. If all of what they said in country songs were true, exactly half the men out there at any one time would be heart-broken, driving away in their pickup trucks with their dog by their side, while the other half were out dancing and drinking it up with the first half's cheating girlfriends. So where's that leave you?"

"Mmm. Well, I've got the pickup truck. But no dog yet."

"But you've still got the girlfriend, duh? And I'm not the cheating kind, either." She nodded. "So what did we just learn here?"

Cal shrugged.

Gayle shook her head. "You still think there are going to be pearly gates up there, don't you. Alright, let's run this thing through. Let's say . . . uh-oh, bummer . . . you just died. No big deal though, we all die. So . . . now you're sitting there, way up in heaven, and you're happy, you're beatific, you're content, you're admiring your new halo, you're listening to all the nice angel music, and there's even some little wings starting to sprout out the middle of your back. Then, all of a sudden, this messenger angel appears, and he hands you a telegram, and the telegram says that three of your best friends won't be making it. That's right, three of your all-time, very best, lifelong friends. They just won't be making it into heaven. 'Sorry, sir,' the angel says. 'Seems there's a slight problem with their paperwork. Some things they got completely wrong, plus a few incompletes on the morality side, and so, well . . .' Hmm. And so now you realize, Cal, right then and there, as you're sitting up in heaven and everything's perfect, that you're never going to see these three friends again. Never, ever, again. That's three of your very best lifelong friends . . . you're never, ever, going to see them again." She watched his face. "How happy are you now for all eternity?"

Cal tipped his head to the side. "I never saw it that way."

"So there you are. Heaven *can't* be exclusive, it kills the whole buzz. And if it's not exclusive, then there's no need for a fence, and if there's no fence, then there's not going to be a gate, because a gate without a fence makes no sense. So heaven is all-inclusive, by definition. It's actually so inclusive, it makes inclusive the new exclusive. Oh yeah!"

Cal laughed at her lunacy.

He gave the idea some more thought.

"So how would you know it, when you actually got there? I mean, if you didn't have to go through a gate, or jump a fence or something, how would you know you were in heaven? Where's the transition happen?"

Gayle thought about that. "Maybe you wouldn't know it at first. Maybe you'd just be walking along, and it would seem like any other place at first, but then, slowly, everything would start to work out."

"Work out?"

"Yeah, work out. Get better. Everything that could get better would be better, and you would feel it. You'd feel it first down in the soles of your feet, and then that feeling would rise up, rise up like a wild fire, rise up and blast out the top of your head, and then you wouldn't even remember a time when you felt any other way but perfect. You would just feel perfect. Just plain perfect. And you would know it for sure then, that you were in heaven."

She lay back down beside him.

"But eventually, you'd even forget that you were in heaven, because it would feel so perfect, you wouldn't want to remember the part about not being there yet. So you'd still be in heaven, but you wouldn't know it anymore because you'd have nothing else to compare it to. It would totally be perfect but it would feel just the same as it does right now." She looked aside at him. "Don't you think?"

Cal grinned. "I do."

Time drifted past like sunlight.

"I bet you we could find it," Gayle said after a while. "I mean for real, Cal, you and me, if we both looked for it, just really looked for it, inside and out, feet to the ground, soul to the world, we would find it, we'd find El Punto del Cielo. The Point of Heaven. Oh yeah. We'd be the ones to find it."

Cal nodded. He leaned over her and brushed her hair aside. He kissed her face all around.

They watched the rest of that day's sky pass overhead through the canopy of the little tree. They spied a tiny lizard, a black and yellow striped fellow with red footpads, inching its way along the top side of the twisted branches, peeking its head out over the edge every few seconds like a wandering game of hide and seek.

They tried guessing where it would show its little face next.

10.

Cal's low fuel light blinked on.

He was driving the edge of the desert, the road skirting a fractured wall of mountains rising high to the right, with sand hills rolling off into the distance to his left. He couldn't see much of what lay ahead for him. He slowed his speed. He figured to get another ten miles or so on reserve, hoping for a station soon. He knew there was nothing behind him for twenty.

He made it twelve.

The truck rolled to a stop on the gravel shoulder alongside a running wire fence that hadn't held anything back for fifty years. The engine ticked down like a spastic clock and died with a final cough. A dry silence rolled in seconds later.

Cal turned off the ignition.

The old man popped his eyes open to the sudden stillness. He looked off into the wider nothing surrounding them, a land as empty as the sky. Two cinder cones rose up in the eastern distance like a pair of earthen teats sucked dry by the sun. He stared there a moment, blinking, then looked across at Cal. "Thanks for the ride, then." He pushed his door open to leave.

"Hey, whoa, old man," Cal said. "I didn't stop here to let you out. I just ran out of gas, so . . . that's what we're doing here."

The old man paused. He looked out at the terrain again.

"I just ran out of gas," Cal said.

The old man tipped his head. "You already said it. So I'll say thanks for the ride again." He slid off the seat onto the ground. He shook his legs awake. He rubbed his eyes. He closed the truck door softly, the latch clicked home. He started walking toward the wire fence.

"Where are you going?" Cal said through the open window. He swung his door wide, stepped outside and walked to the front of the truck, the old man still walking away.

"There's nothing out there."

The old man stopped at the fence, bent the wire lower where it already sagged and swung one leg over, then the other. He stood on the other side and watched Cal in silence.

"There's nothing out there," Cal said again, less sure of it than the first time. He looked around in a half circle.

The old man pursed his lips. "If that were true, you wouldn't be here." He glanced off into the folding distance. "And neither would I." He stared at the two cinder cones. He held his hand up at arm's length in that direction and squinted his eyes like he would figure the measure of distance between them. He dropped his hand back to his side. "We sort of make it up as we go along, don't you think? All of this." He held Cal's eyes a moment. He tipped his head west. "Right now, I got some making up to do of my own. I'll leave you to yours." He turned and started walking away.

Cal watched him go. "Hey!" he called after him. "Hey! Do you know if there's a gas station around here? Somewhere? Anywhere?"

The old man stopped walking. He turned around, he took a look up the road. He nodded his head a bit. "There should be." He turned again and walked away.

Cal watched him cross that dry roll of scrub and dunes until he was no more than a wandering dot among the scatter of mesquite bushes. Then the dot itself disappeared and there was nothing more to watch.

Cal looked down the road in either direction. He stood silent by the truck and waited. "There should be."

He hadn't seen more than half a dozen cars in the past half hour. None were coming his way right now.

He walked up the road for five minutes. At the top of the next rise there was another view, slightly wider, more or less of nothing. Time itself could have fallen down sideways in that road and hindered no one's progress.

He turned and walked back to his pickup.

He climbed up into the seat and shut the door behind him, the windows opened wide to a silence so adamant he could hear his own heartbeat shuffling to get out of the way. He looked off into the scrub hills where the old man had vanished. Twenty minutes had passed, more or less. There was no sign of life anywhere. He looked for the spot where the old man had bent the fence low but there was no sign of that either. The whole thing now seemed more like some vagrant thought blowing through than an actual memory.

Cal looked to the seat beside him. His sunglasses were lying where he'd thrown them, the crumpled flyer for the singer that was nobody's daydream lying beside them. He stared out the windshield at the empty expanse.

He heard a dull rush of sound, like a fast wind rising on the road. A black sedan rolled past him at sixty and rocked the truck with its back draft. "Dammit." He opened his door and jumped out, waved his arms like a madman. "Hey!" No brake lights showed. "Hey!!" The car topped the next rise and was gone.

Two hours and three more cars passed by.

The sun slipped lower toward the mountains and the colors of the day shifted; the stagger of fence posts with their shadows longer than they were tall; the tufts of witch grass bent over in the emptying wind, drawing bulls-eye circles around themselves in the sand.

Cal stood by the side of his truck with his left elbow up on the hood, his right thumb in the air for the fourth time and the last smile on his face that he might have owned for the car advancing toward him.

A young kid picked him up in a plastered old station wagon that made more noise than one car. The kid was just out of high school, one way or the other.

"Out of gas?" The kid coughed into the road dust rising up around them.

"More ways than you could count," Cal coughed back.

"Shit happens. Come on, then."

Cal opened the door and got inside. The kid floored the gas pedal, the engine thundered up and the car pulled back onto the road like an overloaded motorboat.

"Gas station's another twenty miles down the road, if you was wondering," the kid yelled over the engine noise. "Yeah. Some houses there too, trailers mostly, convenience store across the road from the station, convenient for what I couldn't tell you."

Cal stared straight ahead.

"The name's Patch," the kid offered.

The car had no windshield. Their hair blew straight back as they got their speed up.

The kid shrugged.

"Well, what I can tell you is this: it's not just you and your truck and yourself that's totally fucked here."

Cal gave him a short look.

"That supposed to make me feel better?"

The kid shrugged again.

"What difference would it make if it did?"

Cal looked out the side window. Fence posts ticked by.

"You know those old service stations you come on sometimes?" the kid said. "Out in the middle of nowhere, surrounded by the wrecks of burnt-out cars, with most of them taken apart and left for dead? Pools of oil and mud and nuts and bolts everywhere you step?" He looked across at Cal. "Well, here's what. You substitute all them cars with planets. You got that? Planets instead of cars, all of them laying around in the dirt outside some fucked up garage, all of them rusted out the same and just as broken." He nodded. "Earth is one of them planets then, right now, this minute, tipped over on its side like that and leaking shit out all over the ground." The kid spit out of his window. He shook his head. "So you can know just one thing for sure from what all you're seeing, and that's that the mechanic in charge is a fuckin'

fuckin' dim-wit." He grinned over at Cal. "I sure don't know how it got to be that way, but here it is, so there you go. Where was you headed to, when you ran out of gas from the getting?"

Cal nodded to his right. "Up into the Black Mountains."

The kid looked past him in that direction. He shook his head. "Ain't no driving roads up there, Slim."

"I'm hiking in."

The kid's eyes narrowed. "I ain't heard of that one yet. For real? Hiking?" He looked over at Cal. "You ain't prospecting for gold, are you? Because I can tell you straight out, it's been done and done again, and there ain't nothing left up there to find that don't find you first with the first name of trouble." The kid spit out his window again. "You running from the law?" He had the thin slice of a grin going.

"Not yet."

"What's your reason then?"

"I told you what. I'm hiking up."

"Right, right. You're hiking up. That's what I heard too." The kid nodded absently. "That's some kind of death wish you got going on?"

Cal gave the kid a short look.

The kid's grin widened. "Because a man would need some kind of death wish going on, to want to take a hike up there. Either that, or be just plain walk-into-walls stupid."

Cal half-nodded back. "You saying I'm stupid?"

The kid let out a laugh. "Oh that's good, coming from the guy who just dry-gassed his truck out in the middle of sunny bum-fuck nowhere. You want the first answer that comes to mind?"

Cal gave him a cold stare. "Look, I'll take the ride from you since you offered it, but if you're going to bust my balls, I'll just get out here."

The kid smiled like a twelve-year-old.

"That'd be even stupider."

"Fuck you," Cal said. He reached for the door and cracked it open.

"Whoa, whoa, no need for that, friend." The kid slowed down a bit. "I ain't looking to bust your balls for real. I'm just throwing a bunch of words out there." He nodded out to the desert. "Something to fill in the blanks, is all. Having some laughs. Got to go with the flow, right? Like water off a duck's back. No problemo there."

"Yeah. Sure."

About a mile blew past them with its dust trailing like a veil.

"Hell, I wonder if that even happens, for real," the kid said. "You ever seen that happen yourself?"

"Seen what?"

"Water off a duck's back."

Cal shook his head no.

"Yeah, me neither. I don't even know what it means. So what the fuck's with that, then? I ain't going to say it no more." He licked his finger, made an X in the air. He drove on.

"Hey. How's a duck's quack?"

"What?"

The kid raised his voice. "I said how's a duck's quack?" He laughed and slapped at the steering wheel.

Cal gave him a confused look. "I don't understand."

"You don't understand a duck's quack?"

"I don't understand the question."

The kid's face went straight. He gave Cal a long look. "That's because I wasn't asking you a question for real. Jeezus, man."

Cal drew a blank. "What were you asking me?"

The kid shook his head. "I wasn't asking you nothing. It was a joke. You know, like, knock-knock."

Cal looked out through the missing windshield.

"So?"

"So what?"

"So who's there?"

"What's that?"

"I said, who's there?"

The kid frowned. He looked out his side window. "Fuck if I know," he said under his breath.

They rounded another bend and topped a long rise. Taller mountains loomed darker to the right.

The kid nodded in that direction. "That's Apache territory you're seeing up there right now. Yessir. Same as it was in the long ago."

Cal looked it over as it rolled past.

"I got no issue with Indians."

The kid laughed. "Yeah. I had this uncle once, he went off salmon fishing one summer, up in the Yukon, said he had no issue with bears."

Cal nodded absently.

"His ass was never heard from again. What a dumb-fuck." He looked over at Cal a few seconds. "I wonder if he tasted like a dumb-fuck. Right? These two big old bears sitting down by a stream, licking their chops, and one bear looks up and says to the other, "Tastes a bit like dumb-fuck, doesn't it?" The kid laughed. "That nuts, right?"

Cal nodded back.

The kid shook his head. "So there you are." He looked up at the big wall of mountains. "So you're probably going to kill yourself trying to get up there, is what I'm saying. Yep. Or you might just make it up there alright, a big maybe on that, but then getting back down's another story. People have flat out vanished up there, friend. Presto chango. The old disappearing act. So where's that leave you?" The kid waited for any answer. "You some kind of magician?"

"No."

The kid watched Cal and the road about evenly.

"You scared of something right now?"

Cal gave the kid a closer look. "What would I be scared of?"

The kid shrugged. "Take your pick. You don't need me to name your terror, plenty enough of that to go around, all by itself. I was just wondering, is all, why your hands are shaking like that."

Cal glanced down at his hands. He steadied them against his knees.

"It's just the shakes."

"Say what?" The kid let off the gas a bit to hear better.

"I said, it's just a case of the shakes," Cal yelled back.

"Alright then," the kid nodded. "Guess that's just what it is. A regular old case of the shakes." He sat up straighter in his seat. "One case of the shakes, please. You want some fries with that?" He laughed and slapped at the steering wheel.

"Hey, check it out." He reached in and turned a knob on the dash, the windshield wipers jumped up and swept back and forth across the open space where the windshield should have been. "That's something else, ain't it? I rigged them up the other day to do that." He turned them off. "You sure don't want to hit the washer button by mistake, though."

Cal watched the road ahead for any sign of its end.

He caught a ride back from the station with a two-gallon can of gas and a tattooed trucker hauling a load of corrugated roofing up to Chamizal. The trucker worked his way up through the gears. "Where was you headed when you run'd out of gas?" the trucker asked. He grinned over at Cal with a cemetery of teeth and just miles of time.

"I sure was," Cal said. He looked out the side window at the roadway rolling past.

11.

Cal stood beside his pickup truck with the can of gas.

The semi bucked and geared its way down the twilight road until the silence that otherwise owned the place rolled back in to claim it. The mountains to the west glowed a deep rose where they caught the last light from the buried sun, the flatlands to the east sunken to a milky blue. He stared out at the vacant scrub, the roll of hills like waves in an ocean of sand.

He tipped up the gas can and emptied most of the gas into his tank. He popped the hood and removed the air filter and primed the carburetor with the rest.

He started the truck and the pool of silence promptly fled. He clicked on the hi-beams and pulled out onto the road.

He drove back to the service station, returned the gas can and pumped another twenty bucks' worth of gas into his tank. He drove across the road to the convenience store. He walked inside and bought a pack of smokes and paid the girl at the counter. She slid his money off to one side without a look while she flipped through a magazine with her other hand. Her hair was dyed black and tipped in flame blue, twisted into knots on her head and poking out the sides like sudden thoughts exploding. She had a chrome nut and bolt screwed through the meat of her left eyebrow. A barbed wire tattoo coiled around the base of her neck. She was dressed in three or four layers of something black that was shredded once then tied and riveted back together, almost. Metal rings and hoops wound through her ears and nose, some of them chained one to the other and enough bracelets and shackles on her wrists to drown her if she were to fall into any sudden water.

Cal turned to leave but there was something about her that held him. He picked up a pack of cinnamon gum, reached into one of his pockets and laid some change on the counter.

He waited.

He took a closer look at her face. Down past all the surface noise there was something familiar about her. Something about her eyes, and the fire he saw there.

Like the fire in Gayle's eyes.

"Is there something else?" the girl said. She looked up at him and smiled a bit, and shook her head enough to make all her metal parts jangle.

"No. Ah, yeah," Cal said, caught off balance. He looked away. "I, ah . . . is there a restroom here?"

She looked him in the eye. She smirked. She nodded her head to the right. He followed her gaze down the aisle to a large sign hanging above a metal door with the word "Restroom" spelled out in three-foot-high hand-painted red letters.

"Sign's not working at all today," she said. She smiled and looked back to her magazine.

Cal nodded thanks. He walked down the aisle, pushed the metal door open. The door shut tight behind him with a dull whump. There was one stall and one urinal there, and the floor was wet in between them like the last guy couldn't make up his mind which one to use. Cal stepped up to the urinal. The wall in front of him was graffiti covered, half painted over and regraffitied. At eye level, right in his face, was a statement printed in bold letters, with red arrow points added at either end:

WE ARE THE GUN-TOTING SHEPARDS OF THE PLANET, PISSING UPSTREAM OF OURSELVES AND OBSESSED ON A POST CARD OF EDEN. IT SAYS, "WISH YOU WERE HERE," SO WE DO.

Cal read it over and flushed. He stepped back and read it over again. Then once more. He left and turned the light out on the way, the door slammed tight behind him and that thought hung on the wall in the dark like a spider for the next mind.

Cal nodded to the girl on his way past. She jingled something in her left hand and the rest of her jangled with it. He walked on. She popped her gum and watched him out into the parking lot. She folded her magazine shut.

Cal threw the smokes and gum onto the seat. He closed the door and reached for the ignition. The keys weren't there. He looked into the tray on the top of the console: nothing. He patted his pockets down: empty.

"Dammit."

He opened the door and stepped outside. He checked the floor of the cab. He reached in under the seat, down alongside the base of the console where the keys might have fallen: again, nothing.

He walked around to the passenger side, patting his pockets down all over again. He looked back toward the store, down along the ground where the keys might have dropped. He opened the door, bent down low and looked in under the seat. He reached his hand in further, he found other things long lost: a cell phone charger, a favorite glove of Gayle's gone missing two seasons back, a veined river rock she'd found in the Chamas a year ago that she said looked like a heart that was struck by lightning. He held it in his hand.

"Where you trying to hide, Cal-boy?"

The chained girl's voice twisted in the air above him like a corkscrew.

Cal straightened up from under the seat. "What?"

The chained girl stood jangling herself at the driver's side door. "You look like you're fixing to crawl up under your seat like some big old sidewinder."

Cal blinked. "How do you know my name?"

The girl looked back surprised, and she laughed out loud.

"Your name's Big Old Sidewinder?" She looked down at him for as much as she could see from there, then back up, making some sort of appraisal. "Well alright then." She nodded back with a crooked grin.

"No. You called me . . . Cal-boy before. Didn't you?"

She laughed at him again. "So your name's Cal-boy?"

"No. It's just Cal."

They stared at one another.

She cleared her throat.

"I called you *cowboy* before, that's what. You know, as in . . . *cowboy*." She twirled her hand in the air over her head. "You know, as in, *yee-hah*." She glanced around inside the truck. "So. You're Just Cal. You looking for something special?"

He stared back.

She held her other hand up and dangled his keys. Other parts of her jingled along in harmony.

"You found my keys?"

"Mm-hmm. And so now you're going to ask me my name next, isn't that right? Be the nice polite cowboy and all."

"What?"

"Name's Alma, that's what."

They stared at one another again.

"Well . . . hi, then, Alma," Cal said. He stood and gave her a nod. He laid the river rock on top of the dash. He brushed his hands off against his pants. "Where'd you find my keys?"

"Just about where you left them for me," she said. She nodded toward the store. "Back inside there, where you laid them down on the countertop and you took yourself that pack of gum but you didn't pay for it."

"I did?" He looked back toward the store. "I didn't?"

She grinned.

"You did both." She nodded her head, hoops and chains clanking. She pointed to the gum on the passenger seat. She spun the key ring in circles on her finger. "You shy, or just playing cute?"

She dangled the keys a little closer in his direction. Cal reached for them but she closed her fist and pulled them back. She watched his hand shaking in the air.

"Why so nervous, Just Cal?" She looked at his face, leaned her weight to one foot and popped her gum.

Cal dropped his hand to his side.

"Life, that's what. Can I have my keys?"

"Life gets you all so nervous?" Alma said. "Maybe you aren't getting enough of it to fill your tummy up then. You've seen new kittens, right, when they've gone all hungry for too long?" She shook and jangled herself like a nervous kitten. "They shake all over, just like that. Just like you, right now." She cocked her head toward him with her lips pumped. She angled her hips the other way. Her shirt-thing slid lower off of one shoulder and her chains rattled. "Am I right?" She said it just so. She re-hitched the shirt-thing up a half-notch.

Cal stared back like a deer in the headlights.

Alma looked up at the night sky. She took in a deep breath, arched her back and pushed her chest out.

Cal stepped away from the cab and closed the passenger door. He walked around the front of the truck. Alma hopped up on the running board and slid herself into the driver's seat, and she was resting her hands on the steering wheel with her bracelets still jangling by the time Cal stood beside her. She turned and looked up at him.

And he saw the fire again in her eyes.

Like the whole world to her was an interesting toy.

Alma watched him from close range.

"Well? You want to take a ride with me now or what, Just Cal?" She batted her eyelashes. Her breath smelled of watermelon bubblegum.

"Look, ah, Alma. No thanks, I, ah . . . you're a fine looking girl . . . woman . . . it's just . . . I don't know, I don't have the, ah, time, to, umm . . . I just have to get going." He pointed down the road. "I have to keep going."

He turned a vague look out at the crossroads.

The gas station sat across the road in the blue twilight, the cars broken and tangled there in a terminal disorder. Radio noise sifted through the air from some other time long past. Pools of orange light from the streetlamps fell like moats around the scatter of houses. Trailers lay at odd angles across the flats like they were dropped there by a sudden wind and no one saw the need for any correction.

Cal turned to face Alma again but was lost from his words in the look from her eyes.

She watched him the whole while. She nodded her head at what she was seeing.

"I saw the way you looked at me, back inside there. And I see it now too. I'm not blind, you know. And then you go and leave your keys for me, right there on the counter? Hello?" She dangled his keys in the air. "So maybe your mouth's saying that you have to get going, but what I'm seeing in your eyes is that you're just begging for a little taste of me." She rolled her head and laughed away and her bracelets jangled.

The station mechanic stepped out from the garage across the road. He wiped his hands down on a filthy red rag. He looked up at the falling night sky, stuffed the rag down into his back pocket, lit up a cigarette and took a drag. He walked to the edge of the roadway and stood there, watching the two of them.

Time felt bent. It stuttered forward in fits like the hands of a damaged clock.

Cal shook his head.

"I . . . have to go."

"Take me with you," Alma said back. "I've just got, like, oh, all night."

Cal reached again for his keys. Alma pulled them aside a bit, then dropped them into his hand. She laughed and slid herself up over the console like a black cat and settled into the passenger seat. She picked up the pack of gum and peeled off the string, pulled out a stick and offered it over.

Cal shook his head no thanks. Alma shrugged and popped it in her mouth.

Cal sat into the driver's seat. He fit the key into the ignition.

"I want you to get out now. You should go on back to your store."

She looked off toward the store and laughed like she was having a great time, and her laughter shook her all over until she sounded like a collection of wind chimes on someone's back porch.

She focused her eyes on Cal.

"And just where is it that you have to be going to?" She glanced down at her pearly black fingernails, held them up to the light. She glanced back at Cal.

Cal stared away through the windshield, his thinking completely truant.

"Please . . . just go."

Alma cocked her head and regarded him.

"Well why'd you look at me then, the way you did before? Right in my eyes like that." She waited for any response. "Most places I know of, that look says but one thing: invitation. You know that word, Just Cal? In-vee-tay-shun?"

Cal looked back to her face.

"You reminded me of someone else, is all," he said quietly. "I'm sorry." He shook his head and looked away. "It was nothing."

"Nothing?" Alma made a funny face. "Pretty intense look for a nothing." She watched him a moment. "You are the shy one, aren't you."

Cal didn't answer.

"Well," she said. "Shy or not, it's no bother. I got lots more going on for me beside looking like someone else. Not in the way of bragging, mind you. It's just true."

The station mechanic took another step into the roadway. The glow of his cigarette lit his face with a red bulls-eye. The station lights flickered dim and then bright again behind him.

"I should go," Cal said.

"Should, should," Alma said back. She shook her head. "You know what's interesting with that? I was talking with an old Indian a while back, real old school he was, way out past Mescalero, and he asked me what that word *should* meant. We were sitting outside a store on some crates talking a bunch of stuff. First off, he said he liked my decorations just fine, meaning all my chains and stuff. That's what he called them, decorations. He said it showed the kind of heart I had inside me, which was a strong heart, and it was a good thing to show it. Then that word *should* came up and he asked me what exactly it meant. He said he'd heard it plenty of times but he still didn't know what it was supposed to mean. So I thought on it for him, and I told him it was like coming to a fork in the road and you know which fork is the right one to take but you go the other way instead, and so the way you didn't go becomes a *should*. He thought about it awhile, and you know what he said?" She slapped her leg. "He said, 'Well that just explains a shit-ton about how it got all to the mess it's in now.'" She sat back and laughed and looked aside at Cal for his reaction.

He didn't have one.

"I . . . have to go."

"I already know that," Alma said back, sassy. "But you're still here and here I am next to you. You think that's some kind of accident?"

"I don't know what it is."

"Because there's no such thing as accidents." She gave him a closer look. "No such thing at all. We show up when we do, and for a reason too. There's reason enough for all of it, if you take a look. You just have to take the look. The minute you were born, it was written down somewhere that you'd drive in here when you did. And see? You just did, and that's why you're here right now and you can't prove it any different. You think you're someplace else or something?"

Cal watched her face, her shining eyes, her metal parts flashing.

"And the minute I was born too," she went on, "it was all set down somewhere that I'd be waiting here for you when you pulled in. Not that I'd be *waiting* waiting, but all the same, here I am and I'm not about to argue with that either."

Cal looked away. He shook his head slowly.

"No?" Alma laughed. She had a smoky laugh. "You can't say no. Shaking your head like that and thinking the world's going to change its mind because you don't agree with its reality? There's not a single one of us here operating alone, if that's what you're thinking, coming and going like some ship of fools in the night. I mean, really? Alone? Man. That would be like being God or something, but way back before the first day of creation, because that's about the only real *alone* there ever was in this world, or any other, tall story or not." She gave him a long look. "And anyway, we all know *alone* didn't work out too good for him either, because here we are to prove it, for better or worse. So there you go. And here we are."

Cal nodded, a blank to the sound of her words. "Right. I need to go."

"So . . . I . . . hear," Alma said back. She tapped her fingernails against the dash. She picked up the veined river rock Cal had left there. She turned it over in her hands. "Oh. This is real nice." She looked it over more, her face all lit up. "Where'd you find it?"

Cal didn't answer. He watched her face, her eyes. He saw the playfulness in her.

"It looks like a bright bolt of lightning got itself all caught up inside a heart of stone." She set it back on the dash. "A heart of stone." She looked at it a while longer. "Whose is it? Yours?" A sly smile on her face.

Cal looked away.

Alma reached out and turned the stone halfway around for a better angle. She sat back and pondered it. "Well. So here it is now, just like the two of us."

Cal stared out through the windshield.

"Why did you do it?" he said quietly, more like a thought that had broken free into the air on its own.

"Do what?" Alma asked, tilting her head.

"Disappear," Cal said, barely audible.

"Do *what?*" Alma laughed. She turned halfway around to face him.

Cal closed his eyes. He leaned forward, his hands on the wheel like a man driving asleep. Alma watched him.

"It's all wrong," he said, the words draining from him with his breath. "All wrong."

He opened his eyes and reached down, gave the ignition key a sharp twist and started the engine. He looked aside at Alma, at all her metal parts and chains and the barbed wire tattoo strung around her neck. "Why'd you do that to yourself?"

"Do *what* to myself?"

"All of it. The whole thing, the way you look. That barbed wire tattoo twisted around your neck, for one."

Alma laughed out loud.

Then she stopped laughing. She gave him a curious look.

"Damned if it don't sound like you're mad at me right now. And really? For how I choose to look? Well, well. Another voice heard from the fuck-you choir." She shook her head. She sat back in the seat.

"You know what I heard? I heard if you spend this life in judgment of others, you spend the next life in judgment of yourself. Now I'd say that's the ground and the definition of hell itself, the keeper and the kept, the same. So right here, in this life, I'm not about to sit in judgment of anyone. No sir. And maybe I don't know as much as you, but here's what I do know. You're looking at me right now, and you're giving me some serious looks too. And I'm sitting here, talking nice back to you. Now for whatever it's worth, that's a real different path for both of us than if you never pulled in here in the first place, or I never walked outside to hand you back your keys. I could've just thrown them at you from the door and been done with it. Hell, I could've just thrown them in the trash. Then I'd just sit back and watch you crash and burn the rest of the night, wondering yourself into one big what-the-fuck. Maybe that would've suited you better."

Cal lowered his eyes. He said, "I'm sorry."

She gave him a closer look.

"I was just having some fun with you before, that's all. Just to see where it all might go. But I can see now it's not fun you're after." She shrugged. "And so it goes."

Cal looked away.

Alma cleared her throat. "I'll answer your question for you, since I'm still sitting here and all. And you did ask it so . . . nicely. What was it again? 'Why'd I *do* that to myself?'" She pointed out the window to the desert. "You see that world out there, Just Cal? I mean really see it, for real? Life takes, that's what. *Life takes*. This world is a hard case, and a harsh judge, and there's nothing out there that can live for too long that doesn't have spikes, or fangs, or armor, or scales, or poison of some kind to protect itself. Or *thorns*." She pulled her shirt-thing off to one side and bared her neck more into the light.

Cal could see the whole of the tattoo now. It was a flowering vine, like a morning glory, encircled with thorns.

"Thorns," Alma said. "To protect the flower. So the flower can bloom. So the flower can persist." She gave him a quiet look. "So the flower can procreate. Otherwise, it'd all be gone in a flash." She pulled her shirt-thing back into place and looked out at the crossroads. "And if it's one thing I'm not going to be, it's gone in a flash." She shook her head slowly. Her jewelry clanked and chimed.

Cal stared down at his hands. He tightened them on the wheel to keep them from shaking.

"So you can keep your judgment of me, or whatever it is, to yourself. But I'll keep my life, thank you. It's all I've got just now, so I'm sort of partial to it."

She reached out again for the river rock. She turned it over slowly, felt the fit of it in her palm. She placed it back on the dash.

They were both quiet a while.

"The world is full of choices," she said. "Every second, another one shows up. And there's one right here to be made now." She tapped one of her rings against the door handle. "You can go off down the road by yourself or you can take me along with you. I'm not scared of living, and following that, I'm not scared of dying either, just as long as I get to do some living first. And we might just find us a little something nice out there. Something that stays put for a while."

Cal sat motionless.

She gave him a long look. "You know what? You act like someone who knows what's coming for him. But you can't know that. None of us can. The world does what it does and you've got no say in that. The only thing you do have say in is what you already know, and so you speak what you speak because of that knowing. That's the best you can ever do. You speak your knowing. The only other choice is silence." She shook her head, her metal parts jangled. "But boy, I can sure tell you, there's enough of that out there already. And besides, it's not much like a living thing to be silent. A rock, maybe, but not a living thing."

Cal stayed silent.

Alma sighed. She looked away through the side window, back toward the store.

"I've got a question for you." She waited a bit. "What is it that you dream of?"

The truck's engine idled. The mechanic across the road flicked his cigarette to the ground. He turned and walked back to the garage. The street light above them flickered on, flared bright and went out again.

Cal looked into her eyes. His voice was quiet. "I don't dream anymore."

Alma looked at him a good long while. She nodded her head, her jewelry clinked.

"That's your dream, then."

She opened the door and stepped to the ground. She looked up to where the sun had fallen behind the mountains, a purple-red rim to a jagged black outline.

"I'm a whole lot better than this place, you know."

She looked suddenly alone standing there, improbable against that backdrop. Impossible even.

"I know that," Cal said. "I can see it."

Alma smiled. "You can?"

"Yeah. I can." He gave her a straight look. "You're a whole lot better than this place could ever be."

Alma nodded. Her posture softened. "That's the first nice thing you've said to me." She looked back at him a while. "I guess we might as well leave it there." She stood waiting by the door.

Cal nodded toward the dashboard. "Why don't you take that river rock for yourself. I'd like you to have it."

"Oh yeah?" She gave it another look. She reached in and picked it up, turned it over in her hands. "Alright then. I'll keep it for you."

She walked a few paces from the truck, leaving the door open behind her. She turned to face him.

"My name's not really Alma. It's Juliet, for real. I just don't tell most."

Cal gave her a puzzled look. "Why'd you tell me?"

She shrugged. "You're not like most."

Cal managed a half-smile. "Juliet. That's a good name. You know the play?"

She nodded a bit. "Yeah, I do. I did a paper once on it, back in high school. I copied the whole play out in long hand, word for word, except I changed the title. I called it *Spineless in Verona*. It got me an F."

She gave him a long look. "So I guess I've got one last question for you. Where is it that you're so set on getting away to?"

Cal looked away. He took in a long breath. "Up into the mountains." He paused. "Down south a bit from here."

Alma tilted her head. "What are you looking for up there?"

He shook his head slowly. "Not looking for anything, I guess." He paused. "I'm going there to disappear."

"To disappear?"

"Yeah. To disappear."

"For real?"

"For real."

She was quiet a while, watching him.

"Why?"

He didn't answer.

"C'mon. Why?"

Cal sighed. "Why's a question you can't ever ask."

She laughed a little. "Well, I sure know that one. Boy-o-boy, do I. But I'm still here anyway, asking you all the same."

Cal didn't answer.

"Someone disappear on you?" she said.

He blinked, but that was all.

Alma nodded. "Fighting fire with fire, huh?"

A silence rose up between them, antique and set adrift with the radio noise in the air, and the dying twilight above.

"Well," she said. "If it all goes real well for you up there, like you're planning, I guess I won't be seeing you again, right?"

Cal nodded. "Guess not." He tipped his head farewell. He hit the gas once, hard enough to make the truck jump forward, and the door swung shut by itself.

Alma dropped the rock in her pocket and walked back to the store.

Cal sat idling a moment and watched her in the rear view mirror. He saw her standing behind the counter, flipping through a magazine, adjusting her shirt-thing up across one shoulder. Like it all never happened, or he hadn't been there at all.

He pulled out into the violet night, turned west onto County Road 17.

12.

He drove another two hours up into the mountains, into the turn of night. The road twisted back and forth on itself like a heaving drunk. The night sky had drained to black, an inky black that erased all sense of direction or feeling of distance gained. He pulled off the road at the top of a long rise. He shut the engine down, and then the lights, and the blackness rushed in to claim the space around him. He stepped out of the truck.

His eyes adjusted, and the sky filled with stars in their bright order, until the whole canopy blazed full. He lay back against the warmth of the hood.

It felt like years ago that he had slept beneath those stars, ages ago that he had slept at all, a different lifetime altogether. To shut his eyes, to drift into the quietness that gathers, that grows fast into sleep like vines grown luxuriant, curtaining up the expanse of a treetop and weighing it down, drawing it slowly back to earth in a tangled soft web. Like a breath inhaled and held, where all falls into namelessness.

The world slept every night.

They lay on their backs on a mountain trail, watching the stars. Different stars, back then.

Gayle had been distant and withdrawn lately, silent in the way that a furtive desert creature silences itself to remain undetected. Days had drifted by like that.

Her art would do that to her sometimes, or her writing, or her dance; would cause her spirit to falter, or fall into doubt.

"The infernal quest," she had called it. "The one step you can't not take. The one step you can't untake once you've taken it."

She needed to walk near the edge sometimes, she would say.

"To see how different the world can be. To see how close I can come to falling right over the edge, back into creation itself."

It was a cosmic dare she'd invited with arms held open, and could not refuse.

A night beneath different stars, Cal listened as she tried her best to put words to it.

"I need to see the proof," she said.

"The proof of what?" he asked.

Gayle didn't have the exact answer. She struggled with the words.

"The proof of what is. The proof of what I can believe." She hesitated.

"I need to see the hand behind everything. And if there isn't a hand there, or some force, or something that sets it all in motion, then I need to see that too. Either way, I need to see it. I need to see the authenticity. The authenticity of what is." She was quiet again, searching for her answers.

"Sounds like a tall order," Cal said. His words sounded small and weightless against the night. They slipped away into the darkness.

Another night beneath stars, side by side in the refuge of the mountains.

"What if there are no mistakes here," Gayle said. "No mistakes at all. What if everything has the right to be?"

"The right to be?" Cal asked. He gave it some thought. "If it's here, then it's here, right?"

Gayle had difficulty with her words. She searched the stars like she might find an answer there.

"No, I mean all of it. All of the good and all of the bad, taken together. What if all the horrific things that have happened in history have the right to be, just like the rest of it? What if evil itself is not a mistake? Not just some passing aberration, some momentary negation of good? What if evil is a legitimate condition all on its own? Something that's built right into creation." Her voice got smaller. "Something that's written into the script."

Cal wondered about that. "I guess it would depend on your definition of evil."

She shook her head. "Evil doesn't need my definition to be what it is."

There was a tear that rolled down her cheek. She lay so still beneath those stars, like the smallest of movements from her would shatter a fragile wall, and whatever resided on one side of that wall would annihilate the world that resided on the other.

"I have searched my soul," she said. Each word stood alone and singular as she said it. She began to say more but her voice broke and her words trailed off to a whisper. She wiped the tear from her cheek. "It's no longer a choice for me. Not like it was. It's nothing I can control anymore. And it's right here in front of me, right here, all the time. The bottomless truth." Her hands were shaking. "And boy, I sure asked for it, didn't I? All that time I was searching, searching for the truth, inviting it in, and now I couldn't undo it if I tried. Lesson #273: You can't unlearn to see what you've already seen." She shook her head. "Guess I blew that lesson."

A breeze stirred around them. The grasses all rattled, then hushed. The stars winked above.

"What I used to call my *inspiration* . . ." She sighed. "Oh god, I found it alright. Or it found me. It owns me now, controls me completely. And my *choice* . . ." she laughed at that word, "my *choice* is extinct. I'm a fucking puppet." She shut her eyes. "Inspiration, indeed." Another tear broke free and rolled down her cheek. "Dream come true for an artist, right? All the inspiration you can eat, and me with my big fat mouth." She was silent a while.

"You know what the word means, Cal? *Inspiration?*"

Cal lay beside her in the dark. "More or less."

She sighed. "More or less. What luxury vagueness is. I wish I could afford it." She shook her head. "Inspiration. It's from the Latin, from the root word *espiritu*. It means, literally, to breathe in your spirit. In-spir-ation. To inhale your spirit. But I don't think I can breathe in a world that holds evil as an equal to good. That's like breathing in poison. And I feel it, Cal, I can *feel* it, that I've backed myself into some kind of corner here, with all of my, my what, my cleverness, if that's what it's been. Or my what, my tenacity? My insatiable quest for vision? Oh boy! And so this . . . this thing, this elusive thing that I was reaching for, all that time, all that time, and now I can't put it down if I wanted to, it's taken hold of me instead, and it's more than I can handle. I feel cornered, and . . . I . . ."

Her voice trailed off. Seconds held in silent suspension.

"I've become doubt," she said. She was trembling. "I *am* doubt."

Cal turned and he reached his arm out around her. He began to speak but she cut him short.

"Sure, sure, and I guess that's fine too, if that's how things are, if that's what's really going on here, and there are no mistakes. Who am I to argue with reality, huh? I'm a momentary spike on the vigilance meter, that's all. The rant of an ant against a hurricane." She forced a laugh from herself. "I'm just a grudge-bearing nobody in the face of that reality. Take a number, lady, and get in line . . . welcome to the Complaints Department, Division of Spirit."

She took a few breaths.

Cal tried pulling her closer. She eased herself away.

"I'm a freaking Humpty Dumpty here."

"Humpty Dumpty?"

"Yeah, Humpty Dumpty. A self-righteous raw goddamn egg. He had no right climbing up onto that wall for a better view of the world. And neither did I. What was I thinking? Have you ever tried picking a cracked freaking egg up off the floor?" She nodded her head. "Yeah, that's me alright. All over the place. Fuck the king and all his horses."

She was shaking.

"Gayle," he said.

"I'm afraid, Cal. I'm afraid." She shook her head. "Such a big strong girl, huh? Wow." Another forced laugh from her. "Whatever it was that I claimed to be, that I worked so hard to be, to be the one who gets to peek behind the curtain, who gets to see what's real and what's not . . . I'm done with all that. I've had enough. I'm afraid to see it. I don't care what's there anymore. I don't want to know."

Cal strained to see her face, but she was no more than a profile against the starry sky. He reached for her hand in the dark, he held it tight.

She shook her head. "There's no off switch, not for vision. Once you learn to see, you can't unlearn to see. You just see . . . more."

She stilled herself. Time measured in quiet breaths.

"I've been an artist," she said.

There was a finality to the way she'd said it.

They lay on their backs at a mountain pass, watching the stars. Different stars in the sky that night. A different time in a world, unmeasured in days or months, or years.

His arm lay beneath her head like a pillow. They watched a shooting star plunge down from the north, flare clear across the length of sky and split in two, each half speeding away from the other in a shimmer of sparks. Two glowing trails hovered in place a moment longer, then thinned away and were gone.

"What would you do, Cal, if one day this all came to an end?"

"If what came to an end?" Cal asked. "The world?"

"No," Gayle said. "Smaller. A single moment of the world. The time we've had together. Everything we've become. Who we are right now, you and me."

Cal turned to face her. "Why would that ever come to an end, Gayle?"

She hesitated.

"That's not what I'm asking you right now," she said. "I'm not asking for the why of it." She shook her head. "Why is too big a question to ever ask." She scanned the stars. "Or the answer, if we ever got one, would be too big for us to contemplate." She was quiet. "So the question is if. Just . . . the if."

"Just the if?"

"Right. The if." She turned to face him. Pinpoints of starlight reflected off the curve of her eye. "What would you do, Cal, if it came to an end between us?"

Cal gave it some reluctant thought.

"I'd try my best," he said.

"Your best?" She waited. "Your best to do what?"

"Well. Not so much the what. I don't think I'd know about that ahead of time, about the what to do. How could I ever know that? So, yeah, just . . . my best. I'd try my best."

She was silent.

"That's it?" he asked her.

She sighed. She nodded her head. "Yeah, I guess."

They watched the stars turn.

"What about you?" Cal asked after awhile. "What would you do if it came to that, if it came to an end between us? Jeez, I can't believe we're even talking like this."

"Yeah. Weird, huh? What the hell's wrong with me?"

Cal gave her shoulders a little squeeze. "I didn't mean it that way."

They were quiet a while.

"I would hide," she finally said.

"Hide? Hide where?"

She thought about that. "Not where. There would be no where to it at all. No one place better than any other." She shook her head. "Just, hide."

Cal turned onto his side. He cupped his body closer to hers.

"Why are we talking like this, Gayle? What is it?"

"Nothing. It's just spooky dark-of-the-night kind of talk." She tried for a laugh. "It's the vacuum of my philosophy, sucking at the rug of my disbelief. Something like that. You know me."

"Yeah, I do." He brushed the hair from her neck, he nestled his face there. "I like what I know. But why that question? And why now?"

'Why . . . why." She took in a long breath. She let it out.

"That shooting star," she said. "Burning up like it did just then. Breaking in two and burning up."

"It was just a meteor," Cal said. "That's what they do. Thousands of them burn up every day. We just happened to see that one."

"I know, I know," Gayle said. "But we were meant to see it too, because here we are and we saw it, right? So now it no longer exists out there, but we know that it did once. So it only exists in here." She touched his forehead with the tip of her finger. "That was its destiny from the start, and ours too, woven to its cloth and into ours, at the moment of creation."

Cal thought about that. "But if that was its destiny, and ours too, then nothing's really changed. It was a cold rock out in space, and then a sweet fire lighting up the sky, and we laid down here just in time to see it all. So, destiny accompli."

Gayle scanned the sky from one end to the other. "But it left an empty space where it used to be."

Cal pulled her closer. "But we're still here, Gayle. You and I. With the memory of all the beauty it left behind. We're the keepers of that beauty."

Gayle nodded to that.

He could feel her body relaxing into his arms.

"The keepers of the beauty," she said, and then again, like a soft recitation. "I like the sound of that."

They fell asleep in each other's arms.

Cal saw the stars fallen to dusty pools in the hood of his pickup truck. He watched them bend their way across the curve of the windshield.

He climbed into the cab, pulled the door shut behind him, heard the latch click home. He started the engine and snapped on the lights. The stars above swirled back into blackness like the memories within, as numbered and as numb.

His tires grated over the loose gravel, skipped back onto the asphalt, and he drove on. The road toyed at the edge of the mountains, grew thinner in its twists, longer in its dusty turns.

❖

Dissolution.

1.

Six weeks earlier, or seven. Another lifetime ago.

Cal was away at work on a deadline installation with Angel Fire, down at the big Scottsdale Office Park project in Arizona, pulling double shifts each day. Exhausting nights of restless sleep in a roadside motel after a few beers and dinner with his crew. He called home after hours when he could. Most nights Gayle was out with her friends. She didn't like the home alone thing very much. Wednesday night he called in late, near midnight, and she picked up. She was in bed. She sounded tired. Or sad maybe. Not so happy to hear his voice.

He said, "What's wrong?"

She said, "Nothing."

He could hear the opposite. "What is it, hun?"

"It's nothing. I don't know. Maybe I'm just coming down with something." She paused. "A bug of some sort."

"You don't feel well?"

A longer pause. "I don't know what I feel," spoken quietly.

"You want to talk about it some?"

She said she didn't want to talk about it.

"My mind hurts," she said.

It all felt awkward, it was late, they were both real tired. He let it go.

Friday night, he called in late to tell her that the project was wrapping up and he'd be home late Saturday night. The house phone rang without answer. He tried her cell, the voice-mail picked up and he left his message there.

An hour past midnight into Sunday morning, Cal pulled up to the curb at the house, dead tired from the eight-hour drive after a ten-hour workday. He shut the truck off and sat back, his eyes dust dry, his brain coffee-edged and burnt from too many miles of driving.

Gayle's car was absent from the driveway. The house was dark. He checked his watch. He grabbed his duffle bag from the seat and walked up the driveway to the side door. He swung the screen door aside and stepped into the kitchen and set his bag down. He flicked at the light switch on the wall. Nothing. Again. Nothing.

"Bulb must be out," he mumbled.

He crossed the kitchen to the hallway. He hit the light switch there. Again, nothing.

He walked back into the kitchen, stood at the sink, looked out the window to the street. He saw the neighbors' houses up and down the block in total darkness. He hadn't noticed.

"The grid must be down."

He turned the faucet handle, the water gushed out as always, he turned it off. He turned it on again, cupped his hands to the stream and drank. He splashed the water to his face, around the back of his neck. He drank some more.

He turned and looked again into the darkened room, he felt around for any dishtowel below.

"Hello?"

He heard nothing back. He failed to find the dishtowel, his face and hands dripping.

"Hello?" he called again, louder this time. A slight echo was all that answered.

He crossed the kitchen to the hall and opened the closet door. His foot kicked something and it spun away into the living room with a hollow sound. He reached for the flashlight sprung in a bracket on the backside of the door. The bracket was empty. He waved his hand deeper into the closet but it seemed there was nothing there at all.

He tried the light switch in the living room twice.

He stood in the dark, waiting. A car rolled down the street and the side-wash of its headlights swept in through the room, showing nothing there, the room empty of furniture. The light faded last in the far corner on a stack of boxes and a wooden chair. The room went dark again.

Cal felt his way back into the kitchen. He stood at the screen door but there was no car pulling in the drive, just a pair of taillights moving away down the street.

He found the phone in the dark on the wall near the door and he lifted the receiver. No dial tone to it, the phone as silent as a toy. He laid the receiver on the counter. He found his cell phone in his duffle bag and flipped it open and the light from the screen half-lit the kitchen, showing it as empty. He dialed Gayle's number. Seconds later he heard her phone ringing from somewhere further inside the house. He heard her recorded message in his ear.

"Hello?" he said again, as loud as he could without shouting. His own voice bounced back to him in echo, returned to his ear with all the gathered sounds of a house that held nothing.

He pushed through the screen door and crossed the drive to the garage. The door cracked a flat sound behind him and a distant dog barked back its protest.

Into the garage by the side door, he flicked at the light switch thereto no effect. He stumbled over some boxes on his way to the shelves at the back wall. He found the canvas bags he was hoping for, the ones filled with camping gear. His fingers traced down through the shapes in search of a flashlight or a headlamp. None. Matches, candles, a cigarette lighter. Anything to shed light. Nothing.

He stood in the street by the door of his truck. He climbed inside and started the engine and threw the truck into reverse. He backed into the street, then slammed the truck into forward and drove toward the house, his front tires bounced over the curb, then his rears, and he hit the brakes. His high beams clicked on, the front of the house lit up, the engine idling. The emergency brake pulled tight.

Cal stood again in the kitchen, in the space where the table should have been.

He stood in the living room with his shadow against the wall from the headlights blinding in through the front window.

He walked down the hall to the bedroom and opened the door there, and stood silent in the near total darkness, where his eyes failed to tell him what his heart could already see clearly without any light.

2.

The first glow of dawn lit the mountains to the east, the night air hung cool and wet over the rooftops and it amplified the scatter of crow calls hovering for the break of day.

Cal rose from the corner of the living room floor. He crossed the room and looked out the front window, his truck parked opposite him in the front yard, the lights still on.

A power company truck had been prowling the neighborhood all night, its spotlights searching the wires street by street, the yellow lights flashing, the crack of the dispatch radio haunting the stillness in waves. It rolled by again.

Cal stepped outside. He walked up the driveway to the street. He watched the sky lighten by degrees. He saw the outline of his house falling into place, the details filling in one by one.

His house?

He turned and walked off down the street. Twelve blocks later, he stood outside of Billy's house.

He let himself in through the kitchen door. Billy almost never locked his doors. He had stickers affixed to the windows that read:

> Warning: Premises Protected by Two Dogs and a Gun.
> Break Glass for More Details.

No one ever did.

Cal walked in through the kitchen. He turned down the hallway and stood outside Billy's bedroom door. He could hear the man snoring on the other side. Cal pushed the door open and took a few steps inside. He stood without a word. He sat into a corner chair padded with cast off clothing and sank further into the quicksand of his thoughts.

Billy awoke dry-mouthed with the first lick of sunlight slipping through the blinds.

"Jesus!" he said when he saw Cal sitting in silence beside him like a ghost. He jumped up, or tried to, from the tangle of blankets that wrapped him tight. "What the hell are you doing here?" He rubbed his eyes, then held his head steady.

"Were we . . . did we . . . when the hell did you get here?" He sat forward. "How long have you been sitting there like that? Jesus, man. What the hell time is it?" He looked around for any sign of a clock. "This is just . . . weird." He stared back at Cal, his mouth slack.

"Gayle's gone," Cal said in monotone.

Billy tightened his eyes for more focus. He moved to the edge of the bed.

"Gayle's . . . gone?"

Cal was staring down at the floor. He nodded.

"Last night. I got in late. The power was out. It's still out. So I, ah, I didn't . . . I couldn't see, but . . . there's nothing there, the furniture, it's gone, and I . . ." He looked up at Billy. "I don't know where she is." He shook his head. He looked back down at the floor. "I don't know where Gayle is."

Billy blinked. "You mean she left you?"

Cal looked up. He looked away.

Billy pulled some clothes together from another chair. He found one of his boots down the hall and the other in the living room.

They stepped outside and got into his truck.

The Sunday morning town was still and soft asleep, as quiet as a painting of itself. Rose-tinted sunlight smoking over wet tile roofs, the sky a denim blue. Pink clouds chasing up the sides of purple mountains and dissolving away. Land of Enchantment, Santa Fe.

They pulled up into Cal's driveway and stepped out.

"What the hell?" Billy said, when he saw Cal's truck parked up in the front yard. "You miss the driveway or something?"

Cal stopped short at the kitchen door, hollow-eyed. He stared in through the screen.

Billy edged around him and stepped into the house. He did a slow walk-through, his low whistles echoing back from the empty rooms, one then another.

He rejoined Cal outside, a blank look on his face.

"Damn, Cal. I don't know what to say." He looked back at the house. "I always know what to say. Don't I?"

Cal had no response. He looked like a second-hand copy of himself, staring down at his own hands in the rising light.

3.

Billy drove off down the street.

He reappeared a few minutes later with two giant cups of coffee and a mixed bag of donuts. They sat down at the picnic table on the back deck.

Billy tore the bag open and spread it out flat. He arranged the donuts like they were on display. A magpie flew past and wheeled in a fast half-circle and landed at the edge of the roof.

"We should make us some phone calls," Billy said. "Grace will know what's going on here, right? She definitely will."

Cal nodded absently.

Billy nodded to himself. He picked up a powdered donut and broke it in two. He ate the first half and washed it down with a gulp of coffee. He broke the other half in two again. He looked at the bird on the roof.

"That looks like the same bird that hangs around at my house," he said, nodding up toward the bird.

Cal gave it a vacant look.

Billy tossed a chunk of the donut toward the bird, the magpie caught it in one bounce off the roof and left with the thing wedged in its beak. Billy grinned.

"Yeah, that's him alright. Piehole, I named him. I feed him most every morning. He must have spotted me here. Or followed us back, maybe. Damn, how's that for loyal."

Cal looked away.

Billy sat a while in thought.

"Someone's going to know where she is, Cal, so I don't think you should worry too much about that part. About where she is. I mean, it's not like she's lost here, like off in the wilds or something." He sipped at his coffee.

Cal glanced back. "So what do you think I should be worried about, Bill?"

Billy had no immediate answer. He checked his wrist for the time but there was no watch there.

"Well, it's still real early, but we'll make us some phone calls once everyone's awake. Then we'll find out."

He picked up another donut and offered it over to Cal. Cal shook his head no thanks. His own coffee sat off to one side, the lid still on.

"Did you try her on her cell phone?"

Cal gave Billy a tired look. He pulled out his phone and hit Gayle's number. A few seconds later they heard her phone ringing from inside the house. Billy's eyebrows went up.

"On the shelf, in the bathroom," Cal said.

"She left her phone here?" Billy sat forward. "Man, this just got weirder. Why would she . . ." He stopped short and gave Cal a close look. "Did you guys have a fight or something?"

"No."

Billy cocked his head. "You sure of that?"

"I'd sure know if I had a fight with my own wife," Cal said. "And the kind of fight it would take for all this to happen? I sure as hell would know about it, don't you think?"

Billy watched him a minute. He nodded.

"Well, yeah. You would. I was just asking. I mean, you know how it is with people, right? They cover up stuff. They don't really say what's going on. Not all the time."

They stared at one another.

"Not that I'm saying you're covering stuff up here. It's just, well, I was just thinking, is all. Thinking out loud, you know, about what it might be that could, ah . . ."

Cal gave him a hard look. Billy stopped talking.

A few minutes passed.

Billy leaned forward, his elbows on the table. "So, things have been alright between you guys?"

"That's the same damn question, Billy."

"No, it's not. It's totally different."

"Yeah? How's it different?"

Billy thought about that. "Different words."

Cal looked away. "Yeah, well." He waved his hand aside. "I thought things were good between us."

Billy nodded. "Yeah, me too. I mean, from what I could see of it, anyway. You guys always looked okay. The perfect couple. And now . . . wow. Talk about waking up in the wrong pair of socks."

He leaned in and quartered another donut.

Cal spun his coffee cup in place, in slow half-circles.

"She was sort of distant lately."

"Distant?"

"Yeah. Distant."

"Not around, you mean?"

"No. Around. Just not all . . . here."

Billy nodded back. "Where was she then? I mean, like, the rest of her."

Cal sighed. "Jeez, man. What?"

Billy shrugged. "I'm just trying to get the full picture here."

"And you think I have the answers? Do I look like the answer guy right now?" Cal shook his head. "Christ. I don't have the answers."

Seconds unwound.

"Gayle would just . . . she just gets like that sometimes. Just gets distant."

Billy gave that some thought. He nodded.

"Right. Like maybe she gets mad at you for something you did, and she doesn't want to talk about it, so she gets distant instead. Hell, it might even be something you didn't do. That's the one that always gets me, and the worst thing is, you can never know for sure what it was, because you didn't even do it in the first place, so then it becomes this whole insane blame game, and I tell you, that's where it always starts to fall apart with a girl, where the exact thing that drove you crazy about them at first now just starts to drive you nuts, so you end up . . ."

Cal was giving him a shut-up kind of look.

"What the hell are you talking about, Bill? Because I'm talking about Gayle here. Gayle. Gayle doesn't get mad. I've never seen her get mad once. Not once. Not about anything."

"What does she get?"

"Get?"

"Yeah, get. When things don't go her way, what does she get?"

Cal gave him a tired look.

"Gayle doesn't have a way that things have to go. She's not like that. She's . . ." He shook his head. "She just goes the way things are already going."

Billy leaned back against the deck railing. He looked around at the yard. He looked toward the house. He looked again at Cal.

"So you're saying this is the way things were already going?"

Cal exhaled. He looked off to the mountains in the west, to the morning mists hovering the Rio Grande and dissolving away with the rising light.

Billy stared down at the deck boards between his feet. He ran the toe of his boot over the top of one of the deck screws that had worked its way up.

"I might be off base with this, Cal, way off base, but . . . well." He hesitated. "You don't think this is about another guy, do you?"

Cal winced at the words. He lowered his head.

"If I knew that, I'd know something. But I don't." He thought about it. "What would it change anyway? What difference would it make in there?" He nodded toward the house.

Billy looked in through the back door. He looked down at the remaining donuts. He broke them into smaller pieces, laid them out along the edge of the table. He looked absently overhead for any sign of the bird.

"There's no note she might have left for you? Somewhere? Anywhere? Did you look?"

"I looked."

"Nothing?"

"You saw what's left in there, Billy. For christsakes. You think she'd write me a note, and then hide it somewhere so I couldn't find it?"

Billy nodded. "Right. Hey, what about e-mail? You check your e-mail yet?"

"No. I didn't check my e-mail."

Billy arranged the donut pieces back into circles.

"What about a forwarding address?"

"A forwarding address?"

"Yeah. A forwarding address. We could check in with the Post Office, tomorrow morning, first thing."

"And just what would I do with that, huh? Drop her a postcard? "Yo, Gayle! It's Cal, your husband. Where the hell did you go?""

His eyes flared, his jaw set rigid. He banged his fists down hard on the table, the coffee cups bounced up and tipped and spilled their contents across the table, down through the boards and away through the deck. He stood up and stormed away into the house.

Billy trailed him a few minutes later. He walked quietly through the emptied rooms again, looking for any clues.

They met up in the living room.

Cal stood beside the small pile of his belongings, his clothes, some pots and lids, a box of books, some CDs, a handful of photos, and a small rug rolled up and tied with a piece of twine.

"This is the stuff I had when I lived at your place," he said.

Billy looked it over and saw that it was. He looked around the room.

"All the other stuff? The furniture? The TV?"

"That was Gayle's stuff. Nicer stuff, so I chucked mine when we moved in together. Sold it off for the bills."

Cal crossed the room to the front window. He pressed his forehead against the cool glass. He stared past his truck in the front yard, past the houses across the street and the block of houses after that, then the next after that, to the highway in the distance, silent with its cars flashing against the sunrise.

"Erased," he said. His breath fogged the glass and he turned away from the view.

"What did I get so wrong, Billy, for it to end here?"

Billy shuffled on his feet. "You didn't get it so wrong, Cal. Not wrong enough for all this to happen. Maybe it's not really the end, too. Maybe it's . . ."

"So I've lived, what, seven years now? I've lived with her under the same roof. All that time. And I'm not saying I got everything right. Who could? But I sure don't know what I got wrong."

Billy shoulders sank.

"You're asking the desert about the rain right there, bro. I still can't live with women." He thought a minute. "Not one at a time, anyway."

The lights flickered on in the house just then, the refrigerator bucked alive in the kitchen. It shuddered a few seconds later, the lights dimmed, went out again, and they heard a muffled boom in the distance as another transformer blew.

Billy shook his head to all of it.

"Jeez, Cal. This is just nuts here. Let's go back to my place. We'll make us some phone calls, right? I'll fix us a proper breakfast. And we'll figure this thing out together."

Cal stared at Billy across the hollowness of the room.

"Figure it out? What difference would it make? What difference would it make if we knew every damn detail. If we had a whole goddamn proper video of the entire thing in progress." He pointed to the four walls around them. "This was my living room here, Bill. It was right here." They both looked at the remains. "Do you see it now?"

Billy was silent.

"No, you don't see it. You don't see it, because it's gone. So it looks like things have already been figured out. Just somewhere else, not here."

Cal turned his back to Billy and stared out the window, leaned his weight on the sill. He watched a power company truck lumber past, heard the scratch of its dispatch radio trailing it down the street.

4.

Back at Billy's house, they made some phone calls. No one they called knew what was going on.

Grace claimed total surprise. She said she hadn't spoken with Gayle lately, a month or more had passed since they'd talked last. She had no idea why she might have left like that, or where she would have gone. She told Billy to call her back the minute he found out anything. Her two-year old was crying then, something had fallen over, she had to go.

Cal spent the night at Billy's house, in his old bedroom, lying on a spare couch, with the lights on, staring up at his old walls, the tack holes and tape marks still there from the posters and pictures he'd once hung, the view out the window like yesterday, the ceiling fan with its lopsided spin and the dull ticking sound it still made.

A stack of hours unwound, Cal wide awake as the whole of the night slipped by.

He watched it growing lighter against the windowpanes. Houses staggered awake in a muffled frenzy, the hurried slam of doors, the coffee showered exodus of the working world, the tires spun down gravel drives, the shift of gears on up the road and gone like so many storms spawned by the turn of a clock and set free. One by one by one.

Billy yawned awake and shuffled down the hall. He opened the door and saw Cal lying on the couch just about how he'd left him last night. He stepped into the room and sat down at the edge of a desk.

"You sleep okay?"

"No."

"You didn't sleep?"

"No."

"At all?"

"No."

"Whoa. You must be beat."

"I don't know what I am."

Billy glanced out the window.

"You going to work?"

Cal sighed and sat up. He took a slow look around the room. "I'll call in sick."

Billy nodded.

"I could call off work today too, if you want. If you need some help with . . . stuff. Or some company."

Cal rubbed his hands together, folded his fists tight, unfolded them. Again.

"I think I just need some time with this, Bill. Just, some time alone with this thing."

Billy waited for anything more to be said. Nothing was. He stood to leave.

"Well. There's food in the fridge. Anything else you need, feel free. I'll see you tonight after work. We'll get us some dinner, alright?"

Cal nodded vacantly. "Sure." He lay back on the sofa, fixed his eyes on the ceiling fan, the four blades spinning in a circle, ticking like a clock.

Billy left for work.

Cal stood a long time in the shower, the hot water pouring down over him like it might dissolve the shell of hours he stood within and carry it all away. He watched the water in its easy hurry, falling past, twisting away down the drain.

The water ran cold after a while, like time itself raining past a life, curling down a dark hole, and gone.

5.

The gallery where Gayle worked was closed on Mondays.

Cal called anyway and left a rambling message on their voicemail. He called again and left another one that made less sense than the first, until the message timed out and the machine beeped.

He called the post office at nine. They could find no record of a forwarding address. They told him to give it more time, a few days maybe, that it would show up in the system by then.

He left and walked the twelve blocks home. He saw the neighborhood in ways he hadn't seen it since his first days in Santa Fe. Things looked unfamiliar again and adrift, cut free from the surround of everyday habit. His house looked the same way, foreign and removed. His memory of it seemed secondhand. His truck parked in the front yard was no more out of place than the rest of it.

The driveway was still empty.

He stood by the kitchen door, looking in through the screen. He noticed the bottom hinge freshly broken, the fresh gouges in the paint. Movers.

He entered the house.

The last time it had looked that way was the first time he had seen it. Cool and empty. He and Gayle had filled it instantly with plans for what went where and why, their imaginations alone furnishing the place in seconds. It ceased to be a collection of walls and floors and empty rooms and became a home, right then and there, by power of thought.

Cal wandered through the new vacancy. It was just walls and floors and ceilings again. Geometries of division. A small piece of desert, stolen and boxed.

He stepped out the back door. He walked across the drive to the garage. He found the flashlights he'd been looking for in the dark last night, and the candles, and the lanterns. All he could ever use. He pulled a sleeping bag down from the shelf, then an air mattress to go with it.

He found Gayle's hiking boots in another duffle bag. They looked smaller now than his memory of them. He stuffed them back in the bag.

He crossed the yard to the house, stood in the living room with his handful of gear. He stood there a long time.

He slumped eventually against the wall where the couch had been, and pulled his knees up tight. He watched the rectangle of the front window and its fill of daylight, until the sun went dust red and was nearly gone.

Billy showed up at seven-thirty with a bag of fried chicken and a six-pack of beer.

They hung out at the picnic table until ten. Billy offered his place again for the night. Cal said he needed more time.

He spent that night on the floor of the living room, watching his thoughts and the side-sweep of light from the cars passing by on the street. He lit a candle at one point, but he and Gayle had made love so often by candlelight that he blew the flame out before the light could settle, and the wick smoked a thin stream that scented the air like a memory.

The sounds of night wandered in through the open windows. Dogs barked in a rise and fall of interest over other dogs barking further off. Canine talk-radio, on the air.

Someone whisper-called for a cat.

A trashcan bounced on its side and rolled in the street a block away, maybe two.

Distant sirens howled.

A far train lumbered by, its low whistle echoing like a voice from the past, if the past would choose to have a voice.

The house still held her essence. He caught Gayle's scent more than once, drifting by, then gone.

He fell nearly to sleep, only to be yanked awake each time. The sound of footsteps in the next room, a voice calling his name and he would rise and wander through the house but there was no one there. Nothing but a fog of thought that seemed like an interrupted dream but was not.

The early morning birds sang out before the first light showed. In the near dark their calls met with no response. Half an hour later they tried again, and this time the answering calls spread out in concentric rings, until the trees rang alive with chatter.

Crows called in from above it all like tone-deaf referees late for the opening action.

6.

Cal watched the sky lighten outside. He watched the neighborhood crack to life in fits like some vast machine hatching itself from the ground. He stood at the front window and stared out from his box of insomnia, saw houses shed their inhabitants one by one onto conveyer belt streets.

He took a cold shower and left for work.

Inside the truck, into the silent procession of minutes in the stall of traffic and the blur of details, the whole world talking itself awake by phone or radio and inching forward, crawling past.

Into the warehouse with its smells of metal and vinyl and coffee, the good-morning work-faces good-morning bright, the brisk trade of small talk at every turn like a tin-ear currency, and Cal nodded a silent complicity and slid by like a ghost.

Into the work van with the new guy, the trainee he should have been told about but wasn't or he couldn't remember but there he was anyway with the paperwork in hand to prove it, a young kid as eager as a box of puppies and all the questions Cal couldn't care less about or not focus on enough to answer, back into the crawl of traffic and the scratch of the dispatch radio like a razor slicing his brain in near meltdown now from the lack of sleep and the checklist of calls mounting, mounting, the kid's questions as endless at his ear and there were greater things in the world that mattered more but that was a wholly different world than the one that was passing before his eyes so where was the reason? Where was the reason?

He made it until noon.

He returned the van and the trainee to the warehouse without explanation and drove across town for home.

A car passed by him at one point and it looked like Gayle's car. He didn't see the driver and he missed a clear look at the plates, but he was sure it was her car and his heart raced. He made an instant u-turn at the next intersection, horns blasted him from every direction and he cut through a corner station to avoid the red light but there was no catching up to her, if it even was her. If it ever was her.

He pulled over to the curb, his heart pounding, and he waited, but he didn't know what for.

He stepped out later that night with Billy for some burritos and a few beers at La Cabra Borracho's. He thought he would pass out right there in the booth. They talked some but their words settled nothing, and the shadow play of his thoughts crowded the meal for its flavor. He was yawning almost constantly now, each yawn folding right over the next like those hollow Russian dolls that fit one inside the other. Billy told him that. Cal had no idea what he was talking about. For him, the motel room three days ago in Scottsdale was still this morning.

"It's like a freaking bad dream I can't wake up from," Cal said as they stepped outside into the cool of the night.

"That's because you're not sleeping," Billy said, then regretted saying for the look he got from Cal and the long silence that followed.

Cal drove home weary. He stopped at his usual parking spot at the curb outside his house. His truck idled. He looked at the empty driveway. That was Gayle's parking spot. He rolled forward and pulled in the drive.

In through the kitchen in the dark, down the hall to the bathroom, the light clicked on, new toothpaste pulled from a box, his face a hollow mask in the mirror, his hands cupped with water from the faucet, splashed to the back of his neck, to his ears, his face, the water never cold enough. His mouth to the faucet, drinking. He clicked off the light.

He walked down the hall in the dark like a thief, like a second-rate burglar haunting a house already stolen bald.

He settled onto the floor, pulled his sleeping bag up and yawned another yawn to end all yawns. He closed his eyes, held his body still, trying to lower the volume on his thoughts.

The idea of sleep like a lost memory. The philosophy of sleep in hollow words. The habit of sleep, fallen out of. Hold the posture and it will come, he was told.

To fall into the blankness of a clear sky, a sky of singular blue, silent and swept clean from edge to edge. A featureless, endless, quiet blue, stretching away in every direction, rolling gently like the surface of a lake, rising and falling like a breath. A sky constructed of dots, of thousands of blue dots, of millions of them. Of dots within those dots, invisible and folding in on themselves and folding out again, swelling up and collapsing ever deeper into tiny silent explosions of blue, careening tighter in circles like tiny blue drunks driving tiny blue cars in pursuit of other tiny drunks driving blue cars in pursuit of the million blue dots nearly trance-like now in roaring waves of sleep breaking silent questions, chasing translucent answers down vanishing sub-basement somnambulant dream worlds stretched taut like rubber-band memories thinned to transparency and about to snap . . . blue haze of silence pulled skin fucking tight, hollow-eyed silence of the chattering walls, restless dead silence laid out straight up un-lidded in the blue insistent mirror-dome darkness of night, darkness of day, darkness of mind, darkness of how or why or is it not yet why or not yet how, or again, or not yet again.

Eyes unopened, eyes unclosed.

Birds singing long before dawn, their songs swallowed by the dark.

Crows calling in, from the west they come, as dissonant as spit.

Trash truck growling two blocks away. Cans tumbled like dull thunder under dawn's damp lid.

The first rays of the morning sun sliced red through the dusty window glass.

7.

Wednesday.

Cal looked like a bounced check crumpled to the floor where the couch once stood. Billy told him so when he saw him sitting there at day's end.

"Whoa, you didn't sleep again? How's that even possible? That's three days running now, hombre. So what's with that? Who can do such a thing?"

Cal gave him a worn out look.

"Hell, Cal. I pictured you sleeping it up here all day. You should've seen yourself last night, yawning like you were. You barely made it across the parking lot."

Cal slumped further against the wall.

"So, no sleep, huh?"

Cal shook his head.

"I kept hearing stuff, Bill. Seeing weird stuff, stuff that wasn't there. I couldn't make it happen."

"You didn't go to work then?"

The question hung in the air without answer.

"I tried calling you on your cell. Straight to voicemail. You got it turned off?"

Cal nodded toward his cell phone plugged in the charger, the charger plugged in the wall.

"The battery's cooked, or the charger's fucked up. I don't know which."

Billy wandered a slow circle through the empty room, shaking his head.

"Well you need to get some sleep here, bro. That's the first order of business, I'd say."

Cal nodded back.

"This is some serious shit here, Cal. I mean, look at you. You're a train wreck."

Cal gave him a short salute back. "Thanks, much."

"You're welcome." Billy stopped pacing. "We need to get some sleeping pills into you. Something to knock you out for a spell."

No response.

"How about we go see a doctor tomorrow? I'll set it up, alright? I know a guy I can call. We use him at work a lot, like when bits of fingers get cut off, or crunched. He's a good man for the price. I'll try for tomorrow morning, okay? Cal, hey?" He snapped his fingers. "You with me here, or what?"

Cal held still, staring at the floor. Billy watched him and waited.

"What do you . . ." Cal started to say. He shook his head. He took a breath. "Where do you think she is right now?" He looked up at Billy. "I mean, like right now, at this moment. What would you think about that? About where she is. About where she might be right now."

Billy glanced out the front window.

"Jeez, Cal, I wouldn't know."

"Do you think she's still around, like right here in town somewhere? At a hotel or something?"

Billy shrugged.

"I wouldn't know that, Cal. I couldn't guess. I couldn't say."

Cal nodded back.

"I know she quit her job, I did find out that much. I drove up to the gallery this morning, I caught up with the owner. He told me she turned in her notice last week, Tuesday, of last week, just like that." He shook his head. "That manicured clown knew she was leaving before I did. Damn."

He sighed. He rubbed his eyes in slow circles.

"My guess is, she's somewhere else by now. Just, somewhere else. Hell, I don't know what to think anymore. You think that you know. You think you know what your life is about, at least. Like who you are. Or what's happening. But all of it, you don't know it, not for real. It's all just a masquerade."

He scratched his head with both hands and his hair poked out at odd stiff angles. Real bad hair day.

"And then there's the why. That's another question altogether. That one that will bring you to your knees for any answer." He stared back at Billy. "Why?"

Billy looked away. "I don't know."

Time slinked by.

"So what the hell did I miss? What was it that I got so wrong, Bill, to get it all here?"

Billy sighed.

"Cal. You've got to get your mind off your head like that, man. You didn't get it so wrong. Not wrong enough for all this to be happening."

Billy paced the floor up and back. He stopped at the window, leaned his hands down on the sill.

There were two boys outside on the asphalt, skateboarding in the red twilight beneath the orange streetlamp, practicing the same move over and over, trying to ollie a trashcan laid on its side and damned to get it right. Their boards slammed against the can, pounded it like a drum. They saw him at the window and they gave him the 'gnarly' hand sign. He nodded and gave them one back.

He turned to face Cal.

"I know you're really feeling this thing, Cal. This is a hard hand, a real hard hand that she's dealt you here, and it's just not right, if you want my take. She should have talked to you. She sure should have told you what for. But not this. Not just . . . this."

Cal was staring at his hands. "Yeah, well. It's done. Either way, it's done."

Billy sat down on the floor opposite him.

"I think we need to get you some sleep, Cal. Before you try dealing with this thing, before you try dealing with any of it, that's what you need to do, is get some sleep. We'll get the answers later on. We'll get all of them, I promise you that. I'm with you on this thing, one hundred percent, okay? But right now, what we need is to get you some sleep, I mean some real sleep, because things can go bad here."

"Bad?"

"Well, worse is what I meant. This thing can get dangerous, going on for too long. You need to let go of it. Just for now. You need to put it down and let yourself get some sleep. Then we can deal with all the rest of it, okay? So I'll set up an appointment for tomorrow morning, right? Cal?"

Cal looked at Billy like he was watching his mouth move but nothing more. When it stopped moving, he looked away.

8.

Thursday morning.

Billy set up a doctor's appointment for ten-thirty. He swung by at ten to pick up Cal.

Cal was standing at the end of the driveway in the same clothes he'd had on last night and the same look on his face. He opened the door, sat onto the seat and shut the door quietly behind him. He rolled the window up and looked straight ahead and waited.

"Cal. I called in to Angel Fire this morning. I talked with your boss down there. Hank's his name, right? That's still your guy down there? I hope it's alright with you, that I did that, but, well, I did it anyway, so you're covered down there for now, for the rest of the week, okay? So no more worries from there. You can sleep this thing off till Monday morning if you want to."

Cal looked up.

"You didn't tell him, did you? About Gayle leaving?"

"Nah. No way. I . . ."

"Because I sure don't want those guys down there knowing that. That's none of their damn business."

"Yeah, no way. I totally agree. No, what I told him, Hank, was that there was this family thing, like an emergency, and there'd be a funeral coming up, and that it kind of hit you hard and sudden, and you had to attend to some of the details and stuff. Settle the family matters. So I told him you'd be out of town for a while, and you asked me to make some calls because you were already on the road. So you're clear down there for now, okay? Until Monday morning. Hank said it was no problem, Cal. That's what he told me. Said it was no problem at all, so not to worry."

They pulled away from the curb and rolled down the street.

Cal stood at the same curb half an hour later with a small vial of pills in his hand. He nodded to Billy.

"Okay."

Billy nodded back. "Alright." He drove off for work.

Cal watched his truck until it rounded the bend and was gone from sight. He watched a mangy dog a block away pulling trash backwards from a can tipped on its side. Coyotes. They came down from the mountains, to eat trash.

When he sat on the living room floor with his back to the wall it was just past noon. The bottle of pills sat on the floor next to him and a glass of water next to that. The day was warm. The windows were open but there was no breeze to move the air.

A car went squealing down the block with a loose fan belt.

Cal held the pill bottle in one shaky hand and steadied it with the other hand against his knee. He read the small print that told him how much to take, what to expect and when to expect it, how much alcohol he shouldn't consume and which heavy machinery he shouldn't operate.

He twisted off the cap and rolled two pills into his palm. Little pink pills with a slice down the middle. He tipped them into his mouth. They didn't taste pink. More like metallic gray. He washed them down with water and waited. He stared out at the room. Five minutes passed. He picked up the bottle and read the label again, shook another two pills free and swallowed them down.

He settled back to wait for the what and when to expect it.

Forty-five minutes later and no sleep yet, no magic bullet. The day the same as it was earlier, his mind in a tailspin, his back to the wall, the room before him sparked with dust motes falling through the slanted sunlight.

His mouth felt thick, coarse and dry inside like burlap. He needed to stand, he needed to get some water. It took forever for that thought to reach his legs.

He stood and steadied himself at arm's length from the wall. He bounced down the hallway, one side to the other, pinball-style.

He stood at the bathroom sink with his hands on the faucet knobs. He bent low for a drink and missed and nearly broke a tooth, his upper lip split and bled nicely and he cursed the faucet for the shape it was. He drank until he felt like a bagful of water, but his mouth was still dry.

He straightened up and took a long look into the mirror.

His face looked like guacamole. There was a sound at his ears like air escaping a punctured tire.

He thought he heard his name being called.

Silence.

He heard his name being called again. A woman's voice, distant sounding, or like a milk-colored snake entering his head and slithering away.

Silence again.

Someone knocking at the kitchen door.

"Cal?"

He slid down the length of the hall, his back to the wall. He stopped at the kitchen and held onto the doorjamb.

She was standing outside the screen door, holding something in her hands.

"Mrs. Whitley." She said so herself.

It was the neighbor from across the street. A paper-thin older woman with a shock-top of wind-blown white hair. He thought how well the word *corn* went with the word *stalk* when he saw her.

Cornstalk.

He nodded his head.

He crossed the floor and stood by the kitchen door. He watched her face through the wire mesh screen. Tiny holes that no bug could get ever through. She stood on the other side and smiled, but her eyes looked sad. She said that she was sorry.

Cal shrugged.

She said that she brought him a casserole to eat.

"To eat," she said again, and raised the thing a little higher in her hands. "May I come in?"

He didn't feel like eating.

He nodded.

She pulled the screen door open with her foot and stepped inside. She set the casserole down on the counter. She brushed her hands off on her apron. She wore lots of bracelets on her wrists. Charm bracelets, dangly things. They caught the sunlight and flashed.

She gave him a mother-like look and said she understood what was happening.

Cal wondered what she understood.

She said again that she was sorry. And she said that she had seen Gayle last week. That she had seen Gayle with the moving van, and with the movers, and they were in the driveway with all the boxes and the furniture and she waved hello and Gayle waved back but she seemed too busy so they didn't talk. And that it was Friday.

"Friday morning," Mrs. Whitley said.

She smiled but her eyes looked sad.

"And I thought you were both moving," she said. But now she knew differently. Now she understood.

Cal watched her eyes.

And she promised he would be okay.

'You'll be okay," she said.

"And call me if you need anything. Anything at all. That's what neighbors are for."

Then she was gone, and the casserole stayed where it was on the counter.

Cal turned and walked down the hall to the bedroom door. He sat down in the doorway.

The bedroom looked like a vacated office, random papers stuffed into boxes, envelopes scattered across the floor, an extension cord snaking through the dust where the bed had stood. Curtains absent from the windows.

The scene of an exit.

Cal fenced with his memories.

9.

It was past sunset when the non-effect of the pills wore off. No sleep had been delivered. More like a congealed fog he had waded through in search of a way out. He was jittery now, overstressed, his mouth dry like sawdust and his skin like it was coated with wax. His hair hurt just lying flat on top of his head.

No chance of sleep like that tonight.

He got in his truck and drove aimlessly through the town. He listened to the radio, he didn't listen to the radio, he turned it off, he turned it on again, he looked absently out the window at the strangers passing by.

Strangers.

"Stranger than what," Gayle used to say to that word. There was a funny face she would make to go with it.

And he drove nowhere in the deeper night, then straight through it, wide awake in the sleeping world, the drifts of cool night fog in the valleys parting like some greater ghost than he to hide within.

Then it was Friday morning.

He showed up at dawn in Billy's kitchen with two large cups of coffee and a pair of ham egg and cheese sandwiches. They sat at the table with the red sunlight streaming in the window and Cal talked himself in circles, wound-up like a lopsided top with a dozen theories as to what was really happening here with Gayle and why she'd gone away, and what the big picture was and what his plan should be to stay in the game now that he totally understood it, and how he planned to stay in it to win it, to win Gayle back, and exactly how he would do it. And he knew that much, he would definitely do it. Because what else was there?

Billy tried to follow the torrent of words but it was too much and way too early, and there were still more words coming from him and more ideas and Billy pointed to the clock and was pulling his boots on and walking for the door. He apologized but he had to go to work, and they could definitely talk more later, and Cal nodded, and Billy left.

At eleven a.m. Cal drove to the doctor's office. The doctor was booked up and busy and he expressed a mild disinterest in Cal's reaction to the pills. He said, "It happens sometimes," and prescribed another class of sleep inducers, one that he promised would knock out a horse, with no extra charge from him.

Blue pills this time, triangular shape, no slice. Another page of warnings in small print, another sixty bucks at the pharmacy.

An hour before dawn the following day, in the blue underwater light oozing in through the window, his face nearly focused in the bathroom mirror, Cal was forced to conclude he wasn't a horse.

10.

Saturday morning.
It was a week ago that the alarm clock bolted to the nightstand in the Motel 8 in Scottsdale buzzed Cal awake from his last sleep. It sounded like a pissed-off bumblebee trapped in a plastic drinking cup in half an inch of water. He stood in the dark with his work boot in hand and smacked the clock back into silence. He knew then why it was bolted to the nightstand. He dropped the boot to the floor. He stood at the window, parted the curtains and let the sunrise bleach the remains of sleep from him. He stared out to the parking lot, to the company trucks parked all in a row and the highway rolling alive with traffic beyond.
A Saturday morning in Scottsdale. One more day of work, then home to Gayle.
Saturday morning in Santa Fe, a week later and still unarrived, a shadow man in transit on a living room floor. Cal sat back against the wall with his elbows on his knees and his head in his hands, beside him a bottle of beer half empty and a pint container of pork-fried rice one day old, the cardboard top torn away, the rice gone stiff, the pork turning gray. The slip of paper from the fortune cookie lying face up on the floor, read twice over and tossed aside:

~ *He who journeys without a home has wings, but no feet.* ~

11.

Cal walked past the receptionist's desk just before noon, unscheduled, uninvited, and way past tired, with a hundred and twenty bucks worth of the drug industry's best efforts to sing a convincing lullaby held in his fist. He hadn't been convinced. He stepped into doctor's office and slapped the pills down on his desk.

"No sleep, doc. What the hell did I just spend my money on?"
He sat heavily into the chair opposite the doctor.

The doctor looked over the two vials of pills. He checked the big watch on his wrist. He looked into Cal's face. Looked closer into his eyes. He seemed intrigued. He had some questions.

"Does your vision seem to jump or bounce about the room?"
"It did today."
"A roaring sound in the ears at times?"
"More like hissing. Comes and goes."
"Do you have the waking visions?"
"The what?"
"The waking visions. Dreams happening before your eyes, but while you are still awake."
"Like hallucinations?"
The doctor half-nodded. "I call them waking visions."
Cal half-nodded back. "I see things."
"Things that are not there?"
Cal gave him a look. "They're there when I see them."
"I see. And how long since you last slept?"
Cal had to think about that. "About a week."
"A week without sleep?"
"Yep."
"No sleep for the whole week?"
"That's why I'm here, doc."
"And why is this?"
Cal stared at the floor. "I can't get to sleep."
The doctor nodded. "You are thinking too much at night?"
"I wouldn't call it thinking."
"What would you call it?"
"I would call it not thinking."
The doctor checked his watch again. "And before last week, you would say that you had a good sleep each night, or an average sleep, or not so good?"
Cal shrugged. "I never had to think about it before. A good average, I guess. Not so bad, considering."
"Considering what?"
"Considering I never had to think about it before."

The doctor jotted down some notes in a blue pad. A range of diplomas hung on the wall behind him. On the desk was a framed photo of the doctor standing at the rim of a smoking volcano with a younger woman. He was smiling, she look worried. A younger wife perhaps. Maybe an older daughter. It could have gone either way.

The office smelled of disinfectants and lemon candy.

The doctor stood and walked to the front side of his desk. He sat at the edge. He folded his arms across his chest.

"In clinical studies, a brain deprived of sleep for too long will fall into an R.E.M. state of sleep for moments at a time."

Cal looked up.

"The initials stand for Rapid Eye Movement." He swung his eyes back and forth beneath his closed lids to demonstrate. "The sleep-deprived brain will have its moments of this sleep while still being functionally awake. The dreams fragments, the waking visions, will occur while the other characteristics of normal sleep are absent. With some cases of chronic sleep loss, a patient's brain can be found to counteract any substances introduced for the purpose of the diminishment of consciousness."

Cal said, "What?"

"The condition is known as *hyper-vigilance*. As it seems in your case, the brain is outsmarting the drugs."

It took a minute for that to sink in. "I have a condition?"

"It would seem, yes. If indeed you took the pills as directed and experienced no sleep as a result, yes." He looked appraisingly at Cal. "Very few individuals are capable of this counter-reaction. It is a rare accommodation."

Cal stared at the diplomas on the wall. "That's a pretty lousy accommodation."

The doctor agreed. "Unfortunate, yes." He sat again at the edge of his desk. "It could be said that your brain is guarding the off-switch to your consciousness. It refuses to give up control. It refuses to allow sleep."

"Refuses it? Why would my brain do that? I'm dead tired here, doc, and I can't think, and I need sleep."

The doctor backed away slightly. He held his hands apart. "Your brain would do it to survive. The organism does what it does to survive. It is always about that. It is always about the survival."

"The survival."

"Yes. The survival."

Cal glanced again at that photo on the desk. Billows of steam and lava were rising from the volcano. There was a third person there, further in the background, that he hadn't noticed before. A person slightly blurred from movement. Running away, perhaps.

He rubbed his eyes.

"I can't think straight here."

"Exactly," the doctor said. He brought his hands together. "With this condition, if left untreated for too long, the mind becomes lost."

Those last words took a while to focus.

"The mind becomes lost?"

"Precisely. The brain insures its own survival by losing the mind first." He gave Cal a sincere look.

"First?"

"Correct."

"Why?"

"Primarily the brain is a regulatory organ. What we call the mind is a luxury of interpretation, a side effect of the much larger process, which of course is the process of survival. You can live your entire life without a mind. You cannot live at all without a brain."

Cal stared back at the man.

"It is called a mal-adaptation by some researchers."

"I, ah . . . I'm not getting any of this."

The doctor nodded appreciatively.

"There are many mal-adaptations we don't fully understand."

Cal shook his head. His eyeballs ached.

"So I'm going to go nuts?"

The doctor leaned back. "Why would you do that?"

"You just said I would."

"I'm sure I didn't."

"What did you say?"

"I said the mind becomes lost if the condition remains untreated."

"That's the same thing."

"Not at all. One happens to you while you are not realizing it. That would be the losing of the mind. The other happens while you know it is happening, then, as you fight to stop it happening and are unsuccessful, that would be, as you say, the going nuts." The doctor smiled. "It's a funny saying." He waved his hand aside. "More directly put, an aggregate loss of sleep extended over a prolonged period of time amounts to a death sentence for the mind. Not so much for the rest of you, but for the mind, indeed." The doctor inched closer. "But there are interventions available to treat this condition. Electro-shock therapy, for one."

Cal stood immediately to leave. "Not for this one." He was walking for the door.

The doctor curved around to head him off.

"There is also the controlled administration of morphine. This allows the brain to reset."

Cal stopped. He gave that some thought. "You can do this?"

"We would check you into a hospital for that procedure. There is round-the-clock monitoring necessary."

Cal shook his head. "I'm not going to any hospital."

The doctor gave him a confused look. "You don't believe hospitals are good places?"

"They're good places for dying."

The doctor looked into Cal's face.

"Belief is one of the hardest conditions to cure."

Cal stared back. "So that's where we are now?"

The doctor smiled. "There is also a promising group of sedatives being developed now. GABA inhibitors, they are called. They are in the final stages of evaluation for FDA approval. They will soon be available to the general public. Another year, perhaps. Preliminary tests show these drugs to be most effective."

Cal laughed. "Another year?"

"Maybe less. These drugs target the neural receptors, in the medulla, in the reptilian cortex of the brain. Here." He pointed to the base of his skull. His phone rang but he ignored it. "Here the drugs can block signals coming from the upper brain, which causes an almost total shutdown of what we call consciousness."

Cal waited.

"Sleep!" the doctor said, his hands open, his palms up.

"These are pills?" Cal asked.

"Yes, pills."

"That's what you've got for me? More pills?"

"A very different kind of pill."

"Haven't we been there already? Look, I need to get some sleep."

"You will."

"When, next year?"

"Now." The doctor nodded to a side cabinet.

Cal gave the cabinet a blank look.

"You said they weren't available for a year."

"To the general public, yes. For you, now."

Cal stared back.

The doctor tilted his head. "You must be assigned to the survey first. Once you are assigned, you get the pills immediately."

"How do I get assigned?"

"A participating doctor may assign you. I am a participating doctor." He smiled. "You sign a waiver, then you are assigned."

"What am I waiving?"

"Your right to future complaint from any possible side effects the drug may have. It is a legal protocol. Standard practice with new drugs."

"What are the side effects?"

"These are being evaluated as the survey moves forward."

Cal turned again to leave.

"As you sign the waiver, you will receive the drugs cost free as a consideration for your participation. You are asked only to keep a record of your experiences, a list of your reactions as you take each dosage. There's a checklist supplied, you fill in the blanks, it's all very simple. And very safe, I assure you."

Cal sat in the chair. He looked over the waiver. He signed it.

The doctor began filling out forms, asking endless medical history questions.

Cal stared at that picture on the desk. The blurred person in the background was definitely running away.

The doctor produced six large pills in a small zip-lock bag. Inflated-looking pills, the shape of a pillow, the color of a daffodil. The word Pernasom etched across the face of each. He told Cal to go home, to eat lightly, to have no alcohol. To use no power equipment. To hide his car keys to prevent any accident while driving under the drug's influence, which happens quite suddenly. He handed Cal a small notebook, showed him the layout of the checklist inside, the questions he would have to answer.

"Do you need a pen?"

Cal gave him a tired look. "I have a pen."

He turned to leave.

"Don't forget to write," the doctor said. He laughed. He showed Cal to the door. The receptionist looked up expectantly as they passed, then looked away.

12.

Saturday night, eight-thirty pm, Santa Fe time.

"Saturday night in a hard-drinking town," Billy would've said if he were in the room. He would've said the same thing for any other night. In any other room.

Cal sat on the floor with his back to the wall. He watched the last of the sun's afterglow pull backwards out the windows, over the mountains to the west and away.

His hands shook, his vision bounced around the room like a bagful of frogs. It'd been a week without sleep now. Seven days joined to seven nights, like sections of some bleak pipeline welded into one, with nothing to block the wash of details from one day to the next.

He held a Pernasom in his quaking grip, his hands on his knees, his knees to his chest, and he tried to remember how it felt when the sofa sat where he did now and the TV sat opposite, snarling and jingling, enticing and admonishing, lying and crying and urging another purchase while he and Gayle ignored it and traded their own stories of the week with that first glass of wine or a pair of cold beers, Gayle searching the listing for a movie with the smell of popcorn already in the house from the microwave or nachos from the toaster oven a dozen times over with the phone ringing for friends to meet later for drinks or his head down inside the fridge sorting through the leftovers for another snack to spoil dinner for two at nine, then home for sex.

The memory of all that.

The struggle for memory. The details of when or once why, lying puddled in haste before his very eye. Before his very eye.

"Fucking horse pill."

He tried swallowing it down and almost choked. It dislodged from his throat at the last moment with the whole glass of water weighing in.

He sat back and became one with the emptiness of the room. The notebook and a pen on the floor beside him.

He raised his hands in the air. Like two shuddering udders.

"How am I going to write with these things?"

He pushed the pad and pen away.

He waited for the effects of the drug to kick in.

13.

Pernasom . . . the grand finale at a Fourth of July celebration held inside a coalmine. Electro-shock therapy administered by needle-fingered ghouls in fat white robes, faceless frenzied creatures carved of shards of blizzard-flown ice caressing his brain with hot greedy hands, squeezing it blind for its last drops of daylight, turning thoughts away homeless into the vagrant vacant night, howling out loud through the chemical roar . . . Pernasom.

After its promised delivery of eight hours of deep natural sleep, beware the under-mentioned delivery of a six hour hangover unlike any of alcoholic familiarity: imagine a huge block of cold black steel suspended directly above you and the feeling that it's about to drop, that it's always just about to drop, and crush you flatter than a page in a book.

Cal slumped with his head back to the wall and the sun rising against all belief out the window, the fireworks he saw in the room that night exceeded in their ferocity only by the ones he saw inside his skull when he tried closing his eyes.

Just another night, this one pinned to the wall by explosions in a visual cortex chemically unplugged and electrically short-circuiting. His reptile brain rose up and screamed and writhed its signals across circuits meant for much less.

The organism does what it does to survive. It's always about that. Always about the survival.

The sun was rising in Santa Fe.

A gorgeous Sunday morning.

14.

Cal, when he finally could stand up without falling over, took the remaining Pernasoms out to the garage. He poured the pills from their little plastic bag and laid them in a tight circle on the cement floor. He pulled a sledgehammer down from its pegs on the wall and smashed the pills and some of the concrete below them with a single ringing blow. He hung the hammer back on the wall and returned to the house.

Billy showed up at ten. He came in through the kitchen door eating a peach. The screen door slapped shut behind him with a loud crack. Cal winced from the sound. Billy stopped up short when he saw Cal's face.

"Whoa! You look like warmed-over shit."

He tossed the second peach he held over to Cal. Cal caught it, just barely, and set it down beside him. He sat on the counter, close by the sink. He would retch occasionally from the vertigo.

Billy watched him a few minutes. He took a seat on the floor.

Cal told him about the night. About the drug and how he'd signed up like a goddamn test monkey to take the goddamn drug. Told him about the rage of nightlong fireworks and how burnt his brain felt, how his skin felt like plastic and the taste of metal in his mouth sucked so he couldn't stop drinking water and puking and how he smashed the pills in the garage with the sledge and he'd do the same thing to the doctor if he thought it would do any good but he knew it wouldn't so what was the use.

"What's the damn use, Billy."

Billy shrugged. "You could pay someone else to do it for you."

They were quiet a while.

"I am beat," Cal said. He looked the part. "What is it, Billy, that I just can't sleep here. That I could want it, need it like I do, and it won't come. It just won't come." He looked up at Billy a few seconds. "You ever hear of anything like it?"

Billy glanced around the room. He shook his head.

"Nope. My own sleep's never more than a blink away, most times. Two blinks, if I've got company." His face brightened a notch. "Wait. There is something I heard. More like I saw it with my own eyes. This guy I worked with, an older guy about sixty, sixty-five. I worked with him a few years back, ran into him on some carpentry jobs every few months or so. We were sitting down having lunch one day and I noticed his hand, all the fingers on his right hand, and it looked like there were no fingernails there, just none at all. So I tried for a better look without getting right up in his face, I didn't want to embarrass him or anything, you know, like bring up some bad old memories because maybe he was in some prison camp once or something, where they do that kind of thing to make you talk. Who knows, right? But the more I thought about it, the more I figured he wouldn't mind me asking, because it wasn't like he was trying to hide it, his hand was right out there in plain sight, holding onto a sandwich. So I said, yo, Uncle Bill, what's with the missing fingernails?"

Cal looked up. "This guy's your uncle?"

"No, no. That's a job thing. Whenever there's more than one guy on a jobsite with the same first name, you call the older guy uncle. Saves on the confusion, right?"

Cal gave Billy a look. "So if there's a younger guy there named Bill, they call you Uncle Bill?"

Billy shook his head. "No way."

"Why not?"

"It goes according to size too. You never call the bigger guy *uncle*. Or if there are two guys named Tom, you don't call the older guy Uncle Tom. That one just doesn't work out."

"What do you call him then?"

Billy shrugged. "Cuz. Short for cousin. So anyway, I asked Uncle Bill where all his fingernails went. He held up his right hand, he showed it off a bit, gave me a real good look. And he held his other hand up alongside it and the fingernails were all there like normal. But his right hand, nothing. It was just skin, like on the rest of his fingers, just skin, all the way up, over the top and back down the other side, slick as can be. So Uncle Bill sat back and said, 'it's the damnedest thing.' And he tells me how he used to work with his brother, his older brother, and they worked together since he was fifteen or so. So that's about fifty years by the time I met him, right? So they started out in carpentry and had themselves a cabinet business for a while, and they did some flooring and tile work and some other odd stuff like stucco walls, fences, etc. But they always worked together, and he said his brother more or less ran the show and lined up all the jobs, and it usually worked out pretty good, so that was that. Then he said there was a day when they were out working a job like always and his brother fell down dead of a stroke. Bam. Just like that, dead and gone. So they had the funeral a few days later and Uncle Bill buried his brother. And that was that."

Billy gave Cal a long look.

"So he went back to work the next week without his brother, and it was sort of the first time for that, and he said it didn't feel right, not right at all. Over the course of the next few days, he says, the fingernails on his right hand turned mushy, like they were being dissolved in acid or something, and then they fell out, one by one, for better or worse. And never grew back." He shook his head. "Talk about losing your right-hand man, huh?"

Cal stared at Billy a while. "What's that got to do with me not sleeping?"

Billy shrugged. "I didn't say it had anything to do with you not sleeping. You asked me if I'd ever heard of anything like it. That story sounds pretty much like it to me. Same basic what-the-fuck, just a different end result."

Cal thought it over.

"Look. We know that something's keeping you awake, right? So it must run pretty deep. What did the doctor say? Did he tell you anything?"

Cal nodded his head, then held it still for the dizziness that followed. He waited a moment to speak.

"Yeah. The doctor . . . he gave it a *name*."

Billy waited. "So what's the name?"

"*Hyper-vigilance*," Cal said. He stared at Billy. "That sound good to you?"

Billy raised an eyebrow. "Sounds like some kind of jungle snake you don't want to mess with."

Cal thought about that. "Yeah, well . . ." He shook his head, winced and held it still again. "Do I look hyper-vigilant to you?"

Billy gave him an appraising look.

"No. You look more like, well . . . I already told you what you look like."

"Yeah. Shit. Thanks."

"*Warmed-over* shit is what I said. That's different."

"Yeah? It's better?"

"No. Worse. Fresh shit's better."

They were quiet a while.

"The doctor said I could lose my mind."

Billy stared, then laughed out loud. "You? Lose your mind?" He shook his head. "No way. He doesn't know you like I do. That's the last thing I'd say you'd ever be losing. I'd bet more money on your balls dropping off in a bookstore."

Cal nodded vaguely.

"He said I would lose my mind if this thing went on too long. Something my brain would do to save itself."

Billy made a face. "Save itself? From what?"

Cal gave him a tired look. "That's what I said."

Billy thought it over.

"Well the hell with it anyway. You ask me, you lose the thing that you're thinking with, how are you going to know that you lost it in the first place? That's like saying *it feels good to be alive.* Feels good compared to what? What the hell else do you ever know?"

Awkward looks passed back and forth between them.

Billy stood and paced the length of the kitchen, twice, three times. He stopped at the screen door. He swung the door wide and looked out on the street.

Two houses down, a large man with a small leaf blower was raising a huge cloud of dust from his driveway, dust that drifted down the street to settle elsewhere.

"What the hell's the point of that?" Bill said. He watched it a while longer, shaking his head.

He pulled the door closed. He noticed how it missed the jamb at the bottom. He fussed with it a bit, trying to make it fit. He saw the broken hinge at the bottom and gave it up. He pushed his hands into his pockets, watched absently as the yellow dust cloud grew larger.

Cal stared at the tile floor, his eyes focused on a single spot, a brown stain about the size of a nickel. Coffee spill, he guessed. Coffee with cream.

He drank his black.

Then he could feel his heart pounding like a jackhammer, hollow and loose inside his chest.

15.

Monday morning, eight days of free fall, no sleep, more silence than he knew existed in the world.

He tried his hand again at work. Billy said it would do him good to get out there, back in the routine, back into the flow of things.

"You get to the bottom and you down the nut, right?"

"I don't know what that means, Billy."

"Yeah, that's, ah . . . I don't either."

But at work he was more scattered than before, dangerous now like a loaded thundercloud. Climbing ladders, dropping his tools, transposing his numbers, making electrical misconnections. Forgetting standard procedure.

He kept trying. Time after time.

That was all of what he had left to him. Time and the trying.

He was home after an endless Tuesday at work, completely fried. He had lost his wallet. He noticed it gone when he reached for it at noon to pay for a sandwich. He backtracked the rest of the day searching for it, two times, three times, that stupid lost feeling of knowing he had just looked everywhere but doing it again anyway.

The wallet stayed lost.

License, cash, credit cards. Identity. He'd lost enough already. Proofless now of who he was in a world that always demanded proof, so who was he?

Thursday afternoon his foreman Hank stopped by the job site near Rio Rancho. He motioned Cal aside for a talk. He offered condolences for the death in the family the previous week. Cal mumbled his way through a sketchy response. Hank nodded. He thanked Cal for the great job he had managed the week earlier in Scottsdale.

They stood alongside Hank's truck.

Hank suggested a leave of absence. Cal's stomach twisted and his heart stumbled involuntarily but he could find none of the right words to reverse the course of events. He more or less agreed with the decision.

Hank handed him an envelope, his two-week paycheck inside with the travel bonus for the Scottsdale job, plus a good faith, two-week-in-advance check as well. Hank assured him in every way he could that it wasn't a severance check. He told him to get some rest, told him to get some help with it if he could. Told him to call in when he felt better, to stay in touch, to hang tough.

He said they were friends.

"That's still in place, Cal. We're friends here, good friends. You've been a great team member, one of the best. Hell I don't like this one bit. No I sure don't. But it's down to business now, the way things are going, and it's not my personal feelings at all. You well know that. But I do have people to answer to. We all do." He gave Cal a long look. "We all have people to answer to."

Down to business.

His joint bank account with Gayle never held much of a surplus. She'd taken her share of it with her when she left. Cal cashed the two paychecks into twenties, kept the cash in a plain white envelope in the glove box of his truck.

First Bank of Cal, he said.

Then another weekend blurred by, Billy in attendance as best he could but the man was seriously miscast in any such role as attendant.

Cal wandered the local streets, wandered all of Santa Fe trying to exhaust himself or whatever it was left in him that wouldn't let go. He waited for a phone call from Gayle, for news of her from any quarter.

He kept his sunglasses on more than not, the daylight harder on his eyes than he could remember.

He passed more for a shadow of a thing than a thing casting a shadow.

The organism does what it does to survive. It's always about that, about the survival. Every hour, it's about that. Every minute.

He thought of taking a drive to California to see the ocean. He hadn't seen the ocean yet.

Then what, when he got there?

Turn around and drive back?

What was the point?

His hands shook like two dispossessed animals trapped at arm's length. He tried his best to regain control there, to will his hands back into stillness.

No such luck. No such will.

He stood one day outside the gallery where Gayle had worked. He stared in through the plate glass window.

What would he say to her if he were to see her standing there? What on earth would he ever say? What possible combination of words to redress the ruin of space between them?

He saw one of Gayle's paintings hanging on the back wall. The Contract, she had named it. A price tag of six thousand dollars was tacked up beside it. Gayle had laughed when the gallery owner set that number there. But she would have laughed at any number. For her, the payment for art was all in the doing. Any further payment was cake, she said. Just, cake.

In the painting, a woman stood at the edge of a cliff, off to one side. The figure was turned away from the viewer. With descending brush strokes, Gayle had created the feeling of unabated erosion, like a rain of time itself, or of gravity. It looked as though the figure had been standing at the edge of the cliff from the beginning of creation and had seen it all, the whole panoply of the world and all of its history, crashing past, bearing down. And that figure would soon be worn away to nothing.

"Fragility as a Stone" was her original title for the piece, but the gallery owner hadn't liked the title, and it was his gallery. His wall.

Gayle and Cal had been out hiking a wild section of the Sangres Mountains without a decent map. They'd run up against the edge of a dead end butte, looking for a way down where there was none. Cal said they would have to backtrack a few miles. Gayle stood a moment at the edge of the cliff, perched against the wider view, and she asked Cal to take a picture of her there before they left. As he pointed the camera, she said, "Wait," and turned away from him towards the desolate view. "Like this," she said and held the pose, and he snapped the picture. She really liked that picture when she saw it. She said it defined the dimensions of her soul, or at least pointed in that direction. Cal wondered how so. She said that more words would never get them there.

That photo eventually became the inspiration for the painting. It was a self-portrait in that respect.

There was the painting now before him on the back wall. And there was Gayle standing in it, turned away from the viewer. Wearing down, forever wearing down.

The new girl at the desk was looking at him like he might be trouble. She was reaching for the phone, she was dialing. Cal saw his own reflection in the plate glass. He had to agree. He nodded a vague compliance and walked away.

One block, two blocks, a dozen blocks aimlessly he walked.

The Contract, Fragility as a Stone, his silent conversations unraveling.

16.

Another sunrise. Another week draining past. The neighborhood shifting its gears from weekend to work and he stood by silent and watched it all through the glass.

At nine o'clock, he placed a call to the New Mexico State Police. He waded through a list of possible options, punched the number that matched his need. He was connected to the Missing Persons Bureau. He had a pad and pen ready.

The officer on duty said he would need some information about Gayle.

"What was she wearing when last seen?"

"I couldn't say."

A description of her car. The plate numbers. The date she went missing. Her relationship to the caller.

"And you have reason to believe that she's still in New Mexico?"

"She was here last week. Two weeks ago. I don't know where she is now. That's why I'm calling."

"And you have reason to believe she was abducted?"

"No. No, she, ah . . . she left."

Silence on the other end. The reshuffling of papers. The man explained the limits of their jurisdiction. The procedures they were mandated to follow, the circumstances that would allow them to engage those mandates, what the law permitted, what it didn't. He supplied Cal with a list of phone numbers, of family help organizations, of private detectives he might call. The other lines were ringing off the hook, the office was busy today.

"Killer busy," the officer said. He laughed at his own choice of words. "Full moon last night, right? People go nuts." He wished Cal luck. He hung up.

Cal exhaled. He sat back against the wall. He stared down at the pad on his lap, its pages filled now with the scattered and scratched out descriptions of his missing wife, the color of her hair, her height, her weight. Her age. Her eye color. The year and make of her car. All the things he already knew. Or thought he knew. Scattered now and scratched out.

17.

Middle of the third week.

The phone numbers he dialed turned themselves around as he dialed them, the wrong people would answer and hang up.

Traffic signs read backwards, or didn't read at all in the normal sense. Rules of the road were disintegrating before his eyes.

He found himself stopped at an intersection for a red light. He had no recall of how it had happened, he just found himself there. No memory of seeing the light, no memory of putting his foot on the brake.

Does red do that to us automatically? Make us stop? What about that red cape they wave at a bullfight? That red makes the bull go. And what about green? He tried to think of a time where green makes you stop. He opened a container of leftover chicken salad once and found it covered over with a bright green fuzz. That green made him stop. The tangled wall of vines and leaves in a rainforest jungle, there's a green that tells us to stop, stop cutting down trees, stop making the jungle disappear. Just leave it alone. He tapped his fingers at the steering wheel. So red can mean go sometimes. Green can mean stop.

He looked up and saw the light had turned green. The man in the car behind him leaned on his horn. Cal watched him in the rear view mirror. The man blew his horn again and threw his arms out to the side, like what-the-fuck. Cal leaned on his horn and threw his own arms out to the side, what-the-fuck back at you, buddy. They sat there, engaged and enraged, until the light turned red again. The guy behind him threw his hands up one last time, defeated. Cal took his foot off the brake, hit the gas and began to roll through the intersection against traffic. Those cars hit their brakes now and began working their horns, waving their arms out the windows. Cal waved back and his was the only car moving, lawfully or not.

Other driving distractions that nearly caused him accidents: the flattened roadside kill of a magpie, its broken wing flapping like a call for help in the breeze of every passing car; a young girl walking by the side of the road, her face precisely obscured as he passed by, a small child pulling her along by the hand, urging her to hurry; a handprint not his own appearing in the dust on his dashboard; a burro standing atop a ten-foot-high pile of trash, proudly, king-of-the-hill style; a sign that read Breakfast Served All Day 24/7 Six Miles Ahead on Right, Closed Mondays – Forty Miles To Next Gas Open.

He rediscovered his high school dislike of cigarettes. He smoked them again for the slight fog they delivered, the measured sense of time they marked. Twenty smokes to get him through the bright half of a day, twenty or more to get him through the dark side, each day cleaved in two like that, the sun a flaming yo-yo sunk at one horizon and yanked up on the other, the hours in between spinning, the daytime tedious and glaring, guilt-filled and roaring out loud, the nighttime empty and quiet enough to wander, then eventually too empty, too quiet, pressing in against him like a wall of pure vacancy, punctured only by the spark of his cigarette lighter at his face, flash, flash. Flash.

One midnight at a gas station out on Cerrillos, he ran into a friend who didn't recognize him. Who wouldn't recognize him. Who refused to recognize him.

Cal stared the man down until he took notice.

"You got a problem?" the man said.

"What am I, the invisible man here? You just pretend you don't know me?"

The guy gave him a good long look, then shrugged.

"Am I supposed to know you?"

Cal walked closer. He pointed to the man and said his name. He pointed to himself and said his own name. The man took another look and shook his head. "I don't know those names, and I don't know you."

Cal mentioned the history they shared. The man half-listened, his jaw set. He wasn't amused.

"And I'm telling you, you got the wrong guy. Now you best back off, friend."

And the more Cal looked at him, the less he was sure of it. The man reminded him of no one in particular. Cal stepped away at a loss. The gas station itself, then the intersection surrounding it, all of it seemed out of place suddenly, the details unfamiliar, like the evaporation of recall of a dream you wake too suddenly from.

He topped off his tank, got inside his truck and drove away.

He spent the following nights driving further from town, out on the lonely roads, the roads of no familiarity, killing the time, covering the distances, burying his thoughts in the miles behind him. He found one road so long and straight and dark there was no need for his hands to be on the steering wheel. He could have closed his eyes and gone to sleep. But he wasn't sleeping.

He'd pull off the road sometimes, drive down into the hidden wash of an arroyo and lie on his back in the bed of the truck watching the stars parade across the sky in their entirety, until the morning light ate them whole. Some vague form of contest it was for him, watching the whole night sky roll by like that. Cal versus the firmament. He won every time.

He spent that Friday night with Billy and some other friends, trying to get himself drunk. He could feel the alcohol as it bled up inside his head, cool and foreign like some lost tourist wandering his brain without purpose. It did nothing more for him than that.

"Things are okay," he'd answer to any of questions of how he was doing. "Just takes time, right?"

"Exactly," Billy said. He clapped him on the shoulder. "That's why trains have no rear-view mirrors. They can't do a damn thing about what's behind them."

18.

"Blown out of the water."

Cal sat atop the roof of his pickup, parked out at the end of the Hyde Road Overlook north of town. Legs crossed, his hands at rest in his lap, his sunglasses on, looking to the world like some ragged understudy of Buddha, but he felt no part of that serenity.

Santa Fe was fading into the haze of another sunset. It sparkled back to life a half-hour later as a bright electric skeleton, its streets and highways outlined and shimmering. He could follow the lay of the land as it rolled further south, the glow of the highway curving like a snake through the dark hills to the rise of Sandia Peak in the distance, then Albuquerque beckoning beyond like a promised land hatching beneath a lid of orange-brown light.

"Blown out of the water," he said again, each syllable turning like some curious object lifted from a shelf.

He'd heard the saying enough, in films, on TV. Still, it sounded foreign to him. New Mexico didn't have the kind of water you need in place first to then get blown out of, so it was an off image.

"Blown out of the water." He nodded to the cadence of the phrase, felt each word escape him and dive away to silence in the dust-dry landscape.

He would sink deep into a tub of water if he could find one, the steaming hot water of an oversized tub filled to the rim, in a darkened room where no sound could escape, sink further until the water covered him over and he would lay beneath the surface without need of another breath, until all the chatter above him and within him had been stilled.

The sameness of days behind him.

19.

Cal returned home late in the day near the middle of the fourth week. A Wednesday, he knew vaguely. He'd spent most of that day driving back from being lost on the dirt roads and forest trails out past Taos.

There was a police car idling in his driveway. Cal saw it from a half a block off and he drove past. He circled the block trying to think of what it was he might have done wrong, or might not have done right. He had no driver's license yet. He hadn't applied for one, couldn't remember, didn't really care. He ran more red lights than he knew of, he cut people off at intersections, he could barely hold his focus on any busy street.

He pulled up to the curb on the second pass. He took in a long breath and shut off his truck. He glanced at his bloodshot eyes in the rear view mirror, the dark circles below them. He put his sunglasses on. He took them off again, thinking it might look better, more honest. He stepped from the truck and walked across the yard to the driveway, resigned to whatever fate. The officer stepped from the squad car. He waited for him by the hood. He introduced himself.

"Patrolman Hendricks," he said. "Ed." He was about the same age as Cal. He took a step forward.

"Are you Cal?"

"That's me." Cal offered his hands forward to be cuffed, a sideways smile to go with it.

The officer had no smile to offer, his eyes more serious than that. He held some papers in his hand. He spoke quietly to Cal, methodically, to verify some other names, some other addresses. He went over a computer print-out, a list of contacts and phone numbers Cal would have to call and the times of day that would be best to arrange things. To arrange things.

To arrange . . . things.

The officer said he was sorry. He tilted his head slightly when he said it. He tucked the papers into a gray envelope and handed them to Cal. He nodded once and turned away, got into his car, took off his hat and laid it on the seat beside him. He glanced up at Cal. He gave him another short nod; farewell, or take care, or shit happens. He backed out of the drive, drove away up the street.

A few neighbors stood shadowlike in their doorways, at their windows behind curtains, curious at a distance.

Cal sat on the steps outside the kitchen, his back to the street. He read the accident report in the fading light, trying to steady it from the shake of his hands:

> Car traveling southbound, Pacific Coast Highway, twelve miles north of Big Sur, single occupant, 6:35 am Pacific time.
> Road conditions: wet.
> Visibility: intermittent, patchy fog.
> Estimated speed: 60 mph.
> Control of vehicle lost, guardrail breached.
> Estimated time of death.
> Immediate causes . . .

Immediate causes.
A stack of papers shaking in his hands.
Gayle had died.
Yesterday.

20.

Three days later, three dozen phone calls behind him, Cal made the long drive east around the mountains and then down, down, down to Enid, Oklahoma.

He stood with Gayle's family inside a wooden church, then outside in the cemetery beneath a blistering sun, the two solitary trees there scattering their shade just out of reach, any answers he might have had coming lowered into the cooler ground. Words were spoken.

Eyes with questions held, his own answers avoided or spun off in vague response.

"What was she doing in California?"

"Where was she going?"

"Were you all planning to move?"

More eyes peering into his, trying to see it somehow, to make sense of it all. To breach the obliqueness.

Standing in the kitchen of her childhood home, a paper plate in hand, a furtive meal. Feeding nothing in him but the need to move through the next block of time, then the next after that.

The sun angled lower. Scores of people hovered more relative than he, each with a claim to some special memory and eager to offload it, to share the grief, to spill it.

A photograph of Gayle as a child, smiling out from a frame on the wall. Her head wreathed in flowers then, the frame wreathed in flowers now.

An early friend of hers he'd heard of but never met. She steered him away from the crowd, off to one side of the table. Several drinks downstream by then, she needed to talk.

"Gayle was the one," she said. "You know how every group's got one? She was the one for here." She paused. "The old everyday stuff, that couldn't hold her place at a table too long. She lit out from here soon as she could, that's for sure. Just picked up and gone one day, trail of dust behind her. Oh boy."

She laughed some and sipped at her drink.

"And we got us plenty of everyday around here too, if you didn't already notice. You could be sitting down talking with somebody, nod off for an hour, wake up and finish your sentence, and they'd still be sitting there where you left them, happy for the extra time they just had to think it all over."

She tipped her head toward the photo of Gayle.

"Not so much with Gayle, though. She was always real busy trying to get away to something else, even if she didn't know exactly what that something else might be."

Cal nodded. The girl nodded back.

"It seemed like religion sometimes, with her. Not the real kind of religion, of course, but it as well might have been, the way she was always at it."

She laughed at a memory.

"There were some old days, back in high school, where she'd had just about enough of what she could take of being here, and she'd walk on out to Route 412 and stick her thumb out in the air and be gone, just like that. Whoa, huh? And she always headed west too. She said west was her destiny. Call of the wild or what, right? I wished I could've been more like her, but I could've never done something like that. She said she had to do it to feed her spirit. I looked her right back in the eye one time and asked where she got the damn nerve to step away like that and just take off on her own. 'What kind of spirit needs feeding like that?' I said, but she didn't have any real answer for me. More like just a look she gave me that said don't ask."

She sipped from her drink. She turned and pulled a curtain half aside and looked out the window at the miles of sunflowers planted there, the world flat and golden to the horizon.

"When I think back to it, it's almost like there was some kind of treasure that she kept tucked away inside her. Something that she needed to keep secret from the rest of us. I got mad with her at times for that, for the way it made me feel, like I was being left out of something. Best friends shouldn't feel that way."

She turned back from the window, she glanced at Cal.

"I'm sorry. Listen to me, will you? Going on like that."

She was quiet a while.

"I don't know. Maybe she wasn't really shutting me out, not on purpose anyway. Maybe that's just who she was, for real. Someone born with a little treasure inside her. I guess we could leave it at that, right?"

She looked down at her drink, she swirled the ice in a circle.

Cal looked around the room for any near or gracious exit.

"She had herself a pet crow for a time, if you can believe it."

Cal looked back. "I didn't know that."

"She did. Fit her idea of a proper pet just fine, too. She saw there was a pair of crows building themselves a nest one day, down by the creek, up the top of that big old cottonwood." She nodded out the window. "You can just about see it, right over there."

Cal looked out the window. He saw the tops of some trees.

"Boy she could focus on stuff like that when she had a mind to it. She'd get an idea in her head and that would be that. So she got this idea that she could have herself a pet crow one day, and that it would fly up in the sky free and loose as the wind itself but it would still be hers, still be connected to her in some kind of way. And so she started going around asking everyone about what a baby crow might eat, because of what the parents would be feeding it, and she read up about it at the library. She kept watch on those two crows the whole time, binoculars and all, and when she figured the time was right, she nailed some cleats up alongside that tree and climbed right up there, right on up to the top, and she snatched herself out an egg."

The girlfriend smiled. "She wore a football helmet on her head when she did it too. She painted it over in white, but with a couple of big eyes painted onto the back because she read that the crows would be dive bombing her the whole time, trying to peck at her eyes, which those crows did for sure because I saw it, but they just pecked at the back of the helmet where those crazy eyes were painted, and Gayle kept her face tucked down inside the whole time with a pair of swimming goggles on and a bandana over her nose and mouth."

The girlfriend laughed away at that. Cal tried to smile.

"So Gayle got herself a crow egg that day, and she hatched it out a few days later in an incubator that she 'borrowed' from the Science lab. She named that baby crow Gabriel, and that bird followed her around like a puppy as soon as it could walk, and then later on when it learned to fly, Gayle would ride her bike up and down the road out front, and then further on into town even, and Gabriel would be right there the whole while, hovering over her like he was tied to a string. Some folks even thought that's what they were seeing when they saw it, and they'd yell out, "You should let that bird go, he's a wild creature, he's not meant to be kept," and she would stop her bike and Gabriel would land on her shoulder, and she'd take a hold of him and throw him up in the air and he'd fly around free as can be then land just where he was a few seconds ago and she'd yell back, "So how many times you want me to let him go?""

The girlfriend laughed a deep laugh. "Oh man."

Cal gave her a confused look. "I remember Gayle talking about a friend of hers, a boy she said she knew as a kid, by the name of Gabriel."

The girlfriend gave him a confused look back. "There was no other Gabriel around here that I ever knew of besides that crow, so he must have been it." She took a sip from her drink. "Maybe you heard her wrong." She watched Cal over the rim of her glass. She nodded and smiled hi to a guy who came in from the kitchen.

"Gayle ever do that crazy dance for you, the one she called the Gabriel dance?"

Cal half-nodded.

"She'd put us in stitches every time with that one. That was his dance, Gabriel's, she got it from him. He would stand up on a branch or something, get all excited, and he'd step twice to one side, then twice to the other, back and forth like that, faster and faster, his wings held out the whole time like he was drying out his laundry. And he'd tip his head up to the side so he could watch you, first one eye, then the other. Boy, she could make us laugh with that one."

"One day there was a boy from school who killed that bird. We were out by the corner store, hanging out in the street and talking, and Gabriel was perched up on a telephone wire above, just being his bird self, when that boy road up on his bike and stepped off and took aim with his pellet gun and killed Gabriel just like that, one shot, like that's just what you're supposed to do with a bird, right? He said he didn't know it was a pet or nothing, and we all crowded around him and were screaming that it was, and we were just about ready to beat him silly, but he kept saying he was sorry, that he was real real sorry, so Gayle stepped in and told us we should just let it go. What's done is done, she said."

She shook her head. "You ask me, I think that boy knew just what he was doing the whole time, and he was just plain jealous that a girl could have a pet such as that, so he had to put an end to it."

Her drink was empty. She looked down into the glass. She looked back at Cal.

"Gayle said we would have to have a funeral for Gabriel. She took us down beside the creek where she got him, and she set us to gathering up some sticks and brush for a funeral pyre, and we built the big sticks up crosswise like you build a log cabin, then we filled it in with the brush. It was up to about waist high when we finished it all. Gayle said that we would need some flowers too, lots of flowers and leafy vines and such, to cover it all over. She made it feel like it was some kind festival we were about to have. She made it feel like a celebration. She always had that way about her."

"When the pyre was all done, she laid Gabriel down on top with his wings spread out wide and his head propped up with a little twig so he looked just like he was flying. We sang a few songs for him, and she read some of her poems that she wrote. Then we each took a turn saying a little something about him, even if it was just about how he was always pecking at our earrings or bracelets or something, because that bird was just crazy about shiny things."

"So then we were all quiet for a spell, thinking about poor Gabriel, and Gayle turned to me and handed me the book of matches. She asked me if I would do the lighting of the fire for her, because she didn't exactly want to see that last part. She said she just wanted to have her memory of Gabriel the way it was right then, with him lying there on that bed of flowers in all his shining glory. So I said okay, that I would do that for her."

She looked a while at Cal.

Cal looked down at the half slice of orange cheese left on his plate. The half a cracker next to it.

"That was the summer she changed her name too, just before we went back to school. Changed the spelling of it anyway, from the regular old G-A-I-L, to the G-A-Y-L-E. She said it could be pronounced in two syllables if you spelled it that way, Gay-ll. So we started saying it that way. Gay-ll. We all did that, and after a while, no one remembered the difference."

She laughed. "She said I could change the spelling of my name too, just to stir things up a bit, like she said, but none of us could come up with another way to spell it that didn't make it look like some kind of disease or something. I mean, Vera, right? Where you going to go with a name like that? Gayle said that I could tack a silent *h* onto the back end and that might work out, it wouldn't change the sound of it but it would have a different look, but I couldn't see the point of adding a silent letter to it just for the looks. I mean, right?"

She glanced absently at a basket of potato chips and the bowl of dip next to it. She pulled the basket a little closer to the bowl, spun it a half-turn.

"She had a pet snake too, for a while. That was a few summers before. She kept it in one of her pockets, or up in her backpack." She laughed. "We were calling her Eve all that summer, because of her hanging around with a snake like that."

Cal nodded his head. "Eve," he said.

"Yep. Wasn't much of a snake, as snakes go. Skinny little thing not more than a foot long. She named him Pencil, because he was pencil thin and he came to a point at one end, and the other end was rounded off and kind of pink like an eraser. That was the smart end, she said, because that's what she always said about pencils, that they had a smart end and a dumb end, and the smart end was the eraser because it took care of all the mistakes the dumb end was always making." She laughed at that and shook her head. "The smart end of a pencil, right?"

Her smile faded.

"We were just girls back then. Little girls." She stared at the wreathed photo. Her eyes saddened. "I've forgotten how much I missed her," she said, barely audible.

An awkward silence spread like a stain in the wake of her words. She set her drink aside and moved away across the room.

Other people stood before him now, in ones, in twos, actors in the drama of grief, their worn out smiles, their withheld tears, their honest-to-god handshakes endless seconds long and silent. Their best wishes, their implied farewells.

Cal declined the offered bed in the spare room at the end of it all. He left by a side door instead with a liter bottle of water. He drove the eight hours back up into the high country and then down again through the deeper night.

He rolled up to his house and shut off the lights. The clock on the dash showed two-eleven a.m. as he pulled the key from the ignition. He sat in the quiet and stared at the chain of streetlamps curving away down the street, each one ringed with a thin orange halo in the cooler night air.

21.

Billy caught up with him on Tuesday.

He drove past the house for a third time that day and saw Cal's truck parked in the drive. He pulled in behind it.

He'd read the news of Gayle's death in the Monday paper, a single short paragraph, ten pages in.

He swung the screen door aside, poked his head into the kitchen. "Hey," he said when he saw Cal standing silently in the middle of the room.

Cal nodded back a thin hello.

"How you holding up, hombre?" He stepped inside. "Jeez, man. I am sorry. So sorry." He wrapped his arms around Cal. Cal stood woodenly within them.

Billy stepped back. "I cannot believe this. I mean, I just cannot believe this is happening." Tears at his eyes. "I read about it yesterday, Cal. I would have been here earlier for you if I had known. You could've called me. You should have called me."

Cal tipped his head to one side. "I had a lot of stuff to take care of. So I took care of it." He waved his hand at the empty room. He dropped it to his side and stood silent again, staring at the wall.

Billy glanced at the wall. He watched Cal. "What are you doing, Cal? What's going on here?"

Cal shrugged. "She left a while ago. That's what's going on. More of the same."

Billy gave him a hard look.

"What?" Cal said to that look. "You think something's changed here?" His eyes like two dark holes bored in the earth.

Billy backed up a step.

"Cal, look. I'm sorry, man. I don't know how this deal is for you here. I sure don't know that. It's just, the way things keep going here, with Gayle leaving like she did, and then she's way out there by herself, and she . . ." He shook his head. "And you're still here in this house, and it's all so empty, and . . ." He couldn't find the words. "You should leave, Cal. You should really leave this place. It's like a bomb's gone off here. And I think you need to set it all aside right now and leave it. It's no good here. Not anymore. Not like it was. Not like this. And there's no point to it now. Not in the waiting."

Cal nodded to his words.

"Right, right. And that's just what I was thinking too, Bill, just right now, that's what I was thinking, that there's no point to it anymore. Not in the waiting, like you said." He clapped his hands together with a loud pop. "So. Where to go, huh? That's the next question. Where to go? And the answer is?" He stared expectantly at Billy.

Billy shuffled a bit on his feet. "Well hell, Cal, you could move back in at my place, for one. Just for a little while, you know? Until you, ah . . ."

Cal was giving him a cross-threaded look. "You know completely ass-backwards that sounds right now? Because I can tell you how ass-backwards it sounds, if you don't know it already."

Billy held quiet a moment. He looked away. "Yeah, well. We were a good team once."

Cal nodded. "We were. I don't deny that a bit. But once is not now, is it?" He held his hands to the side.

A thicker silence descended.

Cal stared again at the wall where the kitchen table had stood.

"She was driving south, Bill."

"What?"

"Gayle. She was driving south on the coast road when it happened."

Billy didn't know what to make of the statement.

"In the police report, that's what it said. It said she was driving south. They don't usually fuck up details like that. And I called them and checked."

"I, ah, don't . . ."

"You take a look at a map, Bill. She was talking about San Francisco lately, about driving up to San Francisco, to see about it, to see about moving there one day. So you take a look at a map when you get the next chance. You don't drive from here, to get there, and then drive south on that road. North is the direction you'd be driving if you were going up there. North. Not south."

"What are you saying, Cal?"

"I'm saying she was driving south on that goddamn road, Billy. She was driving south when she should have been driving north. That's what I'm goddamn saying."

Billy was lost. "I, ah . . . maybe she, I don't know, maybe she just got turned around or something. I don't . . ."

"Yeah, that would be a great answer, wouldn't it? Maybe she just got turned around."

They stared at one another.

"Or maybe she turned around, Bill. Did you think that one all the way through? That maybe she turned around, that it was a choice?"

Billy blinked. "Cal. I don't understand what you're saying here."

Cal nodded. "Nothing. I'm saying nothing." He exhaled. He turned and paced the floor up and back a few times. "It changes nothing, anyway. Whatever way she was going, she was going."

He stopped his pacing, he faced Billy.

"You see how things are right now, right here? You see how it all is?" He pointed to where they both stood. He snapped his fingers. "And you see it now?" He waited. He snapped his fingers again. "It's the same, right? All of it, it's the same. So it changes nothing. What I think, or what you think, it changes nothing. Thinking changes nothing."

He stared at Billy.

"Try changing the way you think right now, Bill. Can you do that right now?" He waited. He snapped his fingers again, he pointed to the empty room. "Did anything change here?"

Billy scratched his head. "Cal . . . I don't know . . ."

"Right, right, and you don't have to know, do you. I'm the one that has to do the knowing right now. That's exactly why I'm here. And that's exactly what I'm doing, I'm doing the knowing. And right now, right here, what I know is that thinking changes nothing. So you can think what you want."

Billy waited a spell in silence.

"I don't know what to say, Cal. I just don't." He sighed. "Goddamn all of it." He fixed Cal with a steady look. "I'm sorry that this is happening to you. I'm sorry for you, and I'm sorry for Gayle. And that's all I've been trying to say."

There was a gulf widening between two shores, a disconnect in progress.

"Well I'm sorry too," Cal said back. "I look the part, don't I?" He stared at Billy, a dark wall of clouds gathering behind his eyes. "That's what I would think if I were you, and I saw me."

Cal turned away and stepped out through the screen door. The door slapped shut between them.

"So take your pick, Bill. There's sorrow enough to go around. Just depends on where you're standing." He put a foot up on the deck railing, leaned in, fumbled with his lighter, lit another cigarette.

There was one still going at the edge of the sink. And the one before that still smoking on the tile floor near the fridge.

Billy stepped that one out with the toe of his boot and left through the front door.

22.

The weeks of drift from the moorings of habit took their toll, the rain of empty hours falling and failing all account.

His face in the mirror, he stopped shaving one day, stopped halfway through the ritual of it, his arms dropped to his side. He stared at his half-shaven face.

The razor went into the trash.

He stared at himself in the mirror. He could see his entire ribcage clearly beneath his skin. His collar bone jutting out, his shoulder joints knobbed. He had cheekbones now.

"Gaunt," he said. A word he'd seldom spoken. An odd sounding word. "Gaunt." Like some medieval English pronunciation. The past tense of gone. Gaunt.

He looked hard at his face again. Nearly unrecognizable. Where did he go? Gaunt.

157

In the kitchen, the bills and papers were piling up. Pizza boxes half-full, their contents gone rancid, junk mail strewn across the countertops and scattered to the floor, an invoice from a storage company in San Francisco, unopened, unnoticed, shoved off to the side with all the rest. Handfuls of mail littered the ground at the curb beside his stuffed mailbox, were blown down the street, were gathered up by neighbors and returned unseen, laid neatly at his kitchen steps.

Cards and letters kept tiding in, from friends, from people he couldn't remember, from people he never knew at all, all of them offering their condolences. That word on every page. Condolences. Always the plural. Condolences. Not one single condolence offered by itself. "Have a condolence," he said. "I can only spare one, just now. I'll be needing the others."

More paperwork arriving from California. So much of it. Documents, certificates, official looking pages in their endless array, all bearing the office stamp or the state seal, all laced with signatures or requiring his. Return postage required. Notary required. Forwarding address required, if applicable. If not applicable, please disregard.

A gray file-sized envelope rolled up in a tube and wrapped tight with a red rubber band. It sat on the counter for days. It rolled forward and back with any breeze blowing in through the door. It fell to floor for the third time one day and Cal picked it up, snapped the rubber band off it and flattened the damn thing out, just so it would stay put. A report from the Medical Examiner's Office, Auxiliary Department, County of Santa Barbara, California. A red stamp affixed near his name and address with the word "Confidential" bordered within an arrow. The arrow pointing at his name.

Cal undid the metal clasp, slid a finger in under the flap. The flap cut his finger like a razor and he winced.

"Dammit." He brought the finger to his mouth and he tasted blood.

He pulled the document from its sleeve with his other hand. He scanned the clustered blocks of type, not caring to read any of it at all, half-reading it all the same.

Details from the autopsy finding. "For christsakes. What for, clarification?" He sucked at his finger.

One line, halfway down the page, three words highlighted in yellow. He read the words over again and felt the remains of his heart tear to pieces.

> twelve weeks pregnant

He tore the paper to shreds, to jagged bits, swipes of his blood on half the pieces as they fell to the floor. He cleared the whole counter of its clutter with a wide sweep of his arm and all of it fell away. He would have cleared the walls of the house the same and left none of it standing. He left the house instead. The screen door swung wide and slammed shut behind him. A neighborhood dog barked.

And he drove. He drove all the rest of that day. He drove clear through the night that followed it. He drove through half the next day too, seeing nothing at all the whole time save for what was placed there directly before him, immediate in the windshield, between the painted lines, on the vacant roads.

23.

Billy searched the town for him whenever he could. He never found him at home, he rarely caught him by phone. He lucked out one day, he saw Cal a half-block ahead making a hard left turn across traffic and up onto Hyde Road. He followed behind him at a good distance.

Cal was parked up at the Overlook leaning back against the hood of his truck having a smoke when Billy pulled up alongside.

"Hey," Bill said through his open truck window.

Cal nodded back without much enthusiasm.

Billy shut off his truck. He stepped out, walked over and stood beside Cal. He looked out over the view.

"You're harder to find than a skinny fat girl, you know that?"

No response from Cal.

"They're supposed to be a good find, too. All of the appetite, with none of the carrying costs."

Cal nodded again. "Tits on a chicken." He took a drag of his cigarette.

"Yeah. Like that too. Not that I ever looked. So, why don't you tell me where haven't you been yet, and I'll start my looking for you there the next time."

Cal turned to face him. He shrugged and nodded out toward the view. "All over."

Billy watched him. "So how are you for real, Cal? You still on the uphill with this whole thing?"

Cal gave that about a minute's thought. He shook his head. "Not so much now, Bill. It's pretty much leveled off." He pawed at the ground with his foot. "It is what it is, right? So it's going to be what it's going to be."

Billy nodded to that. "Yeah, that's why they say. You could be born with a clown face and polka dot skin, and if you spent two minutes of your life wondering how things could've been different, you just wasted two minutes."

Cal gave him a long look.

"What do you make of time, Bill?"

"How do you mean that?"

"The idea of time itself. What do you make of it?"

Billy gave it some thought. "It's a waste of money."

Cal looked away. "That's not what I meant." He held his cigarette up and watched it burning down, the smoke curling away in the air. He dropped it to the ground and stepped it out.

"The science of it, is more what I was thinking. The definition of time. What your guys up at Los Alamos would say about it?"

"You mean the physics of time?"

"Yeah. The physics of it. What the hell it is, for real."

Billy looked out at the view to gather his thoughts.

"Well. It's not exactly an elemental." He nodded up toward the heavens. "Out there in the universe, you've got this whole world of energy, just all kinds of energy doing crazy-ass stuff, and then you've got matter. Those are the two elementals. And matter is basically a congealed form of energy anyway. An arrested form, you might say. But time is neither one of those two. It's not energy, and it's not matter. It's more like a side effect of the interaction between the two. It's a condition, a flexible component. And then gravity comes in and fucks all around with it. Stretches it out like taffy."

"Gravity?"

"Yeah, gravity. Gravity bends time around. Time speeds up in the locale of matter. Matter more or less creates gravity. And the more matter you have, the more gravity. The more gravity, the faster time flows around that locality. It's like how water in a stream moves faster to get around a rock. Some guys are theorizing that time is actually a subcomponent of gravity, and vice versa. They each create the other. So there's a lot of interest about that, because it leads to the idea that time and gravity can be manipulated, artificially compressed or expanded. If you could do that in a certain locale, compress or expand the flow of time, or gravity, then the matter in that locale would have to vanish, at least temporarily. It would probably look like you were vaporizing it. Just without all the vapor."

Billy looked aside at Cal. "You following any of this?"

Cal shrugged. "Not really." He gave Billy a closer look. "I was thinking more about the past/present/future part of time. How it all works. How one becomes the other. How all of this . . ." he held his hand out to the view, "can be here one minute, then the next minute it's not here. It's like time eats everything up. Time eats reality, swallows it all. Takes it away. Hell, I don't know." He shrugged again. "Where does it all go? The life I had before, the things I thought about. Where does it go when it's not . . . here anymore?"

He waited for Billy to answer.

Billy looked at the ground. He drew a rough circle in the gravel with the toe of his boot.

"Well, there's a theory that holds that all of time, every moment of it, past, present, future, is happening simultaneously, so there's really just one position, one setting for time, and that's all of it at once. All of time at once. They compare it to a guitar string, and if you were to mark a bunch of different points along the string, then plucked the string, all the points would vibrate at once, even though they're still separate points." He nodded toward the town below them. "So right now, right here, all the old west guys, and all the Indians, and all the dinosaurs and everything else before that, plus any future this place might see, it's all happening right now, simultaneously. All in one instant. Bam! But the reason we can't see it that way is because, in our particular locality, there's a sort of narrow perceptional mechanism in operation, a mechanism that localizes and attaches itself to the time string at a single point, and then it moves along the string in single direction. It's gone linear. It's kind of like that little metal thing that rides up and down the zipper when you open or close it. That thing can only be in one place at a time, even though the whole zipper is there at once. Kind of the opposite of Velcro. So that more or less leads to the notion that all of creation, everything out there, is really a vast collection of singularly focused points of organized energy moving in linear fashion at their own particular speed along the string of time. And just in one direction at a time too, the direction we call forward." He shook his head at that. "But we don't really know if it's forward or backwards or whatever the fuck. We just call it that because we have to call it something, right? The real trick, though, if you could ever pull it off with technology, would be to bend the time string around, bend it all the way around until it formed a closed circle. Whoa! That would be like stepping into a giant hall of mirrors, except the mirrors would all be made of time. You'd be seeing everything at once. And so you'd probably be everywhere at once too, because it would get pretty damn fluid in there, matter/locus wise. All the borders would come down." He whistled low. "That would be totally insane."

Cal nodded vacantly. He reached into his back pocket and pulled out the pack of cigarettes. He tapped another one free and lit it up.

"So it's all happening at once?" he asked. "And the past is still here, right now?" He blew some smoke out.

Billy nodded.

"Yeah. It's all here now. That's how the theory goes."

"But we just can't see it, is all."

"Right."

"So we're basically blind to it. Blind to what's happening right in front of us." Cal took another drag of his cigarette. "Blind to what's coming, blind to what's been."

"Well. Not blind exactly," Billy said. He thought. "More like, possessed of a limited perceptual horizon. Or how about this: inhabiting a semi-sequestered processional uptake." He smiled at that one.

Cal nodded back. "Blind."

A few moments passed, silent except for the sound of a light breeze rocking the aspen leaves from side to side, like an entire forest whispering *shhhh*.

"Right," Billy eventually said. "Blind."

24.

A fifth week ground past him, around him, each hour encircling the one following it like an iron chain giving birth to its next link.

He didn't care to eat, or remember to. He lost more of himself, more of his weight, hidden beneath his baggy clothes. His eyes could lie to none of it though. In the bathroom mirror they looked more like two tunnels to a place he would never have chosen to go, but was going nonetheless.

His reflected image stared back at him in quiet contempt.

"So that's it, huh? That's how it's going to be?"

He waded through a long silence, his eyes searching his face.

"That's how it's going to be now?"

The sun-yellow bathroom walls crowding in around him, draining the color from his skin.

"You're not going to sleep again?"

He stared at his face until the placement of his features fell away from any sense of recognition. Like falling through a wall of quicksand.

"You're not going to let me sleep?"

He watched his mouth form the words.

He nodded to the sounds that reached his ears.

He stepped back half a step.

"Okay," he said. "Okay, then." His eyes like thin slits behind which something dangerous could hide itself or seek shelter.

The world notched more from his grasp each day.

On the floor of his living room, his trail maps and mountain guides were spread like cards in a game of solitaire, reshuffled, re-dealt, rearranged. He was making plans for a trip somewhere. A trip to a remote mountaintop, or to some lost corner of the desert. A trip to a place clear of the commotion, clear of the noise of traffic, clear of the chafe of the chattering world. Clear of the spin of his memory, the shreds of his history. A climb back in time if he could manage it, a crawl out from the widening wound of another's purpose. A boiled soul searching for a place to park itself, as stark and singular; a place where the boundary between inside and out might thin to a whisper, where the wind might howl louder than the questions within and clear everything in its path.

A place where the incessant pull of gravity might just hiccup for a second and Cal's timing would fall perfect, his next step to earth stand rejected and that of all the molecules in him to one another, and he would totally blow apart, his last memory an explosion at the edge of some forsaken landscape marking the end of the Cal universe and day one of whatever comes next.

Like a circus dog jumping through its own held hoop, to oblivion.

His options had dwindled to this.

Cal reshuffled the spread of his maps, resurveyed the lay of the land and arranged it to need, adrift in an upended universe that had assigned him now a new purpose.

Purpose: An internal beacon lighting the way; the invisible strings of a marionette that lend the illusion of authorship to any motion that follows; a respite in the shade of a cenotaph to any notion of hope.

Cal again, with a purpose.

25.

Into the sixth week.

Cal appeared at Billy's house near sunset. He hadn't seen him now for how many days. He stepped in through the open front door with a red wash of sunlight crowding in behind him.

Billy was sitting on the couch in front of the TV, rolling a thing he called a *tobaccajuana half-caf*, basically a pipe tobacco cigarette, with some fine-ground high-grade weed dusted across the top half. He sat forward with a start when he saw Cal standing in the room.

Cal could have counted the seconds it took for Billy to recognize him.

Cal said goodbye.

Billy cocked his head to one side.

"Goodbye? You just got the hell here, hombre."

Cal nodded to the irony. He stood his place in tattered silence, his eyes concealed behind shades. Time stood heavy beside him.

"Well, so, qué te pasa, calabaza?" Billy said. No answer came. He stood and gave Cal a once over. "Beard and all, huh? That's a different look." He tipped his head. "You should get yourself a black hat to go with it. Maybe a six-shooter."

Cal took a random look around the room.

"I hear beards itch," Billy said.

Cal focused. "Who do they itch?"

Billy acknowledged the point. "Right. Well. Puff?" He offered Cal the twist.

Cal said no.

Billy regarded him. "Cal, you look . . gaunt."

Cal nodded. "Me too."

Billy cracked a grin. "So, where the hell is it that you've been, bro? But seriously. I drive by your place all the time, no show there. I call you on your cell, you don't call back."

Cal shrugged. "Doing some driving. Out of range, mostly."

"Out of range? Must be a damn big range."

Silence from Cal.

Billy could see the reflection of himself in the mirrored shades.

"Well, you're here now, right? So where is it you're going, that you walk in to say goodbye for the getting to it?"

Cal stared past him like there were no walls there, no structure around them at all.

"Up into the mountains," he said. "Down south a bit of here. Down near the border."

Billy reached for the remote and shut off the TV. He set the joint aside.

Cal went on. "I needed to, ah . . . I just need to get away. From here. Get to, ah, someplace else. Someplace empty. Someplace I can think. So I've made some plans. To set this thing aside. Get past it, all of this . . . what's been happening."

Soldier lies.

He held a hand up to show Billy something, but the hand was empty. It shook from side to side, they watched it shake. Cal dropped his hand to his side. He looked out the window and fell to silence.

"Well hey," Billy said. "Why don't I come along with you?" He arched himself sideways and back like he was ready to pull a pack off the shelf that minute and go. "I could use a good mountain grab right about now. Been too long in the grid, you know?"

Cal set his jaw, he shook his head a slow no thanks.

"Don't need the company right now, Bill. Not for this one. This one is mine. It's just, ah, right now I came by to say . . . to say that I'm sorry, you know, for the way things have been. Because I haven't been, ah, real . . . it's just . . . it's just, I needed some time, before. Time for thinking. And some distance too, distance between the here and now that I've been having. So I couldn't, ah, get a fix on all this, to start figuring it out, what I should be doing next, because of what happened when . . ."

He scanned the space around him. He sighed.

"So I'm going down there, down near the border. Up into the mountains there, to, ah . . . to straighten it out . . ." He stopped in mid-sentence, a long distance gone already, halfway there to where he was planning to go. Billy waited for him to finish.

" . . . to straighten it out, I don't know, with God. Or with the devil. Or maybe the both of them at once." He shrugged. "They're probably the same guy anyway, right? When it comes right down to it? That's what I was thinking." He tried for a laugh. "I was thinking they're the same guy. And they're just messing with us." He shuffled on his feet. "Hell, it's all just words anyway, the stuff we call stuff. We don't need more words right now, the world's full of them already. So . . . it's enough."

He looked to his left suddenly, like something had just changed there, or moved. Billy turned around for a look but there was nothing he could see. He turned back to watch Cal.

They stood in silence.

The familiar space between them had folded up. Or reversed itself to the time before they knew one another.

Cal edged closer toward the door. "Okay, then." He tipped his head farewell.

Billy felt boxed in, out-maneuvered by something he couldn't see, or know of even if he could see it. He felt tired just looking at him.

"Where is it exactly that you're going, Cal?" He stepped forward to stay with him.

"I don't know, exactly," Cal lied. He tried for a grin. He gave Billy a small nod. He turned and walked for the door.

Billy called after him. "Hey Cal?"

"Yeah?" Cal still walking for the door.

"If you do run into God up there, you give him hell, right? I'd say he's got it coming."

"Alright." Cal said. He stopped at the door and turned around. He pulled his shades down. He looked his friend in the eye.

"What if it's the devil I run into?"

Billy nodded back, a half-smile on his face. "You tell that son-of-a-bitch I'm still looking for a roommate."

Cal let that thought sink in. He nodded. He put his sunglasses back in place. He hovered a moment in the doorway. He took in a long breath, then let it out.

"I always felt that I had won her. Like she was a sort of prize for me that night, and I had won her. I won Gayle."

"You felt like you won her?"

"Yeah, I did. That day you played the scratch card game and won all that cash. That night, I won her."

26.

The next morning in the garage, the sun about to rise through the window.

"All I need," Cal said, tired enough of thinking all night of what he needed. He looked down at the floor and time halted right there, nailed tight to every detail like a slice of the world drained of its color, paper-thin and motionless. A blinding light rose up through his skull and he nearly fell over. His face and scalp flushed hot, his blood burned in his veins and he clenched his jaw to the pain.

He blinked that rush away, a sheer act of willpower. He would have none of it.

He refocused on the spread of his gear on the floor.

"All I need," he said again.

He gathered his things one piece at a time, stowed them into their right place in the backpack. He hefted the pack onto his shoulder. He collected four water bottles from the floor and left the garage.

He stood by the truck, dropped the bottles to the ground. He threw the pack into the bed. He climbed up beside it and rolled it tight inside a canvas tarp, against the dust or the dew, against the rain if there ever was any. He looked toward the sky. There wouldn't be any.

He jumped to the ground and felt his bones shake loose inside his body. He felt physically old for the first time in his life.

He took the water bottles inside and filled them at the sink. He capped them each and set them aside. He cupped his hands to his face with water and he drank. He lowered his head beneath the faucet and soaked it all around as the water ran colder.

He shook his head like a dog shakes. He turned to the empty room and leaned his weight against the counter.

His freefall of time spent in that house had narrowed to a few seconds more, so long in coming.

He would leave. Just that.

He saw the kitchen table where it no longer stood, the hook-eye on the ceiling where the lamp once hung. Scrapes of varnish still marked the wall where the chairs had rubbed. The dust shadow of the photograph that hung above the table, of an outlandish sunset in the Chuskas west of Sanostee, with Gayle striking a glamorous pose in the raked light and Cal's shadow stretching out across the ground towards her, the shadow of the camera held high in one hand, the shadow of his other hand reaching for her breast.

How many meals held here? How many laughs unheld?

A bottle cap lying face up on the floor, the last witness beside him to the lives once lived there.

Cal's hair dripped a circle of wet to the floor like a halo fallen to his feet.

He walked a slow pass through the living room. Part prison cell from the light of day, from the habits of a past life. Part sanctuary from the din of a world grown too complex for his fractured nerves to handle. The stack of nights spent there in the dark, the hover of stillborn memory, the infinite recall of things that seemed now never to have happened at all. Dust.

Down the hall to the bathroom, his face like a stranger's in the mirror, his eyes ashamed and defiant both, angry to the point of collapse. Ancient, time-withered, empty.

He reached to his pocket and pulled out his cell phone. He held it flat in his palm. He opened it. He folded it closed again. He opened it once more and pressed Gayle's number, then hit send. Her phone rang on the shelf before him, rang until her message picked up.

"Hi, it's Gayle. If you're hearing this message I must be out of range, but I'm still ready to talk, so leave me a message and I'll get back to ya real soon. Bye."

He hung up. He stared out the small window to a smaller piece of sky.

He pressed her number again. Her phone rang again.

"Hi, it's Gayle. If you're hearing this message I must be out of range, but I'm still ready to talk, so leave me a message and I'll get back to ya real soon. Bye."

He waited for the tone.

"Cal," he said.

Silence on the other end, then the message timed out. He closed his phone and watched its light fade. He laid the phone on the shelf alongside Gayle's phone and turned away.

He walked down the hall.

He opened the door to the bedroom. Time could have flowed around him, or through him, or over him, a millennium or a second the same. Every thought within him stilled.

He said Gayle's name aloud.

The sound of it fell away to the empty well of the room.

He reclosed the door.

He left his house for the last time. The screen door slapped shut to the emptiness held behind it. His boots tracked across the driveway, grinding sand down against sand into dust rising up at his heels this day, the air pink already with sunrise and nothing else alive or awake in the world save for the chatter of crows in flight from the sun, chasing the echo of their calls down the hall of the sky.

He turned the key and started his truck. He opened the glove box and counted out the twenties left there.

He put the truck in gear and spun his tires backwards out the driveway and was gone.

The dust of his going hung low in a thin cloud over the ground, it drifted back towards the house and filtered in through the screen door, to settle on the floor of the kitchen with the dust of other days and other lives, and a bottle cap that slipped once through Cal's fingers and rolled from sight.

❖

Destination

1.

One road leads to another, they say.

From an unbroken roll of asphalt, to graded gravel, to scraped desert dirt, to a winding dust track eroded now to a halt and his maze of choices withered finally to one, Cal bumped to a sudden stop in a rain-gutted rut on the eastern flank of a crumbled mountain range.

His truck idled in the dark, its headlights searching ahead for more. Past the winnowing dust of his intrusion lay a scatter of rocks and cactus, of piñon, ocotillo and cholla, of agave stabbing sword-like at the night sky. Bones laid out flat to the earth where their bearers had finally fallen. The slanted track of a snake's passing in the sand. The imprint of a million stars hovered above, their light a million years coming, the mountains half-worn to dust beneath the churn of time.

His truck idled at the end of that road, hours before dawn. Realm of dream for those who can, heralds of a silent repose free to roam the spirit roads where he now sat grounded, hostage to the silent habits of pain. His emotions gagged and bound, and all the rest of him staring out from a sleepless night-day six weeks old, if it could be counted. Forty-two days. One thousand hours. Three and a half million seconds. Dreamless landscape. Nerve-shaken feast of a bleached memory. The arrogance of time, to unfurl its own design with no regard for those who would measure it.

Dawn lit in through the windshield. The engine of another day idled. The orange glow of another unwanted cigarette arced out through the chill morning air, bounced once to its litter death in the clean desert sand.

Seven week to a lifetime, the night before he left for Scottsdale. Their last night together.

They had gone to bed early. Gayle had been distant and withdrawn for weeks. Unsettled. Her art would do that to her sometimes, as she would say.

Cal awoke at four in the morning. He lay quietly and watched Gayle sleeping beside him. There was moonlight enough through the windows to outline her features like an artist's rough sketch. He watched her breath rising and falling beneath the sheets.

He leaned in and roused her with kisses. Her forehead, her temple. Her cheek. Her lips. He thought he saw tears pooled in her eyes when she opened them in that thin light, glistening. They spoke not a word. They made love for the last time, known then to neither. A dream of two worlds of dreams colliding. Silent, how flesh would dream of touch. How night conceives a dawn and carries it to being.

They drifted back to sleep, back again to their separate dreams, one beside the other.

Cal walked a solitary desert road. There were red sand hills rolling away in every direction, tumbling up to a chain of mountains rising black and jagged at the circled edge of that dreamed world. The sky a deep violet-red, a silver sun pinned motionless above.

He walked on.

A black sedan rolled by. There was no sound to it as it went. He saw Gayle sitting in the back seat. She turned her head as the car rolled past and he watched her face at the rear window. The car slowed to a stop at the side of the road well beyond him. It shimmered like a black jewel in the desert heat.

He reached her after an endless walk, the distance between them stretching as he went.

Gayle stood waiting for him by the door. She was clothed in white, the sunlight pooled around her. She held a small wooden box in her hands.

"This belongs to you," she said, and offered it over.

Cal took the box from her hands. He slid back the lid. Inside was a velvet cloth folded in triangles to the center. He pulled aside each of the folds. Beneath the cloth lay a small collection of bones bleached white from the sun, and a skull the size of a plum lying on its side. He rolled it over with the tip of his finger, the tiny face he saw waiting there.

He gazed up into Gayle's eyes, the blue and the blue-green, as bright as if they were lit from within. Her hair was dyed raven-black and hung straight to her shoulders like a frame, or a pair of wings, folded. She leaned forward, she reached for him and drew his head in close. She kissed him on the forehead, then on the lips, long sweet kisses that spoke volumes, that spoke whole worlds of thought in migration beneath a sea of time, and she held him like that.

They stood apart. Gayle moved backwards to the open car door, the threads of time pulling that world in reverse. She sat in the seat as before, the door closed and she was sheltered within. She raised her hand in a wave of farewell. Cal saw the reflection of his face overlaying hers in the window glass, then the car drove off. He watched it down the road until it was gone from sight. The road dust coiled away and the stillness of the place returned.

He stood alone on that stark road.

He looked again at the collection of small bones, the tiny skull nearly translucent in that angled sunlight.

He refolded the cloth, replaced the wooden lid.

He turned a slow circle where he stood, scanning the view for as far as he could see. It felt to him like the first day of a long journey to him. The sun slipped lower toward the horizon, its light glowing tunnel-like and golden.

He tucked the wooden box up beneath his arm and walked south.

On that long road.

In that last dream.

2.

No roads stretched before him now. He was finished with all that.

Cal waited inside the truck, the windows down, the heat turned up, the antique of any dream left to him failing its grip in the rising light. The last points of Sirius, of Venus, disappeared in the east like shards of melting ice. A crow cracked its raucous call into the blue, complaints newly hatched from a creature with wings that could carry it to the whole wide world and yet brought it here to sear at noon and freeze at night on a diet of dust-blown bugs or less.

Cal with every sinew of thought could not will time backwards from where it spilled itself now into the dust of the desert. His memory alone danced ghost-like upon that ground.

They stood once together at sunset, alone in the million-acre starkness of the Painted Desert.

"We come and we go, and grow our dreams in the shaken earth."

Gayle had said the words aloud to the sky, like an invocation. She bent low then, and traced the words in the sand with her fingertip. They knelt each to leave their handprints alongside.

Cal stood now outside the gates of his harvest, a creature without wings nailed to the floor of the earth, the memories of all of it thrown together in a fog, a roadside stop to stretch his legs, a seven-year marriage to an enchanted girl and all of it had drawn to a close. The road alone had seemed the constant.

Now here, and the road itself had come to an end. Cal's frayed, six-week old quilt of glazed-eyed travel unraveled to threads and scattered downwind like a roomful of whispers.

The sun broke free from the mountains to the east. It spilled a liquid warmth across the land. Cal turned the ignition key to the left and the engine fell silent.

Finished.

3.

A morning breeze drifted in through the windows, the desert air smelled aromatic and clean.

Cal opened the door and stepped to the ground. He stretched his legs. He reached into the truck bed and pulled his backpack free of the tarp and swung it down onto the sand. Any sound he made was swallowed by the stillness.

The air as clear as glass, the sky a deep blue above him and the sun would be hot that day.

He reached into the cab for the four water bottles, for the guidebook lying on the seat. He stowed the bottles in his backpack. He opened the guidebook.

A town named Chloride, the last town he'd passed through at three that morning, lay shuttered asleep in a mountain fog, as adrift as a fading memory, a failed argument against time, the small cluster of streetlamps that defined its limits blinking off and on in some energy-saving malfunction.

From there he drove the numbered forest roads, then further to the unnumbered mining trails and well into the foothills of Black Mountain Range and the deeper sprawl of the Gila beyond.

He consulted the trail map in the guidebook. He checked the elevations he saw, traced the terrain lines he'd be hiking, matched the headings on his compass to the ones he found on the map.

The Anvil Spur Trail should start near there, somewhere, if he had followed all the right roads in the dark. The spur trail would connect to the Anvil Trail proper at an elevation of just under nine thousand feet along a ridgeline of peaks running north/south.

Cal looked to the north. He saw the jagged cliff noted in the guidebook rising off to his left. He steadied the map from the shake of his hands against the hood of the truck. He read the trail description:

The Anvil Spur Trail climbs northwest for four miles in switchbacks across a talus slope to reach a junction with the Anvil Trail. Elevation gain is nine hundred feet. Look for a vertical crack in the cliff face for access at the four-mile mark. The Anvil Trail is found at the top of the cliff. The trail edges southward along the cliff face for a distance of twelve miles with fine views, no elevation gain, then climbs southwest into forested highland and due west into the mountains, away from any longer view. Water can be found there until late spring or early summer in normal years, sometimes dry by mid-July until late September. Up from the forest the trail climbs in stages for three miles to intersect a second ridgeline with open views to the east, south and west. Higher elevations of sparse vegetation, with some snows lingering until late April or early May. An open saddle crosses to the base of the Anvil at the north.

Twenty-eight miles from the trailhead to the summit, the guidebook said. Three thousand two hundred and twelve feet higher than the starting elevation, the guidebook said. A two day hike from the start to the summit, he would figure. Maybe three. Another world away.

The silence of these mountains traces a lineage back to an ancient seabed that rose up in the Paleozoic era. Imprints of long-extinct fishes can be found at altitude, pressed into the rock walls along the climb.

An isolated place, the guidebook said. Visitors numbered in the dozens or less per year. The cross-country flight paths of commercial jets were far enough to the north not to be seen or heard.

A note of interest or caution: Anvil has acquired the reputation as a place where hikers have vanished. How or why this reputation originated remains unclear. This author could find no substantiated evidence of persons disappearing there. Nor have any bodies been found or gone missing, Forest Service reports have stated.

Cal pulled his knife from the backpack and snapped it open, sliced the map page free of the guidebook. He folded it down and slid it into the back pocket of his jeans. He placed the knife back in his pack.

He tossed the guidebook to the floor of the truck. He reached in and rolled up the far window. He snapped the lock down. He did the same with the driver's side. He stepped back and pushed the door closed, heard the latch click home. He watched the keys swaying in the ignition, a small trace of sunlight dancing back and forth across the dash until it stopped.

His pack was propped against the tire of the truck. He grabbed the hold at the top, swung the pack onto his left shoulder, then across his back. He hooked his right arm through the other strap, bounced it all into place. He tightened the waist strap down and the shoulder straps up.

He stared at the talus slope awaiting him, its sprawling disarray of rocks and boulders scattered below the nearly vertical cliff face crumbling above it.

He looked once more at his pickup, the sunrise flaring through its dusty windows.

There were no words left him to speak, no thoughts that would form them if he tried.

He started walking.

4.

He crossed the dusted bottomlands in half an hour's time. The sun climbed higher to his right. The trail before him was barely visible as such, more a series of dry washes that branched one away from the other and meandered back together again. Yucca and cholla crowded every space for a bigger bite of sunshine. He dodged most of the spikes and needles. He cursed the one's he didn't.

He stood at the base of the talus slope. The terrain angled up sharply there, a cracked and broken chunk of earth slanting skyward, shed of any vegetation. He stumbled his way across the scree, then further up among the larger slabs flaked from the cliff face above, the blocks sharp-edged and wedged upright or horizontal or oblique like so many broken tombstones scattered to the earth.

No indication of a trail there at all, no markers or cairns. Nothing to follow but dead reckoning. He climbed on.

His heart raced and the shimmer of the heat and strain of the climb clawed at his will. A drunk-like balancing act he tenuously delivered across that jumble of rocks. Minutes stretched into hours.

He stopped for a breather and dropped his pack to the ground. He guzzled down a half liter of water. He unfolded the trail map from his pocket. Drops of sweat fell like a rain from his brow and stained the page.

He heard an echoing crash overhead, then a vague rumble following it, like a thunderclap rolling back into silence. The sky above him was spotless, the sunlight reflecting sharply from the rocks. He scanned the whole of the cliff face in either direction. No movement showed there, no tumbling boulders, no rising plumes of dust. Sweat trickled into his eyes at that angle and stung them shut.

The mountain crumbled on in secret.

The trail map showed a dotted red line that angled north/northwest across the talus slope. The line ended at a narrow indented notch in the cliff face. He figured to be standing somewhere on that dotted line, maybe halfway across.

The words "Punto del Cielo" showed in tiny red type alongside the notch. He blinked his eyes for a clearer look.

Punto del Cielo.

Right there in print.

He said the words aloud. He shook his head free of sweat. He looked up at the looming wall of stone for any sign of the notch, for any exit from this crumbling mess. There was none that he could see. The sun was two hours up and starting to get busy. Another hour or so and it would threaten any life form foolish enough to be exposed on a slope like that. He had left the truck with four liters of water. His first was nearly gone.

The descriptions on the trail map didn't exactly fit the terrain he found himself in. The distances were off, the directions skewed. The elevations seemed wrong. And there was no notch ahead that he could see, nor further on for what he guessed to be a mile. Nothing before him but a solid vertical rise of stone. If he climbed all the way up there with no way to exit, he'd be fried dead in the sun by noon. Desert harvest. Cal bacon.

His legs felt like lead already. The weight he'd lost in the last few weeks was a liability now. He was well out of shape.

The sun cooked mercilessly overhead. He scanned the sky, half-expecting to see vultures circling. There were none.

He felt like a ghost in that place, a man beyond notice, of little import. His shadow wavered beside him in the rising drifts of heat.

He remembered forgetting to pack a hat.

Time drained past. He cleared his eyes of sweat and stared at nothing in particular.

Purpose called in. Oh faithful beacon, immune to doubt. Its strings reattached.

He refolded the map and tucked it away in his back pocket. He drank to the last of his first liter. He re-shouldered his pack and tread the dotted line again. The rocks beneath him tipped like dangerous playground equipment, the weight of his past weeks upon him like a corpse of himself that he had contracted to carry to heaven. He would have laughed aloud at that image had he not needed the breath more.

Another hour in the balance.

Cal stood high beneath the cliff face, the stones at his feet like iron slabs from a furnace. The soles of his boots had turned mushy, the smell of cooked rubber in the air. Still no sign of the notch ahead, and the bottomlands shimmered below like a spirit world beyond reach.

Nothing more to be done about it. One step follows the next, right or wrong, like one breath follows another. The sunlight cut like a knife.

The mountain grumbled again, a sound so low and deep he felt it first in his feet, the vibrations rising up through his bones like the approach of a train until his skull was chattering down against his bottom teeth and his balance was shaken. He steadied himself against a nearby boulder just as it rolled loose, he made a quick sidestep and the big rock settled downhill with a crushing sound, dust rising around it and the smell of burnt flint in the air, the taste of rock in his mouth. He scanned the cliff above, he watched a football-sized rock banging its way down the slope, careening ever closer like an expertly banked pool shot and he ducked at the last moment as the rock whistled an inch past his head and shattered against the boulders below.

Gravel clicked down the cliff face like a scattering rain. He watched, and listened, and waited. And breathed.

The rumbling quieted.

He climbed on.

Blocks of stone the size of monuments choked his path now, their edges knife sharp, their surfaces hot enough to blister any touch. He contorted his way through them like a man through a maze, lost to the chore of it and the strain of his muscles at every turn, his eyes so stung shut with salt and glare that he struggled nearly blind where time itself seemed as trapped as he to wander this eternity one halting step after another.

He felt a sudden downwash of cool air, like stepping into the edge of a waterfall in a dream. He blinked his eyes, he held his hands out before him, feeling his way forward. He turned his face up into the draft. There was relief enough there to quicken his senses, to steady his step. He kept himself centered to that cooler channel of air and climbed on, his vision nearly burnt, the sun directly behind him now and flashing madly, snatching at his back.

He halted.

Right before him, like a portal to another world, stood a four-foot wide vertical crack in the cliff face running the entire height of the wall. He would have sworn it was not there seconds ago. He blinked his eyes to clear them, he squinted against the metal-sharp glare, but the portal remained.

"Punto del Cielo," he barely said, his voice too shaky to hold.

Cool air gushed past him, wave after generous wave of it. He stood half out of balance, caressed in that welcome current while

his breath caught up with him and the terrain below him flared like some minor version of hell outraged at his pending escape. He climbed further into the shade of that womb-like slice, the rock walls close and cool to the touch, rising high to either side.
"Punto del Cielo."
He repeated the words with each step he took. They echoed like a soft chorus chanted in a narrow church.
He knew there would be another sun waiting for him above. Still hot, but indifferent. Unattached to any immediate outcome.

5.

The fracture widened out, carved its way deeper into the face of the cliff and away from the sun, steeped in its own shade. Odd plants clustered there in hanging gardens, yellow roots like tendons fingered across the sheer stone walls, crowns of spongy leaves held aloft. Fissures in the rock dripped water in strands like curtains of rain falling. Cal stood beneath the showers where he could, leaning in against wet rocks, cooling himself down, soaking his face, his head. He removed his sweated t-shirt and soaked it wet, wrung it out and wrapped it loose and cool around his head.

He climbed on, grabbing at the curve of roots and handholds in the rock where he found them. A slow, halting, tenuous advance, a cumbersome insect ascending.

Inches from his face the fossil imprints of seashells, of mollusks, of impossible creatures cascading across the rock, whole catalogs of them from the earliest chapters of creation, skeletal fishes swimming for release from the rock, rivulets of water rippling across their backbones, stony wet eyes turned blindly to the thin slice of sky above them, a deep sea world of shadow and cold gone long silent, arisen now and haunting the world of air, the world of sun, hidden, insistent, forever. Cal a newest member of that relic world, his hours as ancient, his memories as etched in stone.

He ascended four hundred feet through that jagged sanctuary, every muscle straining.

He surfaced at the upper end, cool and damp now like an emergent toad, his hands and forearms blistered from the baking rocks below, his knuckles de-capped of skin from the climb and bibbed with drying blood. He pulled himself onto a flat stone shelf, back again into a warming welcomed sun. A few feet beyond, a wider trail edged along a shaded rise of woods. Behind him, the crumbling edge of the cliff plunged away, the endless view of browns and yellows there and the pallor of dusty air hovering flat over the earth.

He unhitched his pack and pushed it forward on the ground, crawled behind it and away from the precipice. He pulled up beneath a ponderosa pine in the lee of its shade, rolled over onto his back, the sky above him a faultless blue.

He removed his boots and his socks. His feet felt cooked. He wedged them down past the pine needles into the cooler soil, leaned his weight against the trunk of the tree. His heart pounded, half-triumphant.

He reached for his pack and dragged it closer, pulled a water bottle free, took a long drink.

The guidebook had claimed that water could be found there this time of year, in normal years. He looked around for any signs of normal. He took another long drink.

He lay on the cool padding beneath the tree and stared up through the window of branches.

He would take a nap. The perfect time and place for one, after a climb like that. Just twenty minutes or so, in the shade of that tree, would do it. A short nap. Simple.

He closed his eyes to the web of the day.

Seconds withered past.

He saw the blankness rising within him, a sentinel wall of gray between himself and any notion of sleep. Dull gray like a wall of smoke thickened to stone, insistent, featureless, vigilant. Evicting. Possessive. The sour metallic taste of it in his mouth, the sound of blood percolating through his brain, microscopic bubbles crowding forward, frothing silent contempt.

He opened his eyes from all that. He saw the red blanket of pine needles below him, the tree trunks rising, the flag of blue sky above. He watched the sky cut to slivers by the branches waving in the breeze, small shapes of geometry opening and closing like tiny mouths whispering secrets. Chorus of sifted wind. Choir of silent sky. Speaking nothing.

Purpose called in.

He sat forward, drew in a tired deep breath. He rubbed his eyes for focus. He reached for one of his socks. He reached for the other and replaced them on his feet. He pulled on his boots and laced them tight.

He stepped out from under the tree's shade. The sun's position was high in the sky, nearly noon he would reckon, one o'clock maybe. No matter.

He stepped over to the edge of the cliff, peered down its face. He saw the clutter of giant stone blocks lying far below him, unimpressive from that height, left-behind playthings of a mountain god. He turned away.

He stood atop a high mesa. He saw the Anvil trail tracing away along the edge of the cliff, into the far distance. A good level walk.

"I should make good time now." The words fell away from any meaning, momentary distractions for an unemployed voice.

He lifted his pack, swung it into place and synched it tight.

One step follows another. The trail snaked south and he walked automatically, a small passing disturbance in the greater stillness that resided there.

Something smaller still and hidden he carried within him, an enigmatic creature being hauled to its destination by the duller thing that labored beneath it. The hidden creature was the one with purpose. Cal was just along for the ride.

6.

The trail cut a shallow rut through the crumbling sandstone, it wandered the thin scatter of scrub clinging to the edge of the cliff. The air was cooler, the sun nonbelligerent.

He covered the miles in the company of no thought, a silence of hours measured by the foot.

He pulled up at a stark promontory where a short side trail angled away through a field of boulders. He dropped his pack to the ground.

He followed the side trail to the rim of the cliff and looked out over the edge. He saw the talus slope shimmering far below. Further on, the blue dot of his pickup truck winked in and out of sight through the curtaining heat. Beyond that, the endless roll of hills, the dust-brown earth and the miles of desert he drove through to get there, it all lay before him in abbreviated form, a cauldron of the sun-baked world in miniature. Cal watched the land rising in perpetual waves, the horizon stolen by the heat, the earth blending mirror-like into sky. Stone-heated air lofted against his face in fat gusts. He saw two ravens bank into the thermal below, ride it effortlessly past him and up into the sun. Their daily commute.

He had never felt so small, a singular point in the greater width of the world, the shadow beneath his feet his only proof of presence, his sole trespass without. Time stood silent beside him, unreckoned in that place.

He stepped away from the edge.

He re-shouldered his pack and headed south on that desolate stretch of trail, the measure of its miles irrelevant. The place grew starker by degrees, a view collapsing on itself from the weight of its own emptiness, a failure of nerve on the part of nature to be. The air seemed reluctant to share itself.

He walked on.

The events of his life paraded past, unscheduled, uninvited, one story hitched to another. It seemed now that in each story he had stood within a different costume, that each memory was no more than a play, and he had acted his part well enough but had never seen the entire script, so the costumes were all he had truly known. They fell to the ground now like tapestries torn from their stanchions, each folding down into the dust of its woven story.

He was no greater part of his own history than spectator, and his footsteps dragged. He walked the trail a smaller part of some vast machine, clockworked to it but unadvised of the grand design. He could shut his eyes to it and walk on perfectly, centered to the trail with each step like a dance well rehearsed by a sleepwalker.

He stopped at one point for a drink but the trail seemed to race ahead of him with an urgency he couldn't counter. He felt the animal fear of being left behind, and he stepped back into place, and the balance held, and he would not again tempt it.

To the east one hundred miles rose the Sacramento Mountains. Fifty miles to the south lay Mexico. To the north lay all he had known of late and left behind, one way or another.

The trail turned west now, curving into the forest, and away from any longer view.

7.

Into the mountains, to a lofted forest and a green world held away from the desert by a circle of peaks and a sea blue sky.

There was a different sun at work there, toying through the treetops, tumbling to the forest floor in pools of grace, streaking slanted through the air and sparked with insect wings and spider threads streaming like tiny iridescent rivers. The air was full and generous, and a different rhythm resided. Cal slowed his pace, more now a walk than a march, and he slipped through the woods like a breath.

He came to a halt where the trail split in two before him. A head high boulder lay wedged between the trunks of two Ponderosa pines. The trees had flattened over time, had grown around the big rock to cup it on either side like a giant pair of wooden spoons, like some joke a seldom visited forest might play for its own amusement. The trail detoured around the captured rock and joined again on the far side. Cal walked a full circle around the scene and stood again where the trail split.

He dropped his pack on the spot. He pulled a water bottle free and drank to the end of it. His third liter now gone. One liter left.

Water could be found there. In normal years.

Cal turned a circle where he stood. The forest surrounded him in every direction, more like it had gathered around him than he could have walked so deeply into it, its greenness and shade abundant.

Piñon jays squabbled to life in the canopy above, reshuffled to the lower branches to eye the odd intruder, trading their excited calls back and forth.

More birds were singing, their songs echoing through the woods: peewees, painted redstarts, bushtits, gray warblers. The call of a spotted vireo spiraling through the air.

A red squirrel tacked itself upside down on a nearby tree and picked apart a pinecone for its seed.

Cal removed his t-shirt, brushed the sweat and grit from his face. He sat back against the boulder, let the coolness of the big rock seep in. His hands at rest in his lap, weathered, blistered, his knuckles cut and beaten. He raised them, turned them over slowly for a better look in the shifting light. He watched them in their steady shaking. He hadn't eaten yet today. Or yesterday was it? Or both? He didn't know, he couldn't remember. He didn't care.

He felt the forest waiting, watching him.

He pointed to himself.

"New species," he said, his voice barely audible. He looked out at the forest. "New species here," he said louder. "Runs on Empty."

Until when.

He dropped his hands.

He opened his pack. He reached inside, he felt around for whatever he might have brought to eat. He found an apple. He held it up and turned it around in the filtering sunlight. He shined it against his pant leg and held it up again. He saw the forest and the sky reflected there, bent around the apple's curve like a small planet, with a stem. He took a single bite and set the apple aside on the ground.

He didn't move the rest of that day. The coolness of the big rock at his back, the towering trees around him, the pocket-sized view of sky directly above. The rise and fall of his breath and his heartbeat like a slow drum sounding inside. The shifting songs of unseen birds, their messages crafted of air and shot like arrows through the woods to what target. The greenness of that quiet hidden world.

A passing millipede took an hour to detour around Cal's outstretched leg. A solitary ant inspected the bite in the apple, stroking the odd thing endlessly with its flickering antennae.

The sun lowered through the trees.

An orb-weaver spider fashioned a gem-like web in the fork of a branch an arms length from his eye. The web pulsed forward and back in the shifting breeze.

If he held still and the breeze stopped, he could see the shadow of the spider web on his chest.

"The shadow of a spider web, ladies and gentlemen," he said aloud. His arms held wide.

8.

The sky straight up turned a deeper blue, the treetops alone held the last red rays of the setting sun. The shadows of the coming night filed in across the forest floor.

Cal scraped bare a circle of earth before him. He bordered the circle with gathered stones and set about the collection of firewood. The warmth of the day was fading fast with the last of the light. The mountain's coolness was descending.

It was near dark as he struck a match and the fire rushed to life. He sat back against the big rock, watched the flames rise high and felt the heat at his face and hands like the heat of the sun, and the firelight kept back the night.

"There can be a ritual to it," Gayle had said once, years back. She tilted her head when she said it.
"If you want it so," she added. Like an afterthought.
They had known each other a few months. It was the first time they went camping.
Cal had dropped an armload of gathered sticks to the ground and was about to douse it with lighter fluid and set it alight. The sun was freshly down, its afterglow fading. Gayle watched him with that playful look on her face, a quiet sense of amusement once removed.
"If I want it so?" Cal asked.
Gayle nodded slightly. "Mmm hmm." She hummed a little tune.
He stopped what he was doing. He took a seat beside her. A ritual, huh?" He gave her an expectant look. "Okay. I want it so."
"The choice is yours." She smiled.
She stood and spread her arms wide like a maestro hushing an invisible orchestra. She waited a few seconds. She winked at him and waited a bit more. She knelt then and cleared a two-foot wide circle on the ground before her, scraping the soil and leaf litter aside with a flat rock. She arranged a dozen stones carefully around the edge for a border. She picked through the pile of branches Cal had gathered and selected four small sticks. She broke them above a section where they had forked, so they each looked like the letter Y.
She saw Cal was about to speak, so she held a finger to her lips.
"Shhh."
She smiled and nodded toward what she was doing. He watched the show in silence.
She stood the four sticks into the center of the stone circle, interlacing the forked ends to form a teepee-shaped frame.
"One stick for each of the four directions," she said quietly.

"We can talk now?" Cal asked.

She shook her head no. "Just me." She gave him that playful look again.

She broke more sticks and stood them around the frame, one stick at a time, leaning them in, balancing their weight, building a good sized cone-shaped pile. She left an opening to one side, like a door to the interior. She gathered a few twists of dry grass, a handful of pine needles, and placed them carefully in through the opening.

She dusted her hands off on her jeans and sat back on the ground.

"There. I've just made a house for the Fire Spirits to visit." She looked at Cal. "We can talk now."

Cal smiled. "Oh thanks so much."

He leaned forward, inspected her little creation. He nodded. "It's very nice." He waited a while. He looked at Gayle. He looked up at the falling night sky. "So when can we expect these fire spirits to visit?"

Gayle laughed. She pulled a matchbook from her pocket, struck a match and held it into the twist of grass. The fire lit itself nicely from the inside out, and a steady flame rose.

Cal nodded back. "Well done."

"It's more respectful this way," Gayle said. "You get what you pay for."

He watched the fire crackling to life. "The fire spirits do seem to like it." He nodded and reached for more wood.

Gayle stopped him with her hand on his.

"This is their house right now. Their fire. We have to wait our turn."

"Oh. Part of the ritual?"

"Mmm-hmm."

Cal set the wood aside. He sat back.

"Are we allowed to talk?"

"Sure," Gayle said. "Me first. There are three fires to the ritual. The First Fire, that's this one here, is for the Fire Spirits alone to enjoy. It's their house, so we leave it to them until they burn up all the sticks and the house collapses. And that's the end of the First Fire."

Cal nodded. "Well that makes a lot of sense right there."

She grinned back. "It does. So after that, you can add more wood and coax it back to life."

"And that would be called the Second Fire?" Cal guessed.

"Nope. It is the second fire, but it's called the Heart Fire. That's the one we use for cooking, for warmth, for light, for anything we need. The Heart Fire belongs to us all. It's the people's fire." She stared quietly into the flames.

"Sounds like communism."

Gayle smiled. "It's not a political system, it's just a fire."

Cal nodded. "So how about the third fire?" he asked. "You said there were three fires, right?"

"Right. But you have to ask first about the Third Fire before I can tell you about it. Ritual protocol, you know."

"Well I just asked."

"So you did." She turned toward him. "Well, the Third Fire is a secret."

Cal smiled with anticipation. "What's the secret?"

Gayle gave him a closer look, her face inches from his. The very image of mischief herself. She glanced away, she looked around the campsite, allowing time and her silence to gather.

She looked back and shook her head no.

"No?" Cal tugged at her arm. "Gayle, hey. C'mon now. No?" She was laughing.

"You're going to set me up like that? Tell me this whole story about a secret fire, then you're not going to tell me the secret?"

She took one of his hands in hers. "I'd like to tell you, honey. Honestly." She batted her eyes. "But it's not something I can tell you. It's only something I can show you. And it's not the right time to show you."

Cal waved his hand aside. "You're making it all up. You just love to fuck with your audience, don't you."

"No I'm not making it up," Gayle said emphatically. "And yeah, I do sometimes. But I'm not fucking with you. It's true, I swear."

The first fire toppled over just then, fell away to a rush of sparks that spiraled into the night like fireworks.

"Let's enjoy the Heart Fire first," she said. She reached in with a handful of sticks and brought the fire back to life. "One must be humble and not bumble on the road to Wisdom." She grinned. She piled on more sticks until the fire blazed with generous warmth.

Their night rolled on. A great block of cheddar cheese and a pack of crackers appeared and disappeared. Cubes of steak and sliced peppers on skewers were braised to perfection over the dancing flames. The two bottles of wine they had packed worked their way to empty.

They lay on their backs watching the stars as the last of the fire burned to coals and its light and warmth were dying.

Gayle sat up and looked into the fire ring.

"So," she said, collecting her thoughts, allowing the silence. "The secret of the Third Fire."

Cal sat up beside her. "Right. I almost forgot."

"No, you did forget. That's why I reminded you." She tapped the tip of his nose with her finger.

He blinked. He waited. She sat quietly beside him.

"So?" he said. "What's the secret of the third fire?"

She nodded. "Well. You have to ask first, before I can show you."

Cal threw his hands up in the air.

"That's how it goes with rituals, Cal. You knock at the door before you enter."

Cal watched her. "But I just knocked, didn't I?"

"Yes you did. So now I can show you."

She grabbed a fat branch that she'd kept hidden off to one side. She used it now like a club to break apart the remaining coals. She mashed them methodically, repeatedly, sending bursts of tiny sparks aloft. Soon the coals were broken all to small fiery nuggets. She spread the coals out evenly over the entire circle, out to the very perimeter of the stones. In the still night air, the coal bed flared inward in collapsing concentric rings, one after another. A puffing circle of red light lay pulsing on the canyon floor, beating like a heart.

Cal smiled. "Sweet. It looks like molten liquid. Like lava." He edged himself closer. It was mesmerizing to watch. The heat was generous and soft. "It's like a small sun, lying here face up on the earth."

"I'm inclined to see it as a mirror," Gayle said.

"A mirror? Like a mirror to the missing sun?"

Gayle sort of nodded. "Mmm. Not exactly. But anyway, here's the story." She set the fat branch aside. "All fires are related. All the fires that have ever burned on earth, every one of them, are related to every other fire, just like members of a family are related to one another. No different. This fire is connected to every other fire, way back into time, and all the way back to the very first fire that ever burned. That first fire is called the Grandfather Fire." She leaned in. "So here's part of the secret. The Grandfather Fire, that first fire to ever burn on earth, it's still burning. Right now, right here . . . it's still burning." She almost whispered that last part.

Cal was smiling. "Where?" he whispered back.

Gayle pointed downward, her finger touching the ground. "Inside. The Grandfather Fire is the beating heart of this earth. The earth would be a cold rock out in space if it weren't so."

Cal looked down at the glowing pool of coals.

"But wait, there's more," she said. "As old as he might seem to us, the Grandfather Fire is actually just a child himself. He's a child of the sun. The son of the sun, you might say, if you were into saying dumb things like that."

She nodded toward the fire ring.

"If you still your thoughts, and you look at it the right way, the third fire becomes a window, and you can look down into that window, all the way down, right into the face of old Grandfather Fire himself. And most times you can feel him looking back too, because he's looking up at us, and he's looking way past us too, way out into space, way up to all the other fires burning there in the sky."

Gayle pointed to the stars.

"Those are his family members up there, all his brothers and sisters, his cousins and aunts and uncles and nephews and nieces. All of the stars, all his family."

Cal looked up at the stars. He looked down into the Third Fire.

"See?" she said. "They've invited you to their gathering. And you're always welcome here too, so there's no such thing as alone."

A warm feeling wrapped around him. That sense of isolation that usually came with the wilderness popped like a soap bubble, the stars crowding in all around, the warmth of the fire reaching out. He shook his head in amazement.

"Jeez, woman." He reached out and wrapped her in his arms.

They sat beside one another in that mountain stillness and watched the coals spark and blink away, one by one. Soon there was just a scatter of embers left, glowing soft like orange stars through the clouds.

Cal turned to Gayle. He could barely make out her face in the last of that light, but for a moment he felt like he was looking into a mirror, and it was his own face there in front of him, looking back. The moment took him completely by surprise.

"Whoa! That's . . ."

Gayle laughed. "Like seeing yourself in a mirror?"

"Yeah. And you knew that was going to happen?"

She nodded. "It happens every time. Magic, huh?"

"Totally. Why does that happen?"

She shook her head lightly. "I wouldn't ask magic why."

Cal stared at the flaring circle of coals lying before him.

He leaned back against the curve of the big rock and huddled against the chill night air, his sleeping bag draped over his shoulders. The fire died out one coal at a time and he didn't bother with it.

The campsite fell to darkness. The thin patch of sky above him held a handful of stars, all migrating west. All else slept while he watched, the last eyes on that midnight pool.

9.

The first hint of morning showed in the eastern sky. The last stars blinked out. The first birdcalls met with no response.

A small pair of eyes hovered the ground before him, staring, motionless. Cal could barely make them out at first, more ghostlike than real in the predawn light, through the thin morning fog.

Two yellow dots reflecting the pale window of sky above. They disappeared. He didn't move.

The eyes reappeared, floating low to the ground. They disappeared again.

The sky lightened more.

Opposite him across the fire ring sat an elf owl. Cal watched its outline take shape, its coloration fill in. The owl watched him for long seconds at a time, then closed its eyes for just as long. It reopened its eyes and watched him silently. No other part of the creature moved. A few seconds passed, the owl closed its eyes.

Cal leaned forward. He looked to the branches of the trees above, back to the pocket-sized bird on the ground. He made a small clicking noise to get the bird's attention. The owl opened its eyes a few seconds later, two crystal orbs of pale yellow light, unmoving. It watched him a half minute more, as still as a stone. It closed its eyes again.

Cal sat back against the rock. He watched the owl watching him. Eyes opened, eyes closed.

Daylight evicted the remaining shadows one by one. Songbirds sang again in the treetops, silvery notes echoing through the canopy. A morning breeze slid beneath the ground fog, lifting it in slow waves.

Cal watched the owl. He closed his eyes when the owl did, opened them a half-minute later, matching his timing. Another half-minute passed, they closed their eyes together. Time set adrift in small measures like empty rafts sent downriver. Eyes opened, eyes closed, eyes opened, eyes closed.

The trees above him grew quiet.

Cal opened his eyes and the owl was gone, evaporated like the night before it. A small boat-shaped depression was all that remained in the pine needles. The fire ring was a pool of soft white ash. The sky above held the thickening reins of another day. The forest was silent.

Cal stood, night stiff and bone tired. Columns of mist twisted ghostly through the trees. The orb spider's web stood perfect and complete before him, heavy and glistening with beads of dew. The big rock stood another day trapped between the two great pines, the shadow of a sitting man upon its surface where the falling dew hadn't darkened it.

Cal stuffed the sleeping bag into his backpack.

He drank from his last bottle of water.

He unfolded the trail map from his pocket. He figured his rough location from the lay of land and the distance he had covered yesterday.

Maybe twelve miles of forest trail left to cover, according to the map. A steep climb after that, up an exposed ridgeline about a mile and a half in length. Over the top of that ridge then down into a low saddle, the trail map showed a small dotted square at the saddle's low point. *Cabin or former cabin*, the map legend read. Leftovers from the forestry service of the 1930's, or maybe an old miner's camp. Probably no more than a ruin.

Up from the saddle to the peak of Anvil, a steady stair-like climb to the summit at nine thousand eight hundred twenty feet.

He folded the map away. He glanced up to the high treetops. The first sunrays were entangling there, weaving their way through the branches. He lifted his pack, fit his arms through the straps, bounced its weight into place, cinched the straps down tight.

He stepped away onto the trail.

Massive tree trunks passed him by in silent procession. He was walking through the attic of the world.

The first shafts of sunlight cut their way to the forest floor, hard-edged and abrupt. Cal saw his shadow laboring beside him, step for halting step.

He felt older than anything he could have had knowledge of.

The sun felt heavy this day, made of molten lead, and shackled to the sky.

10.

Near noon.

He crossed most of the forest bowl nestled within the ridges, his focus ten feet ahead and blank-minded. Three steps per breath. Three steps per breath. He spanned a small brook with a single stride and walked on for five minutes, the river of his thoughts and his memories sweeping him blind in its current.

He stopped and let out a long exhale. He dropped his pack on the trail, pulled out the empty water bottles and tread the distance of those lost minutes back to the stream.

He knelt at a stone beside the flow and drank the cold clear water from his hands. He splashed it across his face, he soaked his head dripping wet, the act of trying to wake up from being awake.

He filled the bottles and set them aside. He drank again, his face to the water this time, sucking it in, the water so cold it hurt, until he could hold no more.

He sat back and watched the stream in its quiet flowing, the water in no great hurry, hedging its way around rocks, pooling in circles behind pine needle dams.

Water could be found here, this time of year, in normal years.

So it was a normal year. Now he knew.

He gathered the four bottles and walked that same length of trail for the third time, his footprints on the ground going both ways now before him.

He found his backpack on the trail where he'd left it. He placed the water bottles inside, re-shouldered the load, and he walked on again.

Again.

All of it felt like again: The again of another day, the again of another breath, the again of the memory of all roads that brought him there, the again of every thought that he could ever think or try not to think again, the again of the trail passing silently beneath his feet, the pine needles sucking up every sound at once and the again of his very next step falling, then the next step after that.

The again of a sky torched spotless by another day's sun.

The again of the night that would slink into place behind it.

The again of again. He walked on.

The forest thinned out as the elevation gained, its enormity faltering, the trees shrunken now to brush, huddled to desperate clusters against the shear of the altitude. The trail climbed higher still into thinner air, snaked its way up the bleached backbone of a jagged ridge, stood naked again beneath an iron-white sun. The rocks laid out a twisted path, like steps cut in stone for a drunken demon to climb. A stairway cast to earth from an ancient, careless heaven.

Cal climbed a few steps, then stopped. Then a few more, then stopped. Then a few more, then stopped. The wind would rise. The day would sour. The sun's brightness would be swallowed.

Ascending the stairs of a church, the endless stairs of a church, one heartbeat per breath. Walking, unhinged. One step, one step, one step. The air grown naked and gray, the color of loss, the color of remembrance. Each heartbeat traded for the next.

The god of gravity grew angered, calling in all debts, all payable now, and now, and now. No more climbing on credit. Not a breath of air was given freely. The effort like a shotgun to the mind.

Mental photographs adrift in that fractured air: Cal bent at the knee, his head nearly dragging the ground, Atlas at home at the end of the day, the globe on the couch beside him, the children of Zeus one by one with their fingers in the socket, all of them nodding, all lining up for more.

An army of peg-legged Ahabs parades before a grandstand, beckoning for all to follow, stovepipe hats cocked to one side, barking black smoke in rows.

Ulysses as a child tying himself to a tree, his mother calling him home to supper.

Christmas in the desert lands half a calendar off, as empty, as silent.

Gayle's face at a window, behind glass, beyond touch.

Ballroom lights dimmed, the ocean breezes sticky with salt, an embrace on the dance floor in circles, big band music drifting off into the shadows.

A hall of revelers carved in stone, their glasses raised in an endless toast.

Gayle veiled in light like eternity sitting in a wooden chair, her eyes about to open, about to open.

Cal bent his head low, plow-horse-like and eager to forget. One step, one breath, one step. His hands clawed the silent rock, the bones of earth protruding, the rest of him dead in decades, or hours or minutes, the same. He echoes down the years, cracks the wall of repairs by not moving on, pushing into the crowd of ghosts hovering just beyond the grave or barely still, all begging for a lift.

The sky to the west blackened like conspiracy, like a magnet attracting doom to itself. Clouds rolled forth in waves that each swallowed the next. Straight up the noon sun stood without authority, staring to earth like a convicted god. The sound of distant thunder pounded up from the desert floor, pushed in past the hills to the halls and hidden vaults of the mountain range and took to the air like a sudden war unannounced and unraveling.

Supplicant Cal, climbing the stairs of his church, the religion of rocks and memory and now wind-blown sand rushing east to a point in the sky where the sun had vanished, the altar of mute purpose recoiling in a plume of rising dust.

One step. And then one step more.

A quick end to the species that runs on empty.

~

Eternity waits backstage, patient, attentive, impeccably dressed, holding his hat and coat over one arm.

The curtain quivers, ready for the close. You stand center stage, the house lights come up.

There is one in the audience left. It is you as well. Your eyes meet. There will be no applause.

Eternity checks his watch for the time, suppresses a dull yawn.

You bow to the empty theater save one. A deep, gracious, theatrical bow.

Silence.

There must be more, you think. All those lines learned, all those moves memorized and rehearsed. It took a lifetime to learn them.

"It always takes a lifetime to learn them," Eternity has told you. "Exactly, one."

Face to face with yourself, "How did I do?" you want to ask,

but the air here no longer carries your voice. That privilege has been rescinded.
It is time to leave the stage. That alone is left.
A monumental act, that. Not listed on the program.
The play is over, drawn to a close.
You turn to face Eternity. Eternity smiles benignly, not a hint of encouragement or regret or judgment there.
He simply waits.
The audience of one rises, turns up the side aisle toward the exit, the program left behind on the seat.
Eternity offers his hand. "Shall we?" he says, his voice the richest of baritones.
The next move is your last. You will exit the stage.
That alone is left, the one step more.
There's a rushing sound to the air, it approaches and retreats. A rumbling grows within it, grows then to a roar, to a thunderous explosion.
You turn your head for one last look at all those empty seats.
Is that applause you hear?

~

Cal spun off balance on the last rock of that endless climb. He turned his head toward the roaring sound. The forest lay far below him, draped now in darkness, shroud-like and menacing. He stood high upon a naked outcrop of rock.

The lightning crept up over the rim of the far ridge and shot down into the forest bowl where he had camped last night, striking like the hot electric fingers of some outraged preacher chasing down Satan. A sudden wall of wind buffeted Cal backwards into a stumble. He stared on. Blue-gray sheets of rain closed in over the valley from either side. First drops the size of gumballs whacked at his face and shocked him back to attention. A dozen more and he was dripping wet.

Move . . .

All of it, the wind, the roar, the hiss and flash of lightning, the acrid chemical air, the hair standing up on his neck and arms and the rain punching his face with fat fists of water, all of it telling him to move.

MOVE!!

A lightning bolt cracked not twenty yards away, blue-green then orange in its afterglow. Cal spun with the explosion, was two steps into a downhill run when the wave of its sound caught him from behind and welded each cell of his brain to the next. His legs blurred with new speed.

He watched the trail through his haze of panic and the hail of rain before him, and he saw it in his memory on the map, that small dotted square and the words "cabin, or former cabin," somewhere ahead, across the saddle. The rain pounded him, and his heart pounded back, beyond breath. A lightning bolt cracked and seared the rock where he had just been standing. His downhill run turned to panic-ballet, the act of perpetual falling, suspended. The rocks beneath him grew slick and shiny. Pools of yellow mud gathered in the hollows and splashed with his every third step. Cal danced a frantic descent, charging down the slope with spikes of lightning at his back. There was a taste to the air, like a battery licked. The flashes of lightning froze him in mid-stride, in mid-jump, his arms out, both his feet off the ground, one foot down in water splashing, one look back he'd rather not have taken, ten looks ahead like a prayer through clenched teeth.

He made it off the slope. The downhill was over, the free fall had ended. He was in the flat of the saddle now, he'd have to earn the rest.

His laces were untying and his boots were filling with rain. Water squirted from the welts. His footfalls made a sound like rhythmic burping. The air was dense and sideways with rain, and he could see no cabin ahead. The wind howled over the lower notch and raced across the saddle, flipping plates of rock up one side and down the other like stone leaves blown across his path. He stumbled his way through, lurching nearly to the ground. He came up out of it and out of one of his boots at the same time, sucked from his foot by the mud.

A lightning bolt augured into the rock beneath him that his feet no longer touched and he saw it in slow-motion, razor-fingers of orange fire that spidered off into the stone's face like a cracking windshield and the blush of its explosion shot him forward out of his pack, both arms at once. The pack rolled to a soggy stop on the trail behind him along with his missing boot.

The cabin's outline appeared ahead in the strobing flashes, then vanished again in the curtaining rain. Twenty-five yards remained. A drum-roll of lightning strikes behind him, one-two-three-four, each one closer than the last, and the words he bellowed were lost to the roar. Five more giant steps remained. Half the cabin's face was missing, rotted, long-fallen to the ground. The roofline sagged. Three more giant steps remained. Cal was flying now, diving horizontally through the air like a pro tackle, backlit by a wall of blue-fire in a ring of thunder-rung mountains. In through the gap, the rain pulled away, the silence of a half-second . . . then the crunch of a hundred and sixty pounds of wet panic slammed to the back wall of the half-ruined cabin. The cabin swayed with the blow and recovered, the boards groaned.

Cal lay wet as a dog on the stone floor, tucked up in a ball. The storm raged on like a deranged cat robbed of its plaything. He hugged his knees, he hugged his whole wet self, shaken, his eyes closed, his head buried.

The adrenalin withdrew slowly from his bloodstream, leaving him in tatters, his heart pounding rampant, a buzzing sound in his ears. He huddled down beneath the din of rain on the sheet metal roof and the roar of thunder above it.

There was another sound he heard then, woven in beneath the racket, like a voice was speaking somewhere nearby.

Cal raised his head. He stared into the dark corners of the cabin. There was nothing there he could see, for all his effort.

Voices unraveling in his head, he figured. Nothing more.

A lightning bolt cracked outside, a wash of violet light banked its way through the cabin, into the far corner, onto the figure of a man sitting cross-legged on the floor. The light caught in his eyes like a pair of flashbulbs popping. Cal sat up bolt straight and the cabin went pitch dark. His brain and every muscle held rigid through the retreat.

Another lightning bolt popped, this one closer than the last, its heat immediate and its sound nearly crushing. The other man appeared again. He was speaking, or his mouth was moving, but the roar of the thunder wiped out any sound he could have made. He held out a hand, a thin finger pointing, and the cabin went dark again.

Cal thought that it was Death himself before him, incarnate, and he doubled over, clutched his stomach and retched onto the floor in spasms.

11.

Minutes passed, more or less. Rain pounded at the roof.

The other man struck a match. It flared up to light his face like a sorcerer opening for business. He lit a cigarette, waved the match out and his corner fell again to darkness.

Cal watched without a sound, incapable of any other response and troubled enough with the task of breathing.

The storm lumbered by like a passing freight train, the lightning struck less, the howl of wind subsided. The rain steadied itself into a straight downpour.

Cal felt the man's eyes upon him.

"The name's, ah . . . Cal," he said.

No response from the other man.

Cal straightened himself slightly.

"The name's Cal. Cal . . ." He said his last name but a tumble of thunder obliterated the sound of it.

Silence again beneath the sound of rain on the metal roof.

The tip of the man's cigarette glowed red, half lit his features, then went dark. Again. Again.

Cal glanced through the open cabin wall. He watched the rain falling, he felt his heart pounding. Still alive, he thought. Still alive. He thought that until the thought itself was strange.

The lightning front had passed them by. It was raging further east now, down from the mountains and into the desert, gorging itself anew in the baking heat. The sound of thunder fell back at them without malice.

Cal had the thought of standing, then the very next thought of leaving the cabin altogether, maybe at a full run.

He strained his eyes into the darkness. A thin cloud of tobacco smoke drifted past.

Did Death smoke? Did he read that somewhere? But who would know?

He realized he hadn't been breathing much. He would try harder. And he was shaking all over now, his clothes stuck tight to him and cold with rain.

Not normal. Not normal. None of it was normal. He thought of counting. Counting what?

Time thickened around him.

"I should go," Cal said, half to himself, or maybe just to be reassured by the sound of his own voice. "Go back, and, uh . . . fetch up my gear." He nodded outside. "Seems I . . . ran out of it." He tried for a laugh but the sound he made was more like a choking. "I ran out of my pack. Ran right out of it. And a boot too." He raised his bare foot to show it off. He pointed outside. "Out there on the trail, before I came . . . here." He nodded.

The other man said nothing. His cigarette glowed red, his eyebrows lit, then dimmed.

"Right," Cal said. He rose slowly to his feet. The effort felt second-handed, like he was watching someone else stand up, someone you might root for, like at a sporting event. He edged himself nearer to the doorway. "Well, so I'll just go, now. Go and get my stuff." He skirted the funnel of water running off the sagging roof and walked out into the rain.

He stood a dozen yards off on the trail, shielding his eyes with his hands, looking east after the storm front. He saw it crawling off across the desert like an enormous spider on strobing electric legs. He glanced nervously at the cabin.

He backtracked the trail half barefooted, down again into the flat of the saddle. He found his pack there, tumbled against the brush. Further along he found his missing boot, suctioned down into the mud in mid-stride, filled neatly to the rim with water and ringing with raindrops. He pulled it from the earth like a wet kiss and drained the water away.

He stood there, his boot in hand, his pack half-slung, and stared at the wreck of the cabin in the wet distance. He looked all around himself in a circle.

He slogged his way back to the cabin. He dodged the rain funneling off the roof and stepped inside. He dropped his pack to the stone floor. Water oozed from it in a widening puddle. He tossed his boot down beside it.

He sat heavily against the wall and stared at the ground. He waited for something else to happen. Nothing did.

He removed his other boot and poured its murky contents to the floor. He stopped and looked up toward the dark corner.

"You, ah, don't . . . live here, do you?"

Silence from that corner.

"Because I wouldn't want to, ah . . ." He pointed to the mess he was making, he laughed nervously. He waited.

"Well hell anyway, who could live way the hell up here, right? I mean . . . way up here?" He nodded to the wreck of the cabin.

Silence.

He shrugged. He peeled off his socks and wrung them onto the floor. He pulled off his soaked t-shirt and did the same with that. He opened his pack and reached inside, found another shirt just half as wet and pulled that one on. He settled back against the wall, shaken with the cold and exertion. In shock, perhaps. Lightning-damaged, maybe. He had the thought of checking his pulse. Against what, though.

He glanced to the dark corner from time to time. Minutes coiled passed.

"So, ah . . . what brings you up here?"

No answer.

"To this mountain here, I mean," Cal said. "It's, ah, pretty out of the way, of anything, so, ah . . ."

He strained his eyes into the darkness. A broken roll of thunder stumbled past and echoed off the mountain walls, sounded like a trash can bouncing down a flight of stairs. The corrugated roof rattled and buzzed. The sky was near to black as night. The rain fell harder, louder.

"Are you there?" Cal asked.

No sound came back.

He sat in suspension.

He reached for his pack, dug through the side pockets. He found his headlamp and switched it on. He swept the beam across the dark end of the cabin. There was no one there. Bare wooden shelves ranged across the back wall, a wide board hanging from a hinge that could have been a table if it had any legs. Not much else.

He clicked off the light, sat looking at the dark.

"I'm losing it here," he said. He felt a wash of relief pass through him. He shook his head. "Really, just losing it." He sniffed at the air for any scent of tobacco. None. "Huh." He waited.

The other man appeared at the door, his shadow darkening the cabin before him.

Cal's head snapped around.

The man was dripping wet, his hair stuck to the sides of his head. He stepped in past the thin wash of daylight that might have defined him and disappeared again into the dark.

Cal listened while the man settled in. Then there was just the sound of rain against the roof.

Cal stared through the space that separated them.

"What did you say your name was?"

"I didn't."

A voice finally, to go with the face he hadn't quite seen, or didn't quite want to.

Cal nodded tentatively. Time dragged squirming by its heels, clawing at any detail.

"The name's Cal here." He noticed a burnt scrap of wood on the floor.

"So . . . you . . . said." The three words hung disconnected from the silence placed between them.

Cal looked out at the torrent of rain. Cats and dogs, he thought. Raining cats and dogs. He wondered why, about the cats and dogs. He thought of them slamming to the roof, bouncing of the ground, rolling away through the underbrush in a complete terror, like a total what-the-fuck. And the sound it would make.

"Why are you here?"

"What?" Cal turned and stared into the darker depths.

"Why are you here?" the man said, more distinctly, louder against the rain.

Cal glanced away. He thought it over but his answer was too long in coming. Too complicated. He grabbed some other words instead.

"I just needed to get away. Just . . . to get away."

Rain pounding at the mountain, tiding down through every fissure.

"How's that working out?"

Cal heard the question above the din. He laughed involuntarily at the sound of it, at the idea that there was any answer to it. Sitting barefoot, soaking wet and shivering, in a wrecked cabin, at the edge of nowhere, taking questions from a shadow. From Death himself, maybe.

Maybe not Death. He flexed his fingers open, closed, open.

Death himself . . . wasn't that just too weird? Impossible even? As near to impossible?

He didn't know what that meant.

He could barely think straight. He stared at his bare feet while the rain fell just beyond them.

"How about you?" he said after a while. "What, ah, brings you up here?"

He didn't really expect an answer.

The man cleared his throat.

"Sometimes you get an idea, a powerful idea, and it sticks inside your head, grows there like a tree. Then maybe later, you get tired of that idea, you get real tired of it being up there all the time, and you don't want to be thinking about it anymore. That's like cutting the tree down. You cut it down to the ground until it's gone, and there's nothing left of it that shows. But the roots are still there, and the roots run deep. Deeper than you can know."

There was a long silence.

"That's where your soul goes when you're not looking."

Silence like a black pool of water.

Cal had no other questions that needed answering.

He dropped into that silence like a stone.

12.

One of the first bitter cold days of November, a day damp and overcast, he remembered. A Saturday. Gayle had the day off from the gallery. They had made some tentative plans for a getaway but the weather was uninviting. They stayed home to work around the house instead. Cal built some storage shelves across the back wall of the garage, to relieve the closets in the house that had filled with more boxes of clothing and camping gear and artifacts than they could rightly handle. Gayle was the pack rat when it came to her artifacts. Cal was the same way with his camping gear.

He worked the project late into the afternoon, the day's light fading beneath the cloud cover and the day's rawness chilling him to the bone. Gayle carried the last of the boxes from the house, taped and labeled, and then a hot cup of coffee for Cal. He warmed his hands around the cup as he looked over the spread of boxes. Some of the labels read 'Small Treasures,' others read 'Large Treasures.' He smiled. He asked her where the mid-sized treasures were. She said matter-of-factly that treasures could only come in those two sizes.

"Who'd be happy with a mid-sized treasure?" she asked.

She shivered out her compliments to his handiwork and hustled back inside.

Cal cleaned up the remains of the wood, stacked the boxes into place. He packed his tools away and swept the sawdust from the floor.

He walked across the drive to the kitchen, down the hall to the bedroom door. The heat was on in the house, that first day of the season when the furnace kicks in, the musty warm smell of it, the rumble of the burner through the walls. Gayle was lying in bed with a book and a reading light on over her shoulder, snuggled in beneath a mountain of winter blankets that hadn't been off the shelf since last spring. She lifted the covers aside when she saw Cal standing at the door.

"Come," she said.

Cal nodded back. "Uno momento." He was covered with grit and sawdust. "Shower first."

He dropped his clothes in the hall by the back door. He stepped into the shower. The heat of the water stung the cold from his face, from his hands and his feet and his toes. He found himself turning the water up hotter, a little hotter still, his bones begging for more, the cold that was locked inside him retreating by degrees, melting away, finally erased.

He toweled off and stood beside the bed. Gayle laid her book aside. She clicked the reading lamp off. She lifted the covers and slid over to make some room. The day's light through the window was nearly gone. He climbed in, she wrapped her arms and legs around his body and snuggled in close.

"Oh, you're so hot," she said. She buried her face into his neck. "I haven't been warm all day." Her nose was dog cold. They hugged in that fading light. They talked some. They drifted with the time of day.

Cal looked in her eyes. She was so familiar to him, familiar beyond what could be explained by the measure of time they'd spent together. There was more to it than that. It seemed now that she had always been there, and he had always known her face and the sound of her voice, the words she was about to speak, her velvety laugh. The dimpled curve of skin at her temple, the bones of her cheeks that any sculptor would have fought to claim. Soft transparent wisps of hair edged her forehead like a feathery down. And her eyes, that look from her eyes, so steady and ever still, so disconnected from time.

Like an eternity right there in his arms.

"I could live here forever," he whispered. He thanked her for being in his life, light kisses falling about her face.

Beneath that warmth and the weight of those blankets, there could have been no less space between them.

The light through the window faded, failed all but the world of shadows and dreams. The rain that the sky had withheld all day began falling in cold heavy drops against the panes.

Coiled together in that quiet dark, Cal whispered to Gayle a little story he'd heard as a child. The Legend of the Bird Tribe, he called it.

"A very, very long time ago, there was a tribe that lived at the edge of a great prairie, alongside the banks of a mighty river. They called themselves, simply, the People. They were a hunting folk, a fishing folk. They had lived in that land a longer time than any of them could count, and if you were to ask, they would tell you that they, the People, must have been born on the same day that the land itself was created.

"After ages had passed in the this simple way, a season of change suddenly fell upon them. 'There's something unsettled in the air,' the old ones would say, and then all the People began having the same dream at night. In that dream, they saw that a plague was approaching, a plague that was very different from any others they could remember. This plague would consume the very land upon which they stood. Everywhere they turned, the trees would wither and fall, the rivers would sicken and dry up, the animals and fish they depended on for food would vanish. The earth itself would turn brittle beneath their feet, crack open and fall away.

"The people would awake from this dream in terror. But night after night, the same dream would occur. Some of the people grew very fearful. They wished not to speak of it at all. These people began to sing at night and sound their drums, to feed their fires and dance in endless circles, to tell and retell all their stories, to do anything at all that they could think of, not to fall asleep and have that dream find them again.

"But there were also some among them who felt thankful for the dream, thankful for the message that the dream was trying to deliver. 'Everything that lives speaks to us,' they would say. 'And so must we listen.' These few people put their fears aside and let sleep find them each night like always. And then when the dream returned, as it always did, they asked of the dream, 'Where will the People go to escape this plague?' And each night the answer they received was the same: There will be no land left safe for them to stand upon. Wherever they might turn, however fast they might run, the very ground beneath their feet will be eaten away. Their way of life on the land was truly finished.

"But they also saw that this was not the end. As the plague grew nearer, and the trees began to fall, and the land itself began to crumble, these people saw that they were to stand tall, to set aside all that they carried on their backs, and to let go of all they carried in their hands. They were to hold onto only that which they could carry in their hearts.

"As the ground fell away beneath their feet, these people turned their faces up to the sky and they breathed it in. They inhaled the sky so deeply that, on that day, these people became the first birds; they became the winged ones: all the crows and the doves, the hawks and the eagles, the hummingbirds and owls and larks and swallows, each according to his or her spirit. They rose up across that land in great numbers, their voices raised in joyous song, and they played in the far reaches of the sky, for that was to be their new home.

"After a very, very long time, the land healed itself and was peaceful again. There were new trees and prairies, and new creatures appearing everywhere, and the rivers all flowed clear and strong again. But the Bird Tribe remained in the sky. There were none left that could remember any other home."

13.

Cal busied himself with his wet gear. He pulled his sleeping bag from the pack and looked for a place to hang it out to dry. He found a half-driven nail in the side of a rafter and draped it there.

He found his smokes. He tried pulling the wet cigarettes from the soggy box one at a time, slowly, hoping for some luck. They mostly fell to pieces. He gave it up and laid the box aside. He picked up one of his boots, scraped mud absently from the lugs with a stick.

He stood at the doorway, just beneath the roof edge. Clouds crowded the peak to the north. The sky was the color of wet cement. Another flush of rain pounded the cabin. Hailstones the size of eggs began falling. They bounced from the roof in a deafening clatter, cracked open against the rocks, racketed off into the brush.

Cal held a water bottle to the rain funneling from the roof. He capped that and filled a second bottle, then a third. The water was ice-cold, right from the sky. He caught the water in his hands, splashed it to his face, the closest he could get to a feeling of waking up.

His head ached a gray ache, sodden like a mirror to the lid of sky above. His vision blurred all before him to a dull soup. He closed his eyes to it. A bad dream with no exit. No waking from it. In that smaller darkness he could hear his heart beating, pacing blindly like an animal trapped for life in a cage.

The fall of hail exhausted itself and the rain reclaimed a softer rhythm. Far to the southwest, where the mountains tapered again to desert, he saw a brightness showing beyond the slate gray of the clouds above. There was sunlight there, the storm's end maybe.

He turned his head.

"Hey, could I bum a smoke here?" he said to the dark corner.

No answer from there.

14.

The rain slackened to a trickle. Single drops counted off a cadence from the roof edge, puddles thinned on the ground and streamed away.

A crow landed to a silent hop on the trail. It shuttered its body to shed the rain, shuffled its feathers into place. It lowered its head to drink from a pool in the rock ledge, tilted its head back, tipped the water down. It took a sideways look toward the cabin. It dipped its beak again, swallowed, took another long look at the cabin. It shook its feathers and hopped off into flight, dropped over the rim of the saddle and was gone.

Cal stepped outside and walked the trail to the north. He put the cabin a few hundred feet behind him. The elevation gained, the view a bit wider. He looked to the southwest. A brightness still gathered there, a low fire of sunlight shimmering beneath the iron pan of sky.

He looked to the north, where the trail wound its way higher up through the brush. The peak of Anvil waited there, hidden still beneath a blue-gray shroud of fog. His destination.

Destination. From the word destiny. A place we are meant to go.

He could make no sense of it, any of it. He scanned his memory for a pattern he might have missed, or the slightest of handholds, or a signpost somewhere that might just spell out the word "sense," with a big arrow pointing the way.

He wondered if any sense could ever be made, of anything.

Maybe it was all just a myth. Something we say in the dark to keep the monsters at bay. A bright happy band-aid for a gushing wound.

"Sense. Sense. Sense." He said the word aloud until it was no more than a random shape of air sliding past his tongue.

Silence was better.

Silence made sense.

Or at least it carried less liability.

He stepped backwards down the trail like the flow of time had reversed itself in the world. One step. One step. One step

But the world and all its time stayed just as it was.

He would shelter himself again within the wall of the wrecked cabin, beneath the clock-tick of rain on the roof.

He would watch the clouds thinning at the far ridgeline, racing low to the ground, breaking apart.

A bird sang out a one-note song from its hideout in the brush. All the branches dripped.

The miles of gray distance devoured every other detail.

15.

An hour's worth of weather scattered. The rain ended, the trailing edge of the storm front inched closer through breaks in the southern peaks. Cal sat facing west, perched atop a boulder balanced at the edge of the saddle, staring at the coming rim of sunlight ten miles off. The cloud's edge was sharp there, deep gray to its limits, lined with a bright slice of gold. Beyond that lay a clear blue sky. The cloud's shadow swept the ground beneath it, drawing back like a curtain over the valley. There was majesty to the way it moved, the steady draw of shadow and light together, like a night and day compressed into one. Tree by tree the forest brightened in the rain-sparked sunshine. Their limbs held the sunlight in thousands of quaking drops that sparkled and flurried in sheets to the ground at the first touch of any breeze.

The light climbed up from the forest, spilling now over the jagged trace of the ridgeline, racing across the saddle. The trail opened into the light, rock by rock, all of it glistening.

The sun broke upon him and its heat was instant. A warm breeze followed. The storm clouds overhead pulled back like a sheet of gauze. Details stood sharp-edged and crystalline. Fans of foxgrass bent to graceful arches, heavy with beads of water. Inside each drop, a rainbow. Rocks along the ledge began to steam. The mist rose in slanted columns that raced along the ground, that swept by and curled into greater ropes of fog that chased up the mountain's face. Cal scanned the clearing peak for any signs of life. He scanned all around him in a wider circle. Right now, he was it. He looked back toward the cabin.

16.

The first time he saw the painting, he was standing in Gayle's studio.

"I started it when I was fifteen," she said.

It was a large work, three foot by four foot, propped against a wall.

"It's amazing," Cal said. "When did you finish it?"

He'd known her a few months by then.

Gayle shook her head.

"It's not finished."

He looked the canvas over again.

"Well. It's beautiful. That's you, right?"

"Yep. Self-portrait with Sunflowers. That's the working title."

In the painting, Gayle stood just to the left of center. She was suspended in mid-stride above a nearly endless field of sunflowers. She was barefooted. She wore a white flowing dress, like something you'd see on a prairie woman a hundred years back. Her hair and the dress eddied slightly behind her, hinting at a light breeze.

"So do you think that's a sunrise or a sunset back there?" Gayle asked, pointing it out.

Cal said, "Sunrise," almost instantly.

She smiled.

"How do you know?"

He took a closer look. "Well, it looks . . . fresh. Too fresh to be a sunset. It feels more . . . more optimistic."

Gayle laughed.

"But you have to ask yourself how you got there? Saying that it feels fresh or optimistic, that's a reaction to something, not the cause of it. So what is it you're reacting to? What is it about the sky that made you feel that way?"

Cal nodded. "Good point." He stepped back a step, regarded the painting. He almost spoke out, twice, but fell silent each time.

"I'll give you a clue," Gayle said. That playful look in her eyes. "There's no paint color named *fresh*. No colors for sale out there with the word *optimistic* in their name."

Cal took a closer look. He nodded. "Hmm. I think I've got it. It's the blue. It's this color blue up here in the sky, right?"

Gayle beamed. "You get an A plus! It took me years to get that right." She pointed to a section of sky. "Morning blues have less red in them. That's the secret. They might even drift into green a bit, though you'd never notice it right off. I always intended it to be a sunrise, but in all the early versions of this painting, everyone thought it was a sunset. 'Awesome sunset, Gayle!' they'd say. Like kicking me in the nuts every time."

"Nuts?"

"Figuratively speaking. What am I going to say? Ovaries?"

Cal laughed. He looked the painting over.

"So what's not finished with it?"

Gayle shrugged. "Everything."

In the painting, she floated over the field of sunflowers, her feet hovering inches above the blossoms. The field stretched away in every direction to the horizon.

"The perspective is amazing," Cal said.

Gayle nodded thanks.

"In the original painting, I was standing dead center. Here." She pointed. "I was looking straight out at the viewer. I painted myself from a mirror, so that's what you get from a mirror. And this part, down here, where the tops of the sunflowers are now, that was all a rich brown earth back then. I was standing on the ground, in a cornfield actually, one that had just been harvested, so there were broken stalks and husk litter scattered everywhere. No sunrise yet. The light in that first version came from over here, left, out of frame."

She looked at the painting like she was still seeing the older version.

"You painted all the flowers in later?"

She nodded. "Painted them in over the cornstalks. It had the effect of lowering the horizon, and changing the perspective. It gave me a bit of a lift." She smiled. "See? Now I'm levitating."

"Awesome. Nice trick. What's the key for?" He pointed to an antique brass key she held in her left hand, her fingers closed around it, almost concealing it.

"Don't exactly know yet. I painted that in a few days ago. Makes you wonder, right?"

"Wonder what?"

She shrugged. "That's what I wonder."

He watched her watching her painting.

"So when will it be done?"

She shook her head. "It won't be. Well, technically it will, one day. But I won't be finishing it."

Cal gave her a confused look.

"I've worked on it now for, what, eleven years or so. Long enough that I couldn't bear to see it come to an end. There's a ton of memory painted into it, layer after layer, so it's kind of like my own personal history book now. I figure it will be best finished when I am. That will be its proper end."

That was the first time he saw the painting. He'd witnessed the endless changes made to it over the years, the painting morphing one way or another. New elements would appear, others elements would disappear or reappeared in different places, the mood and the details shifting like the seasons. A work in progress, as she called it. But a work that had always looked finished.

The last time he saw the painting, she had raised the height of the sunflowers directly beneath her. It had the effect of lowering her position, of making her appear heavier. The flowers were touching her feet now, they bore her weight. The petals looked compressed. He could see the faint trail of her passage through the field behind her, winding back to the horizon. He saw that the sunrise there was no longer a sunrise. It looked more like a wildfire. The field was on fire, it was being consumed, and there were clouds of smoke rolling in the distance, darkening the sky. There was a feeling that the fire was advancing.

The brass key was missing from her hand. She held that hand open now, to show its emptiness.

A raven hovered above her right shoulder. She was turning her head, she was about to look in his direction.

At the very bottom of the painting, where the sunflower stalks rose from a dark brown soil, three tiny children had appeared.

They had been painted out of scale, painted in as miniatures, nearly concealed in the shadows. They crouched among the towering stalks like mischievous elves at play in a dark wood. One of them had his hands wrapped around the brass key that Gayle had formerly held. He was dragging it backwards into the shadow, a final glint of light flashing golden from its surface.

17.

Cal sat atop the boulder, willing himself to disappear. He wondered what difference it would make if he did. What exactly in the world would change?

He gave his best effort to find out.

No such luck. He looked aside, saw he still cast a shadow.

He watched the sun slinking lower in the west. The weight of his hours awake six weeks strong now and counting, pressing in like the depths of some private ocean. His face to the coming sunset, the end of something, another sun pushed beneath the rim of sight to climb again with a half-spin of earth, the rush of minutes, of hours, of days and nights in endless rerun like tides drawn and ebbed against a face of stone, temple dog of a shadow world, the shed skin of a snake, the chain link of yesterday curtained across the cast of his character, flattening him with the hammer blows of another dawn, another dusk, the same sun to set, to rise, to set, to rise, insistent child intent of scrutiny, rolling up across the dome of the sky, noticing all but reporting nothing.

A dragonfly landed on Cal's knee, lost of its element at that altitude, blown there from its home in a marsh. Sunlight glistened off its wings, trembled down to tiny geometries.

Gayle's face in a scatter of recall, reflections beyond the order of coherence, a shattering mirror. How did she look? A wind-flickered candle flame playing shadow games on the wall with itself. Hypnotized. Alluded. The thinnest wisp of smoke danced once in circles, serpent-like rose up into the dark of night, then the dark of day. Orange-lit, Cal's face and the stone beneath him, one of a kind.

"You know that saying?" Gayle had asked. "Curiosity killed the cat . . . you know that one?"

Cal sat without moving, a palimpsest of himself imprinted to the view.

"Well, maybe it was so," she went on. "But I'm pretty sure that old cat had the better time of it. I'd rather be him and be curious, than be all the other cats in the world who lived a long life and looked at nothing with interest the whole time."

Cal stood up, the big rock wobbled beneath him. He stood up to stretch his legs, his legs gone stiff and wooden from climbing, from climbing stairs, the ruins of some church or edifice was it? Or entrance to hell?

How many steps exactly, to bring him here?

Every step you ever took, a voice said.

He turned and looked in every direction.

He sat again by default, his balance lost, his head spinning and sick with gravity. He lay back across the curve of the big rock. Behind his eyes, beneath his skin, he could feel his blood pulsing by like wet gravel in his veins, pushed along with each heartbeat, pulled back again, sawing forth in his ears.

. . . and the earth stops . . . and the earth stops . . .

More words grinding past him. Someone forever talking.

"Who's there?" he said.

No one. Knock-knock.

He looked toward the cabin.

He closed his eyes, dropped into the dark jumpiness of his personal night, the fireworks of a depleted brain scanning its entire self in random mode, making unconnections in the frantic lack, sniffing for clues like some harried hound desperate for the scent trail of its missing owner. He fell through a curtain of black silence woven of screaming details, of the kiln-fired threads of his personal history, fragmented, crackling, phosphened. His memories dumped to the floor like a lifetime box of snapshots scattered before an incognate, fat-fingered hand. The fever pitch, the mute swing of a pendulum, the glare of another day too long to be called by any such name.

He opened his eyes.

The hardened blue of sky above, the sun carving each line of creation deeper. Cal felt the curve of the rock at his back, his head angled lower and his blood rushed, the endless loop of questions, the how, the why, the when of it all, chattering in his brain like a roomful of caffeined carnival barkers heard half a lifetime away.

"Step right up, ladies and gentlemen . . . step right up . . . you'll not see this again."

18.

In the mountains once with Gayle.

Her dance across the plain, pirouettes in rows across a mountain meadow, Gayle in a blushing field of spring wildflowers, blooms of yellow and melon-red nearly chest high, floating on long stems to the crystal sun, hung like a painted canvas in the air.

She took to the field at first to wander, and then to dance. Cal watched from a stone seat at the field's edge. A dance for him at first, comic and over-dramatic, onstage like she did so well.

"The Further Adventures of Wondrous Klutz," she called it, the exaggerated feints and flights, the chase of butterflies and demons alike.

Gayle turned inward by degrees, the sweat and momentum of the dance deepening it to a source beyond humor. It was her dance alone then, her breath heaving in the noonday heat, the flowers waved by the breeze of her passage, the rise and fall of bees around her and a single hummingbird that worked the edges of the space with fluorescent darts and dives.

She removed her shirt to the heat of the dance and stalked out her rhythms now, half-naked in spinning circles, contracting within, expanding without, the forces that moved her exploding where there could be no explosion, her body holding its form still against the rage and lash of the tempest rising inside. The Maycolored buds wrought a bright counterpoint to that passing storm of skin on muscle on bone on soul, in motion. She spun and reached for gravity's release, again and again, the field behind her in trampled repose, her wake a widening circle of oneness exited.

Urgent messages from some primal vision, she played them out in pantomime across that hidden meadow, beneath that silence of sky, Gayle at once an angel and a demon, trying each to break free of the other. She spun to the ground and arose, again, her arms held aloft and striking out, embracing within, her long hair flashing behind her in a sweat-soaked arc.

She lifted her voice in chants that grew louder with every pounce, that fell more wounded with each collapse. The earth's heart would beat itself still if she were to cease.

Her voice rang out once more, a finality of sound, a single syllable unleashed birth-like or death-distilled, and beyond all restraint or recall.

"Why?"

That single word, or its question, exited her flesh frame with a rush, like a long-held or deep-buried prayer of hope or despair. The sound of a life and all its woundings, tied in a knot and exhaled. The sound a soul itself might issue in the last moment before all questions go answered.

Gayle dropped beneath the canopy of flowers like a stone.

The stillness she left there. The air filled again with the mild buzz of insects, and the meadow was a vacant womb.

The hummingbird circled the empty stage once more, then whizzed past Cal's face and into the woods at his back. He could hear the whir of its tiny wings, see the sun reflected in its tiny golden eye as it passed.

19.

Cal lay with his back to the big boulder, his face up to the bright roof of sky, a single tear in the corner of his eye and that same question tumbling into the distance of his memory, sucking the slow drain of spirit from him in small bites like ants swarming a feast. That gathered tear broke and rolled down his cheek and he caught it away. He sat up into his endless day.

The rim of distant mountains fell into focus from a jumble of color and shape. If he could just fly there, spirit himself out through his eyes like the act of sight itself, and be gone.

He had the thought of standing but nothing in him moved. How to connect a thought to muscle, to bone? What made it all work? His will a house of mirrors, his body a house of cards, crumbling.

The devil is in the details, my man. Children hide from monsters of their own making. Gayle's voice inside his head.

I know.

He slid from the boulder to the ground, or was pulled there.

By what force?

Gravity mother-hugger.

He felt ancient. He waited for his balance to return.

A hot breeze rose from the west, blew at once over the ridge as if the sun had exhaled a long-held breath. Tufts of grass across the saddle bent low in rustling response, applause and salute to their sun god's return.

Cal took a few halting steps toward the edge of the saddle. Then a few more.

He sat on a weathered rock near the brink, his feet hanging over the edge.

Beside him a large ant toiled in solitude, struggling backwards across the ground with a caterpillar locked in its jaws, dragging the living prize away in fits and starts. The sun sliced in at its lowest angle. The ant cast a bizarre shadow many times its true size across the top of the rock.

A vulture rose from the forest like a kite to the sky. It crossed the ridge where Cal sat, so close he could hear the wind buffeting through its wing feathers. The vulture cocked its leather head and let go a hiss at the intruder. It banked north and flew toward the rise of Anvil.

The ball of the sun sank further through the atmosphere. The forest fell to a pool of shadow, the higher treetops giving up their grip on the light like a roll call in reverse, one by one until the last of them went dark. Songbirds sang to the quiet as it settled thick in that rimmed world. The mountains to the east lit up red like spent embers against a gunmetal sky. Along the ridgeline to the south the light raked. To the west the last lick of sun nested down through the skeletal trees, then was gone.

Coolness descended the peak and a chill went up through him.

Cal stood and gathered the scatter of his belongings. He pulled on a fleece and a windbreaker over that but it did no more than hold the chill inside.

He stood in the cusp of another day, the red silent light fading around him.

20.

He gathered stones for a fire pit. He collected sticks and dead branches from the brush. The peak of Anvil stood sentry-like in a cherry-red afterglow.

He placed a twist of dry grass into the center of the pile and held a lighter to it. The flames danced up, a circle of light spread around him, orange-red like the western sky. Sparks popped and spiraled up against the night.

The firelight pooled on that remote mountaintop, his figure and the shadow it cast huddled against the falling dark, stars waiting invisibly above, silent for the turn of stage.

The unsunned sky caved into shadow.

Cal sat close by the fire, feeding it sticks. The peak of Anvil loomed in the north, a void of darkness now, surrounded by stars.

On a mountaintop once in the San Pedros, their sleeping bags zipped together and the two of them snuggled in close, Gayle told him she'd heard that there were more stars in the sky than there were grains of sand on all the beaches of the world. Cal said he'd heard it was only half that amount. She gave him a quick poke in the ribs and told him to open the other eye. Another night, out in the Mogollon, she said that there was one star in the heavens for every person that ever lived, past, present, and future.

"The real trick," she said, "is figuring out who's who."

Cal glanced to the heavens. He wondered now which star might be hers.

He heard a noise behind him.

He turned and stared toward the darkness that was the cabin. He strained his eyes for any detail, his ears for any further sound. Nothing but shadow and silence from there. The fire crackled but shed no light in that direction.

"I thought you were gone," Cal said tentatively. The words held still in the air as he held his breath.

Well, looks like I'm still here, came the reply. Same as you.

Cal turned away. He stared at the fire. "Yeah. I'm still here." He held his hands closer to the flames.

You might want to watch what you're thinking. That's how beliefs get started.

Cal laughed at the statement.

"I don't hold beliefs anymore."

He heard a shuffling sound. A single board creaked.

No beliefs?

"None. I left them back in the world," he said.

A shooting star streaked across the northern sky and vanished.

Back in the world?

"Yeah. Back in the world."

Back in the world.

The man lit a cigarette and smoked it down. Cal didn't look in that direction but he could smell the tobacco smoke on the wind, sense the cadence of each draw and its following exhale.

Well, so you've got no beliefs. I'd say you've got nothing more to worry about then.

Cal tended the fire with sticks. More stars broke from the eastern horizon and commenced their nightlong journey west.

"I thought you were Death," Cal spoke up. "Before, in that storm, when I first got up here." His words hung in the chill air with the cloud of his breath. "Yeah. I thought you were Death." He looked toward the cabin and waited for an answer.

You thought I was Death.

Cal nodded. "Yep." He swallowed. His mouth was dry. He laughed, a single dry sound escaping him. "Funny, huh?"

A stick popped in the fire, the sparks rose up and twisted away in crazy spirals.

Funny depends.

A crowding silence was gathering, pressing in from all sides like onlookers at the scene of an accident.

"Depends on what?" Cal said.

On where you're sitting.

Cal thought about where he was sitting, not so sure about the funny.

Whose death did you think I was?

A long pause. Another thin drift of tobacco smoke.

Or was it just the idea of death in general that came into mind? Something more conceptual, or philosophical even. Once removed. Was it that kind of death you were thinking of?

Cal huddled closer to the fire. "My death," he said. "I though you were my death, waiting here to take me."

Another stick popped in the fire, a nugget-sized ember arced out and Cal ducked to one side, the ember flew past and bounced away across the rocks and blinked out.

You still think that?

Cal stared into the flames. "No."

So am I then, by you're thinking?

The stars rolled out overhead in the hundreds. Cal fed the fire from his small collection of sticks, one stick at a time, until there were none left and the pool of light that surrounded him retreated into darkness.

21.

Starlight fell across the mountain's fastness. Clouds of mist gathered in the forest below, the tops of the highest trees rising there like scattered church spires through a fog. Beneath that shroud, a lone coyote howled his best for any reply. His voice sounded lost, defeated then by the stillness, swallowed by the night.

Cal gathered his sleeping bag around him against the chill. He watched the stars crowding above, more than he had ever seen. So many present, who could ever begin the count?

The star Vega, hanging low in the north, flashing through the currents of air, the currents of time. He would start the count with Vega. Vega, in the constellation Lyra.

The Judge of Heaven, Gayle called it. She knew most of the stars by name. She would wander the night sky like she was off at a party with a gang of old friends. She introduced Cal to all of them.

"Vega used to be the pole star," she said, pointing the star out. "Yep." She said it like she still remembered the day. "Something like 12,000 years ago, it was the pole star. And it will be again, one of these days. About 14,000 years from now, because the earth has this slow wobble to it."

"A slow wobble?"

"Yeah, a real slow wobble, like a drunk, standing by his car in a parking lot, with a cop watching."

"Been there."

"Right? So the ancients called Vega the Judge of Heaven, because his place in the sky never wavered. His position was true. He was the standard by which the other stars were measured."

Cal found the constellation Bootes.

"Booties," Gayle pronounced it. "But ignore the name, it looks just like a kite."

So it did.

"Bootes was originally an ox," she said. "I can't see that one at all. Then he turned into the driver of a chariot, and his job was to chase that big bear over there from the sky. The big bear is Ursa Major, up there in the northwest. Always making a mess of things. She just doesn't listen."

"I'm not seeing a bear," Cal said, looking for one.

"That's okay, Bones, you don't have to see one. But it doesn't mean she's not there."

He nodded. "Right. Who am I to deny a whole constellation?"

"Exactly, and think of the kind of asshole you'd have to be if you did. You know what Ursa Major means?"

"Not yet."

"Big Bear," Gayle grinned. "So Bootes chases the Big Bear. Isn't that cool?" She said it like it made perfect sense. "You might think it would be the other way around, that the Bear would be chasing the Bootes, so it seems a little backwards at first, but that's what's going on. And that bright star right there, at the tail of the Bootes kite, that's Arcturus. That was the first star to be named."

"By who?"

She shrugged. "The people who first named stars."

Cal laughed. "Now how could we possibly know which star was first to be named?"

Gayle saw his point. "Well, right, technically, I guess we can't know it for sure. But we say it like we know it. 'That bright star right there is Arcturus, the first star to be named.' See how it works?"

Cal gave her a sideways look. "So the next guy believes it because he heard it said somewhere?"

"Exactly. So eventually, we all believe it because we heard it said somewhere, and that's what makes us happy. We like to agree about shit. It's in our nature to be agreeable. Am I right?"

"I agree."

"Of course you do. And don't you feel happy now, because you said that?"

"I do."

He gave the idea some thought.

"So the things we call true might just be statements we all decided to agree upon at some point in time?"

She nodded. "Yeah. The bigger the truth, the longer ago we decide to agree on it. That probably explains why we say some of the dumb things we say too. Things like, 'don't go out without a jacket, you'll catch your death.' I actually believed that one once, when I was little. I figured there was something sewn into the lining of every jacket that was a death repellent, so I cut up one of my jackets with a pair of scissors, looking for the damn thing. And even weirder, I figured it would be purple, for some reason. I was definitely looking for something purple."

Cal nodded. "Yeah. Purple would be the right color of a death repellent. A metallic purple."

"Exactly. Like, a Nascar candy metal-flake purple."

"Exactly. Or how about this one: Don't run with a stick, you'll put your eye out."

"Mmm-hmm. All the kids I knew ran with sticks, no problem there. Me too, all the time. Still got two eyes."

"Right? So it probably happened once, to just one guy, and that was that, they tried to turn it into a truth."

"But it didn't happen. We'd all be missing eyes if it did."

"I agree. So how about this one: Love can move mountains."

"Faith can move the mountains," she corrected him.

"Faith?"

"Yep, faith. That's the statement. Faith can move the mountains."

"No it isn't. When I heard it, it was love can move the mountains."

"Nope. It's faith. Faith moves the mountains. I'm sure of it. That's the statement, everywhere. That's why we say it."

"Well I disagree."

"Well then it's not a true statement anymore. We all have to agree on a statement if it's going to stay true."

"Well, hell anyway, it's a good thing that none of it's true. The mountains would be scattered all over the place by now, what with everyone's faith and love pushing them all around."

"Yeah. It sounds like another one of those dumb guy concepts, anyway."

"What does?"

"Moving mountains to prove your faith, or your love. It's so over the top. So unnecessarily demonstrative. See, the way I see it, guys are always trying to hide something. Doesn't matter what, but they're going to try and hide it anyway. So whenever the spotlight gets a little too hot for comfort, they'll raise up a bunch of dust just to keep the attention elsewhere. You say something to them like, 'So, Charley, you love me?' That simple, and then off they go. 'Whoa, whoa! I'll move a goddamn mountain to prove it!' "

Cal smiled. "Yeah. That sounds about right. So, ah, if that's just a guy thing, what would a girl thing be, to demonstrate your faith, or your love?"

Gayle shrugged. "Give the guy a blow job."

Cal laughed out loud. "Wow. That explains a lot." He inched himself closer. "Makes me feel real . . . optimistic."

"Unbridled optimism leads to disappointment."

"Bummer."

"Hope rules eternal, though."

"Mmm. Hope. Well. So. Where were we? Arcturus, right?"

"Yep, Arcturus. The first star to be named."

Cal nodded. "They had to start somewhere."

She pointed out Deneb and Albireo, the head and tail of the great swan Cygnus, flying down the Milky Way.

"Deneb is the only reversible star."

"Reversible?"

"Yep. If you write the name out in lower case letters on a piece of paper, hold it up to a mirror, it says the same thing backwards. Looks a bit Russian, but there it is. Deneb."

Cal gave that nugget some thought. He laughed. "That's, uh, good to know."

"Yeah, right? It might come in handy some day. Some guy walks up to you, holds a gun to your head and says, 'Name the reversible star, goddammit! And you say Deneb. Done."

Draco the Dragon, spinning his madness in endless circles to the north, forever chasing his tail. Gayle said she didn't know for sure if it was true, but that if you were ever to hear him speak, she was almost certain Draco would have a lisp.

"We should just start saying it then," Cal suggested.

"We definitely should."

Altair the Mischievous, hanging low in the west, glowing sinister and yellow-bright, hastening the end of empires and the vanities of men.

The seven sisters of the Pleiades.

"Coveted once for their great beauty," Gayle said. "Until a jealous giant showed up and turned them all into tiny birds. So they've been huddling close together in fear ever since. Poor little dears. Bad giant."

Pegasus, the winged horse.

"A spring of wisdom would burst forth like water with his every step on earth. Then there's old Perseus the Destroyer, right behind him, seeking forever to rein him in so he could stem the flow of wisdom on Earth and deny us all the clarity. Who do you think won that contest, huh?"

There was old Cepheus, the beleaguered King.

"Father of Andromeda," she said. "He chained his daughter to a rock, sacrificing her to a sea monster to save his kingdom from ravage. Hmm, let's see . . . my beachfront real estate, or my daughter? Oops! There goes the daughter."

Lucky Delphinus.

"The dolphins forever have to do his bidding because he saved Poseidon's favorite consort when she fell from a ship. I think Delphinus was probably boinking her the whole time, then he saw Poseidon coming and made up the 'oh shit, she just fell from the ship' thing as a cover because she was so disheveled looking, and that's not how you're supposed to deliver a consort. Not to Poseidon anyway."

"No," Cal said. "Not to Poseidon."

All the stars and all their stories, locked into place down the ages, traveling the sky as one. The named and the countless unnamed and so remembered, old friends introduced by an old friend.

Cal watched the stars trek across the nighttime sky, until they expired one by one in the light of the new day.

22.

He sat cross-legged atop the big boulder, waiting for the sun.

Small birds flitted across the saddle, flying low to the brush. Half a mile to the north, the peak of Anvil cut the sky like a jagged tooth.

The disc of the sun broke free of the horizon and began its long climb through the sky. The warmth of it felt like a blessing. Overhead a pair of crows winged through the air, light flashing golden off their feathers.

He glanced toward the darker cabin, to its broken geometry, an artifact of some other world, long gone past. Refuge to refuse, a harbor of shadows. A repository of night voices. Boxed confusion.

The sunlight fell around him like a warm rain. He looked to his hands. He turned them over in the new light. He saw the sunlight catching and sparking from the gold of his wedding band. He spun the ring around in half turns on his finger. It was looser now than he remembered. The last link in a chain to some other time, now withered of connection.

He gripped the ring with his fingers, pried it up past his knuckle, twisted it free into his fist. The ring of white flesh it left behind, sunless now these seven years. A pale band of memory, the ghost of a hollow promise that echoed away into the universe or into the halls of time or into the soul itself, or not even there.

He grew tired with the weight of it.

He stood up on the curve of the big boulder, turned his back to the sunrise. His shadow stretched away before him, fell out over the edge of the cliff and down to the forest floor. The ring left his hand then, flying far out over the view, ringing like a small wind chime as it fell away. A red dragonfly met the ring's arc and followed it down in loopy circles, chasing it from sight.

Cal waited. Nothing more moved him one way or the other. No answers had voiced themselves and even his questions had died of repetition in the night. He was finished.

The peak of Anvil awaited. That was all of his plan.

He cast a long look in every direction. The sun at play again in the details, making all the world appear new, so shiny and bright. Then not so new, just beneath the surface. A balance in decay.

How long could it all hold?

He stepped from the boulder to the ground. He stood at the edge of the fire ring, the circle of rocks and the mound of ash within it like an offering left behind for some vacant god.

"The God of Never Shows Up," Cal said. "Never shows up."

He knelt and ran his fingers through the ash, the velvety softness, the act of touching nothing. He held a handful of it to the air and winnowed it away downwind.

He lifted the perimeter stones one by one and rolled them off into the brush where they'd been the day before. He sat down on the trail to watch the new day set its teeth.

The ash tumbled away like snow in the rising breeze. A black circle like a hole bored in the earth was left behind.

23.

The sun grew hot overhead, a desert sun again, migrated to a higher plane. The feeling of it, possessive. It burned away at his eyes, at his face and the back of his neck and his arms and his hands and he stood still as a statue and watched while his shadow shrunk up tight beneath him.

There would be no clouds in the sky this day. The morning breeze was stunned to stillness. The world was vandalized again in the light, the sun a greedy thug.

Cal eyed the cabin, the cooler darkness it harbored within.

"You in there?" he said, his voice like an abrupt bark on the barren mountaintop.

He waited.

"Hey. You in there?"

Silence.

The peak of Anvil wavered in the shimmer of heat. He measured the sun's distance from the horizon with the width of his hands. Four hands high. Four hours up.

"Ten o'clock, " he said.

Ten. O'clock.

He wondered aloud about that word *o'clock*.

"O'clock. O'clock? O'clock."

He shaded his eyes with his hands to stare at the peak. His feet felt cemented to the stone beneath him.

The point of another day sharpened itself against the rocks.

He edged his way closer to the cabin.

He stood a while at the door. Listening. He rapped his knuckles against the boards. A hollow sound, no response to it but more quiet. He knocked again, heard the sound vanish like it was being sucked into a vacuum. He craned his neck for a look inside. Darkness too thick to see through.

He stepped inside. The coolness of the shade wrapped around him and the place was empty. He was alone. He sat down against the wall opposite the door, tired enough already with the length of the day and the immanent rerun of its hours.

He shut his eyes to the demands of sight.

The blank wall would arise within him, the remnants of his dreamworld cut to ribbons and set adrift in the despoiled landscape of his soul-burnt retreat. He could spin his mind there in hapless circles, permitted that hollow luxury to wander the borderlands of fractured thought, to float shadowless over the world like a glass bird, rising higher, veering first to one side, then to the other, half-curious of the hidden places he would find. He could see himself sitting far below, high upon a rise of naked rock like some tattered book written nearly to its finish by nature and then put away on a shelf for good. Sitting back with his legs outstretched and his head tipped to one side and his hands folded in his lap as the last of his minutes unwound and another sun pulled itself across the sky. Sitting there for days, for years, for decades then, undressed eventually by the elements and de-fleshed by the wind and the rain, by the ice and the sun, by the vultures and crows and the swarming of ants all feasting without remorse or agenda, banquet of small ages unfurling. A pile of whitened bones soon left slumped against the wall of a mountain, while another time-distant sunset fingered its light backwards into eye sockets unfettered by the need for sight and free of perception, two circles of orange light cast to the back of his skull like a memory with no one to recall it. A shadow on the ground in the shape of a man who fell asleep and turned to dust. Then no shadow on the ground at all.

A thousand more suns pulled across the sky, by what attraction, to what possible end? The circled face of heaven above, alive with all her night fires cut into the eternal walls of time. Fires that look out from the beginning, to the beginning, back to where the first fire kindled, and how that first fire was, and so still must be, the fire that burns inside a beating heart, for only there can the world be recorded.

He opened his eyes to the dark of the cabin.

Just beyond the door a branch quivered. A small bird was hiding itself from the hammering sun. It piped a one-note song that shivered away into silence like a voice defeated with doubt. The mountain air grew as still as the act of listening.

The cabin was a womb of shade. From three small holes in the tin roof the sunlight angled down to the floor. Dust spiraled upward like tiny lifeforms caught inside bright tubes of glass.

Cal stared down at his hands. Sun burnt, blistered and wounded, familiar and unfamiliar. The ash of his fires beneath his nails.

Any shadows left outside evaporated with the sun's climb, a world forged beneath a hardening sky, the earth the sun's anvil.

24.

That same day in Santa Fe. The realtor had contacted a cleaning service to make the house presentable for the new tenants due Saturday. Three women pulled into the driveway in a white station wagon, the logo *Clean Machine* stenciled across the doors, across the tailgate. They filed in through the kitchen with their buckets and cleaners, their mops and brooms and dust rags and a vacuum.

Four houses to clean today. A good day.

The left-behinds they were happy for: the pots and pans in the kitchen, a drawer full of batteries and four rolls of duct tape, screwdrivers, pliers, an electric can opener, a pair of scissors, some wool blankets and a reading lamp in the living room.

"Hay más aquí!" one of them called from the door of the garage. She held up a pair of hiking boots, they were just her size. There were many boxes of tools, she said, and boxes of winter clothing. And more boxes filled with little treasures.

"Pequeños tesoros!" she said.

"Pequeños tesoros?" the second woman called quizzically from the kitchen window. "Qué tesoros están aquí?" She held up a wet sponge beside her face and watched it dripping. They laughed. The first woman hustled back to the car. She would return a few minutes later with her husband and his truck. This was a very lucky day.

The youngest of them, a girl still in her teens, stood alone in the living room, flipping through a handful of photographs she'd found on the windowsill. She dropped them one by one into a black plastic trash bag. She laughed at some of the photos. These people were very funny. She looked longer at others. These people were very much in love.

She stared out the window to the distance. She wondered when this magic, this miracle of love, would happen for her.

Billy drove by late for work, he wondered whose face that was at the window, he slowed down, but he had no time to stop.

25.

Cal sat with his back pressed to the cabin wall. "What next?" he asked himself. He clapped his hands together. He made a clock-ticking sound with his tongue against the roof of his mouth.

Silence.

The ascent to the peak was next. That was it. That was all of his purpose. He squinted through the door to the outer glare. No shade to be had out there, the sun way too hot for the climb.

He would make the climb later.

"I'll make the climb later," he said.

He took a long breath, he let it out.

How much later?

Another night to fall? Another morning to follow? Another day to burn away, waiting? Waiting for what?

He lowered his head, cradled it down between his knees. He stared at the ground between his boots. The coffee-colored ground between his boots.

Coffee in the mornings with Gayle, more like resurrection than any idea of breakfast, Gayle grinding the beans in an antique hand-cranked grind box carved with jungle plants and small animals peering out, the filigreed brass fittings at the corners and the small drawer in front that filled with the aromatic grounds.

"Who in their wrong mind would start a day without coffee?" she would say.

He just did. He smoothed the ground over with the sole of his boot. He picked up a stick and began tracing lines in the dirt.

They sat at the counter of a diner on the road south out of Moab, the sun about to rise on the lunarscape outside, a red neon light pulsing through the window at their back, their coffee cups before them just delivered, steaming hot and full. Gayle asked the waitress if she had any honey. The waitress looked out the window, then up at the clock, and said, "He's probably still in bed." She turned and disappeared into the kitchen.

Gayle smiled. She looked down into her coffee. She spun the cup around in slow quarter turns. She said that she'd heard that coffee was responsible for the world's current geometry.

"How so?" Cal asked.

"Well, the ancients thought a lot of things back in their day. One of the things they all thought was that the world was flat, and because they all thought so, so it actually was. That's just how it goes. So people sailed right off the edge of that world, all the time. Yessir. All those poor brave sailing people, right over the edge they went, one by one." She dropped two sugar cubes in her cup. "Plunk, plunk, day after day, year after year." She nodded gravely. She dropped another cube into her coffee. "I guess you could think of it as an early form of population control." She picked up her cup and blew across the top of it. "Sailor-ectomy," she said. "Edge of the world-itis. Devastating, right?" She gave Cal a little sideways look.

"Then a day came when they discovered coffee, and that flat old world of theirs just rolled up into a big happy ball right then and there, and it hasn't stopped spinning yet. So yay for us! And no more lost sailors!" She took a first sip.

Cal stared down at the coffee-colored ground between his boots. He had drawn a coffee cup, with a handle off to one side, and a saucer below it, and a few lines of steam rising into the air. He erased the drawing with a sweep of his boot. He tossed the stick aside.

He stared into the distance. He could see the curve of the earth from where he sat.

He lowered his head and rested it on his knees. He shut his eyes, his brain suspended in the usual gray clamorous nowhere, where a thousand voices spoke at once, where slices of time were plucked from the stream one by one and hardened and welded to the surface an iron chrysalis from which nothing would ever emerge.

Looks like you're still here, a voice came.

Cal sat up so fast and straight he banged his head back against the wall. He focused on the dark corner.

"Who's there?" he said, his eyes straining for any detail.

There was no one he could see.

You're like one of those fish skeletons stuck in the rocks up here, the voice said. Just flat out stuck and turned into stone.
Cal looked long and hard into the deep of the cabin.
You're the next fossil waiting to happen.
Outside a flood of sunlight was raping creation, a world roaring its details in lurid silent mayhem. Cal shook his head.
"I'm done with all this," he said quietly. "I'm done with waiting."
But you're still here.
"So what."
So you're obviously not done with waiting.
The silent clock-tick of time.
What is it you're waiting for?
Why are there no windows to this damn cabin, Cal was thinking. Who would build such a place? Why here? What was the reason for any of it? Where was the order? All the questions in the world lined up and chained together like felons, clanging their tin cups against the wall, stealing the interior quiet. The glare outside like a visual scream grown more impossible by the second.
"For fuck's sake," Cal said to all of it. He would have stood up and left then and there but he didn't move a muscle. Or a muscle wouldn't move him.
What would be the point of moving anyway?
Another question heard from.
"What's your problem anyway?" he said into the cabin.
That's another question.
He stared into the dark and waited for an answer.
I have no problem. You said you were done with waiting. But here you are waiting. So how done are you?
That's another question.
He waited for the answer.
Cal was done with waiting. "I'm done with waiting."
He stood and moved to the door, and his eyes were pinned nearly shut by the light outside. The world stood chromed, every detail coated, silver bright.
"Enough," he said. To whom? "I've had enough."
The cabin's shadows ejected him.

He stumbled out onto the trail. He paced in no intentional direction, a blind man walking. Minutes out there passed for hours, the sunlight razor sharp, slicing the air to ribbons. He grew dizzy in the steel pan glare of it, the world dreamlike, or nightmarish, and wavering like a reflection in a funhouse mirror, each breath he took in dire need of replacement by the one that followed it. The cabin rose from the ground and fell again like a thing trying to evaporate. The sound of his boots on the trail like a distant shuffling clockwork, a vague reminder of an echo of the once-learned idea of eternity.

He lasted a few minutes, his purpose lost, his pulse rampant in his ears. He ducked in beneath the cabin's roof and the few degrees difference at the doorway felt like a blessing. He laid himself face down against the cooler stone floor.

What's next? the voice came.

Another question piled on.

Cal had no answer, nor was he sure the question had really been asked.

Time spilled through the sky, streamed away across the rocks, filtered down into the smallest of fissures in the earth, and disappeared.

The sun bore down. It was well over a hundred and twenty-five degrees on the trail, the air as still as a held breath and just as silent. In the cabin the stone floor held its smaller measure of coolness.

Cal lay with his back to the earth, staring up at the roof. Three small round holes punched through the corrugated tin, jagged metal edges pointing outward, sunlight slanting in.

He held his hand to one side, caught one of the circles of sunlight in his palm. He closed his fist around it, opened it again.

You think those are bullet holes up there in the roof?

Cal looked closely at each of the small holes.

"That's what they look like."

The slow unwind of seconds, the circular eddies that hover at the fringe of any greater rushing stream.

So some guy sat here once, like us, and he shot his gun off straight up through the roof like that.

Cal nodded. "That's what it looks like."

What do you suppose he was shooting at?
Cal shook his head.
"I don't know. But he came way up here to do it. And it took him three shots to hit it."
Maybe he didn't hit it.
Cal looked closer at the bullet holes.
"He'd have to be a pretty lousy shot, at that range."
Maybe he changed his mind.
"Changed his mind about what?"
About hitting the thing he was thinking of shooting at.
Cal laughed a thin laugh. "Yeah? What then? He gives up and goes home?"
He doesn't give up. He goes home because he's finished. He's won the battle. He's done with it.
"Done with it, huh? Sounds peachy."
Then there's nothing more to wait for.
"Nothing more to wait for. So why go home?"
Light filtering down through the bullet holes.
Because that's where you go when you're finished.

Cal rolled onto his side and closed his eyes. He pressed his cheek to the cool stone. He wandered the gray quarters of his memory where more voices gathered like smoke and disappeared again into shadow.

26.

The sheet metal roof buckled and snapped at its anchoring stays in the blasting heat. Nothing moved outside, not a cloud in the sky nor a breath of wind to push it. A world evacuated. Cal lay as still in that sole sanctuary of shade, the three circles of sunlight inching across the floor as the sun tracked its greater measure across the sky.
You won't get much further.

Cal glanced in the direction of the voice. He waited for something more to be said.

You can't get there by waiting.

Cal let out a breath and turned away.

Another hour slipped past, more or less, the swelter outside like a coffin lid on the world.

He sat by the door, tapping his foot in the dirt. Dust rising in lazy pools to the sunlight like smoke signals to the trail.

You've gotten real good at waiting.

Cal held a thin stick in his hand. He bent it around slowly, trying to shape it into a circle.

"I've had lots of practice."

The stick snapped in two. He tossed the pieces aside and picked up another one, started bending it around in a circle. It snapped in two.

Waiting's not such a great skill to have when it comes to living.

Cal looked out the door, across the trail to the boulder at the edge of the cliff. To the plunge beyond that, then the next ridge rising further in the haze, and the next after that. The whole width of the world naked and baked beneath an iron white sun. He watched the details as they fell apart, as they broke open and scattered, the known world collapsing upon inspection, unraveling to shreds, to where no sense could be made.

What is it you're waiting to see? the man asked. You expect to see something different?

Cal looked down at his empty hands. He turned them over in the hot wash of sunlight. They shook like caged animals.

The man rose and stood beneath the edge of the roof beside Cal. He shaded his eyes from the knife-glint of light outside.

Cal glanced to his left. He saw the man's boots, weathered and worn away, dissembling like the rest of the world. Like himself. Like his interest in any of it. He looked away.

I think it's already happened.

"What's happened?" Cal asked.

This thing you're waiting for. It's already happened.

Cal stared into the west, the stretch of empty distance before him like a drug he would take in overdose if he could get his hands on it.

"No one here gets to keep anything."

His words sounding as hollow.

Well if that's true, what are you still holding onto?

There was a flutter in the light outside. A shadow swept the ground and a raven slid low over the trail and landed atop the large boulder. It reshuffled its feathers and then stood compact, unmoving, its head tipped toward the cabin. A two-dimensional bird cut from black paper, another empty detail.

Why are you still here?

Cal rested his arms on his knees, his head heavy in his hands.

You have some unfinished business to attend to? Something to prove, maybe?

Time was stuck thick and immobile, the cabin, the world and his every memory of it like a clear crystal of stone he sat within while the light played its endless tricks of movement around him. Nothing really moved, or could move. It was all an illusion.

Cal lowered his head further, he shut his eyes to all of it.

"I came here to die," he said, or those words came from his mouth in that order. Or he just heard them that way.

He heard the shuffling of boots beside him.

Not much I can say about that. We all come here to die. Each one of us, one way or another.

Walls of gray silence crumbling around him like thunder, crashing to the ground within him. Cal raised his head, he squinted to the outer glare. The world exactly as it was before. As it still is.

The thin shadow of the man beside him.

I came here to die once, the man said. But I died with all the love I could hold inside me. That made all the difference.

Cal turned to face the man.

There's no gatekeeper here, the man said. There never has been. You let yourself in.

The raven took flight from the boulder. A puff of air, the first breeze since morning, slid in across the cabin floor.

27.

Cal stood in the doorway, his back to the jamb. Blind theater of rock in attendance, the silence of sky yawning wide, the sun-struck world with its measure of time warped in endless circles, winding down. Forever winding down. The boulder balanced at the edge of the cliff like a sentinel to the view beyond it. You shall not pass.

He stood beneath the unblinking eye of the sun, staring up at the hard shell of sky above him. He walked to the edge of the cliff. The air felt heavy and liquid-like. He was crossing the floor of an ocean, the mountaintop not tall enough to breech the sky.

He climbed atop the big boulder. The rock wobbled in its place.

He stood there a long time.

Always that, he thought. Still standing. The last man standing, he thought to say, but the words never formed. His allotment of time there awake or adrift would not slip away. The world was more insistent than that. Stones go on being stones. There was the sun above, the engine of countless days. There was himself below it, a small plain thing balanced on a rock and the boundaries all dissolved, the mountains were so tired they could barely stand, and time fell through the sky like rain.

Before him the saddle plunged in a near vertical drop to the forest floor. Six hundred feet, seven hundred to the bottom? Would the air hold him up if he trusted it? Fledgling named Cal, his arms spread wide.

Nothing moved. Not a breath within him, not a breath to the world. Not a heartbeat to count against the silence.

What is it that nails everything down to where it is?

To what it is, or whom?

That wraps each thing separate and bound?

Why doesn't it all fold backwards into the lovely nothingness from which it first came? Why doesn't it all just fly apart?

Maybe it does, and we just don't see, because we fly apart with it. So all seems still.

Cal exhaled. He slid from the boulder to the ground. The thought of fried eggs in his mind. The sound they make in the pan when they're cooking. The way they slide to the plate when they're done.

He was searching for something under the brush. A rock the size of a melon and nearly as round. He found one, he lifted it and held it close, cradled it to his stomach like a stone infant. Pulled it in tighter still, felt the heat of the sun seeded inside it, seeping in through his skin. If he could only draw it into himself complete, swallow it whole to the emptiness within.

The distant mountains swayed, seductive, siren-like in the lucid heat. He watched the world in its incessant unfoldings.

He walked back to the boulder with the round stone tucked to his gut. He dropped it to the ground and kicked it tight beneath the curve of the bigger rock. He watched waves of blue earth rolling in the distance, rising without rising, curtaining perpetually aside for whatever next act. He whispered words to the sky that were ushered off into silence, that fled like thieves into thin air. Who could ever know their meaning, or gauge their weight?

Trembling now like a body tearing itself apart in uncivil war, he bent forward, he bucked the large boulder hard with his shoulder, it rolled forward a notch, he kicked the round stone tighter beneath. Tears rimmed his eyes too ancient to be his own and he turned them away.

He planted his feet, wedged them firmly into a fold in the ledge, he bucked the big rock again, it rolled forward another notch, he kicked the round stone tighter beneath.

Gayle in a sudden uprush of memory, scattering mirror-like to the surface like sunlight on a wind-ruffled lake, her voice, her face a million times alive. His two hands pushing, his shoulder slamming harder against it, the big rock rolled further, he kicked the small stone tighter beneath.

How she could seem so strong, so impossibly fragile at the same time, like a single steel thread to the roaring fabric of the world. Her face once, and that look from her eyes . . .

"It's not safe," she cried out. Meaning the world. Meaning life.

"It is safe," he would say, and hold her tight. "It's home." He would hold her so tight. "It's our home."

That feeling of home, that he was finally home, with Gayle at his side. How much time allotted for any breath here? For every heartbeat to sound? Who measures such things to their end and pronounces them finished?

He shoved his weight against the big rock, it inched away further, he kicked the small stone tighter beneath.

Gayle's face at the window, that look from her eyes so ever still. The world he had fallen into. Water splashing down clear and cold over rocks to disappear as suddenly in the desert sand.

A sound split the air above him, a voice or cry rising, one of a kind with the breath of the world. His voice or not his voice, the sound disconnected from him, louder now than possible in its rush outside and free of containment, he slammed his weight against the rock, it rolled forward, he kicked the small stone tighter beneath. Echoes of the cry racketed back from the mountain above, they howled along beside him, he slammed the rock, he kicked the small stone tighter beneath, he cried out again the whole ring of mountains around him now, howling out loud.

Tears streamed down his face as he stepped back, and he breathed, and the howling stopped and the mountains breathed with him, and the big rock rested in its place, but there was another cry rising, the mother of the first one, right behind it. This one split his head in its piercing exit, it felt like birth itself gone wrong and the sound would tear his throat and lungs apart from the inside out, his heart nearly jumped from his chest, on fire now and burning he leaned back and slammed the rock, with all the rest of what he had left, he slammed the rock, slammed the rock, the wall of time, the prism of remembrance, he slammed the rock, slammed the rock, slammed the damn rock. Rolled it off into thin air.

How it tumbled past the sky . . .

The boulder shattered at the base of the mountain, a small thing made of dust. There was no sound to mark its ending.

Cal stood at the edge of the cliff a long time. He could fall away now, slip over the curve of the earth and be gone. There was nothing left to him but tears, more than he could hold, so they fell. Blood seeped from his shoulder and streamed the length of his arm, dripped from his fingertip to mark the ground where the boulder had once stood.

He sat at the edge of the mountain and buried his face in his hands.

~

Gayle wrote once, of life:

> Pages of a book turning backwards in the wind,
> the unravel of any stories left unspoken.
> The incessant turn of earth or choice of any heart to beat.
> The weight of a sigh, or the web of thought that binds us.
> A roll of dice or call of soul,
> the play of light on the hand of a child
> tracing pictures in the air.
> All the passing of shadows, spilling themselves in the sand.
>
> The tap of the baton aside the podium,
> the orchestra still of breath and the next note hovers,
> about to sound aloud.
> Again.
> And again.

~

28.

Hours passed like another day's storm, or the same one raged in a different realm. A storm of emotions set free to level to the ground anything in its path.

Cal stood shaky on the trail, his left shoulder bruised and caked with blood. He stared at the peak of Anvil towering overhead, intrusion of earth into sky. He looked to where the big boulder had stood. The view there was unobstructed now. The world had changed a little then, had rearranged itself.

"Damn . . ." he barely said. His voice was damaged, cracked like unearthed pottery. "That . . . was a . . . big . . . rock."

He turned a slow circle where he stood. The mountains spread out all around him, the arc of sky above and the stretch of desert lying far below like a golden sea, a dreamy haze erasing the horizon between the two.

He was standing on the roof of the world.

The sun notched itself further west, grandfather clock of ages set to measure another day to its end.

Cal was overtaken by a yawn that seemed to generate from his very roots and he surrendered to its tidal flood. He felt each cell of his being partake. He'd forgotten that simple release, that simple pleasure. A yawn.

"Alright," he said. He could think of nothing else to say. That word fit the occasion like a surgical glove. "Alright," he said again.

Another yawn arose within him, a seeming hundred years in its delivery. It crested and broke over him like a wave, washed over him from the inside out. His balance nearly lost.

"Alright," he said again.

He had fallen through a wall of time. He felt transparent. Almost not there.

"Ephemeral."

He nodded.

"Alright."

He staggered to his backpack and unstrapped his sleeping bag and mat. He stepped inside the cabin and spread his gear out in the cool darkness. He laid himself belly down, his hands and a fleece tucked up beneath his head for a pillow. He pulled the sleeping bag close up around his shoulders. He watched that small slice of the world before him and waited.

On the east wall of the cabin, against the ancient weathered boards, the circles of sunlight rose like three small sunlets as the sun lowered itself in the west. He closed his eyes.

He was afloat on a green rolling sea, beneath a golden sun moments away from setting.

Almost gone.

Almost gone.
Almost gone.
Sleep.

The mountains rolled away from the sun, slid into the turn of night and the dream-shadowed world. The sky drained as black as velvet, the stars rose like so many diamonds uncut in their thousands, hordes of suns themselves migrating each to their own realm, flashing remnant sparks on the spokes of that ancient wheel, river of small lights winding past, measuring time in decimals of eternity, the silence of their passage sealed with a wink. Winding past. Forever winding past.

The eastern rim of the sky grew a violet slice, herald of new day. The first balance of sunlight feasted the world again with its brilliance. The wind rose to the day's warmth, tiding over oceans of desert, over mountaintops, pulling trick clouds from thin air and floating them downstream like so many bottles to be uncorked and savored. The play of day again in full dress, the endless rehearsal of the sunlit world, wound up like a clock and set forever to begin. Sun against sky, the ocean of air it swims eternal, all winding past. Forever winding past. The pageant of day and night, the pulse of the world, the shadow and light of it the same thing and no different, like a breath is not two things but one.

29.

He stands in the foyer of a large building surrounded by stone columns, a marble dome rising high above him. Windows round the base of the dome like portholes. The sunlight is pouring in, slanting down through the air to a polished marble floor.

He walks to a door at the far end, his footsteps echoing.

A man stands by the door, a pool of light upon him, his hand at rest on an iron ring at the door's center. He speaks quietly to Cal.

"You know what is required of you?"

"I do," says Cal.

The man recites his words formally.

"You may ask no questions. You may speak only when spoken to. You must speak the truth at all times. Be clear in what you say. Keep your eyes lowered in respect for those assembled. The invitation awaits you, as you accept it."

Cal nods his acceptance to the man.

The man steps aside, pulling at the iron ring, and the door swings wide.

Cal stands at the end of a long hallway. Paintings are hung at intervals down the length of the hall into the distance, each one bathed in a pool of light.

He walks down the hall.

The paintings are scenes from history, pictures of other times and places. Pictures of lives, pictures of moments of lives, important and ponderous. Some of them unknown to him, some of them familiar. They pass by, each one like a dream of itself unfolding. No sound but the rise and fall of his breath, and his footsteps falling upon the stone. Time is suspended.

He walks the length of that hall. A doorway stands at the far end, a pair of massive doors opened wide to either side. A bright wash of light floods toward him. He enters a great chamber, the marble floors polished to a mirror gloss, limestone walls towering high to every side, stone benches rising in tiers. A chorus of people is assembled there, hushed and attentive to his entrance. He lowers his eyes as instructed. He steps to the center of the room, and waits.

A voice rises from the silence. "You have come to make a statement."

"I have," Cal says.

In the surface of the marble floor, he sees the wavering reflection of all those seated above him.

What is it he has come to say? What is it that has brought him here, to this lofted place?

He begins his statement. "I loved Gayle."

Silence greets his words, then a slow stir of voices above him, a ripple of sound passing through the crowd. One voice speaks out for the rest.

"You may only make statements of truth here."

The chamber echoes with those words. The echo ebbs slowly back into silence.

Cal considers the words he had just spoken.

"That is the truth," he says. He says it with certainty.

The voice speaks again.

"Truth exists in the present moment alone. It is much like life in that respect. To speak of a particular life in a past tense implies that that life is no longer. So to with truth. To speak a truth in a past tense implies that that truth is no more."

The sound of the words echoes, their meaning hovers.

"In this place, you may speak only the truth."

Cal sees his own reflection in the polished floor below, a perfect double of himself, peering up from another world.

He re-begins his statement.

"I love Gayle."

The sound of his words fills the chamber, the echoes return to his ear from every direction.

He listens until the hall grows quiet again. He has never felt as still. He has nothing to add to that statement.

The gears of time re-engage. He looks up and sees there is no chamber surrounding him, no ceiling, no walls, no benches. No one sitting in judgment. He stands alone beneath the stars.

30.

Cal lay on his back on the cabin floor. A disc of sunlight flared in his eyes and he awoke. He rolled out from under the glare. His sleeping bag was wrapped around him in a tangle. His neck and his back were stiff with sleep. He saw the broken wall of the cabin to his right, the blue frame of sky beyond. From the three small holes in the cabin roof, three circles of sunlight were cast to the floor. He held his hand out to the side, caught one of the circles there. He felt its warmth. He closed his fist around it, he opened it again. His hand was rock steady.

Outside two birds sang like finalists for a choir tryout.

Cal rose to his feet, wobbling like a rusted machine remanded into service. He balanced himself by the cabin door, his hand against the wall. He squinted to the outside world, to an orange sun hanging low and fat above the fold of mountains to the west. He yawned a wide, luxurious yawn.

The sun was rising in the west. He yawned again.

He stepped away from the cabin, stopped, took a few steps more, then sat clumsily onto the trail. He rubbed his head in his hands to wake more sense into it. His left shoulder ached. He saw the stain of blood down his sleeve. He glanced to where the boulder had been. He stared again at the orange sun riding down the western sky. Clearly it was setting. Still, it felt like morning to him.

He shrugged. "No one here to argue it any different," he said. "Morning, then."

He looked down the trail to the south, across the open saddle. He saw the nameless stone peaks in the distance, the bowl of forest huddled below, tucked already into the shade. He remembered the stream he had crossed, it's bright water flowing. His face and hands to that water, his entire head beneath the surface now and he's falling down through the sparkling depths, the sunlight flashing in golden ribbons across the sandy bottom where he comes finally to rest, his face up, and he drinking it in, drinking it all in, the sky so far above, beyond reach, the water so cold and clear.

There were no rules left for him to follow. Nothing left in the world but thought itself.

He thought of walking the quiet forest path home. The silent churchyard of giant trees, passing by. All of them, passing by.

The thought of home. The idea of home.

The peak of Anvil rose to the north. The sunlight was working its magic there, the jagged bone of rock a deep orange-red now and veined with purple, edged with gold. The air above it screaming blue.

"I am home," he said.

He measured the sun's distance from the horizon with the width of his hand. One and a half hands, an hour and a half until the sun set. He looked again to the peak.

"Next."

He stood over his pack. He found the four water bottles, nearly empty now, a few swallows left at the bottom of each. He opened them and tipped them back, drank what each would deliver.

And he started walking.

The trail wound its way up through a low tangle of brush and crossed to the north end of the saddle.

He paused at the base of the peak. He placed a small stone in his mouth for thirst. "Water from a stone," he said.

The grass and other vegetation had reached their end. Above him the trail rose steeply, jacked nearly straight up across a bare monolith of weathered rock toward the summit. Below him, the cabin sat softly in its long turn to ruins. Sunlight flashed golden-pink from its metal roof.

He stood at the juncture of two worlds. A thin path lay at his feet.

How silent those worlds can be.

31.

He edged his way across a crumble of rocks fallen from above, a solid wall of stone at his back and the open sky before him. The trail narrowed to a thin catwalk no more than a foot wide, carved into the face of the stone by some ancient hand. It cut across the sheer wall and curved away from sight. Gravel scattered at his feet and rained away through the measure of sky beneath him.

He took a deep breath, then a careful step sideways, then another deep breath. He balanced his way across the ledge like that, one step, one breath, one step.

Halfway around the curve, the path narrowed further, down to inches now. He could see the whole column of rock rising up from below, soaring like a buttress from the forest floor. That was the view between his boots. Above him, it just soared.

Seconds more placed him around the curve. The path widened again, there was a broader shelf in sight, a platform of stone held high to the sky, secret from the world. A stick-figure of a man was at rest there, his back to the wall of the mountain, his legs outstretched before him, silent and still. Cal stood a long time and watched him. There was no movement he could see.

A few halting more steps brought Cal to the shelf. His heartbeat was released from suspension. The view to the west had opened up, the bowl of forest lay far below, the ring of mountains surrounding it folding away into the distant haze, the sun hanging over it all like a rosy translucent ball.

The stick-figure man was crumpled in a gangly heap, his head tipped slightly to one side. There was almost nothing left to him. His clothes were worn away to rags, to loose weaves of thread in some places. His skin was weather-darkened, leather-like. The white of his bones showed through at his knees, at his shoulders. His hands were curled together in his lap, his fingers claw-like and withered.

He had been there a very long time.

Cal sat to rest alongside him. No other place to sit.

A short breeze rose up from the forest floor. Cal could smell the life smells it carried, the scent of oak, of piñon and fir. The cool dampness of the shadows that dwelled there.

He looked out over the awesome stretch of view before him.

"This was one great place you found to die," he said to the stick-man. He looked down the tattered man's boots. The same brand of boots as his.

He nodded slowly.

"One great place you found to die."

He watched the shadows of the trees lengthening below as the sun sank lower. He stretched out his legs and settled back against the rock wall.

Way out west at the end of the world.

There were no remains at rest beside him. No other shadow on the ground but his.
"Gayle would have found a place like this," he said.
"Oh yeah."
His memory flooded. He dissolved into quietude on that high platform of rock.
He said Gayle's name aloud, a few times over, like an incantation.
They sat together for a while.

You said it once, that if it came to an end between us . . . that you would just want to hide.
Gayle shook her head.
You can't hide from what you carry inside. It's waiting for you when you get there.
Every detail before them alive.
And you said that if it came to that same end, that you would try your best. Just . . . your best.
I did.
So you did.
The sun hanging in the sky like a pendant of fire.
My life fell apart, Gayle. I was powerless to stop it. I tried dealing with the pieces, but they just fell to more pieces. All the way down to dust. I was left holding handfuls of dust.
He gave her a long look.
Time became a merciless wind that blew the dust away. I was left with emptiness. A gray emptiness.
Gayle looked away to the ground.
And now?
Cal gave her question some thought. He looked off to the west.
Now is better.
They were quiet a while.
She brushed her hair aside and spoke.
There was a sinkhole that opened inside of me. Everything I knew, or thought I knew, started falling into that bottomless pit.

And then there I was, falling in right behind it. I just had to know, right?

Cal nodded. You and the truth, huh?

Yep. My battle. Mine to lose, anyway.

Well, maybe not. What about now?

Now? She looked off into the distance.

Now I'm here.

So you are.

There was a long look between them.

I turned around, Cal. I was coming back. I was coming home.

He nodded.

I know that.

Time has no preferences; it runs in every direction. According to need sometimes. Sometimes, by invitation.

Remember that time, out past Sedona, we were camped up on Walnut Creek, and you woke up in the middle of the night just laughing your fool head off?

Oh Cal, yeah. That was nuts. There I was, sound asleep, just having this regular old dream, and then out of nowhere a TV announcer's voice says: *This just in* . . . *Dracula's sleeping bag is down for the count.*

Cal laughed.

Where's a thought like that even come from?

Boy, I sure don't know. Maybe the universe is just plain sillier than we could imagine. You didn't even get it at first.

Yeah I did.

Oh no you didn't. You said, what the hell's that mean? And I said, Cal . . . a *down* sleeping bag . . . *Count* Dracula? *Down* for the *Count*? Then you got it.

Well hell, woman . . . it was the damn middle of the night.

Well hell back, Calawishus, it was the damn middle of the night for me too, but I sure got it. Woke me right up.

Yeah, well. It still makes no sense.

Sure it does. That's exactly what his sleeping bag would be.

He wouldn't have a sleeping bag.

How do you know that?

Hundreds of small birds flew past on their way up from the forest, their separate songs weaving together into a river of sound that filled the air. A last few notes, then silence.
 Well. So here we are.
 Cal looked out at the grand view.
 Yep. Here we are.
 So it looks like we both found it, right? The mountain named for heaven. El Punto del Cielo.
 Her words on a breath of wind.
 Do you think that's what this place is, for real?
 He watched her eyes.
 She nodded. It is, if we both say it is.
 The magnificent sunset hovering before them.
 So it is then.
 So it is then. Settled.
 She sat back and hummed a little tune.
 Oh, here. You dropped this.
 She reached out and handed him his ring.
 Cal smiled. He folded his fingers tight around it, rested his head back against the wall of the mountain, and closed his eyes.

32.

 He's climbing the rocky steps to the summit. So many of them to the top. One step, one breath, one step. The wind rising at his back, hair whipping at his face.
 Then there are no more steps to climb. It's down in every direction. He turns a full circle to the view. Around, then around again, but there's always more to see.
 The seeming war of then against now, of was against is, quiets itself into stillness. The costumed wall between inside and outside stands as transparent, the shadow of any thought that would

parry that brightness vanquished like it never was, or could ever again, be held.

He takes off his boots, then his socks, and he sets them aside. He removes the shirt he wears and folds it down, and lays it across the top of his boots. He does the same with all the rest, until he stands naked on the last rock of that long climb. He holds his arms out to the sky. The earth crumbles away beneath his feet.

Two ravens fly west, winging silently through the air. Erased eventually into the red glow of the sun. Their shadows trace the world below them like a memory, a pair of phantom birds at play in the borderlands between earth and sky.

❖

⟡

He's driving down a high desert road, the windows open, the day clear, the air a perfect seventy-one degrees, and Gayle is sitting beside him in the pickup. They're both laughing hard at something she's just said, so hard that Gayle has tears from her eyes and Cal has trouble catching his breath. The view before them opens further, it stretches out long and wide and big enough to swallow them whole, and then again with every next second.

And they barely notice.

"God, woman," Cal says, when he finally can speak. He looks to her eyes.

Gayle nods back. "Oh, *God woman*. I like the sound of that. It has a nice ring to it." She's laughing. "What can I do for you, fella?"

Cal shakes his head. "I don't even know, girl. It's just, sometimes, it seems like my soul itself has gotten all mixed in with yours. Just, all mixed in."

Gayle smiles at that. "Well I should sure hope so, Bones. By now, I should sure hope so." She laughs at the look she sees on his face. "You're not thinking it's a bad thing, are you?"

Cal shakes his head. "Nope. No way. Nothing bad about it at all. It's just that, sometimes I have a hard time figuring out exactly where it is that I end, and you begin. Or maybe it's vice versa."

Gayle laughs out loud. "Well I'm afraid it's going to be all *versa* for you on that one, buddy, because I don't end anywhere." She leans over and flexes her bicep in his face. "I'm all beginnings here. One hundred and ten percent." She sits back and wipes the laugh tears from the corner of her eye with the sleeve of her flannel shirt.

Cal thinks about what she just said.

"Wouldn't that be the *vice* then, not the *versa*?" he asks.

"Nope. The *vice* would be the exact opposite of everything I just said." She gives him an amused look. "Why would you want to do that to yourself anyway?"

"Do what?"

"Try to figure out exactly where it is that you end and I begin? I mean, if that's even possible in the first place, which I don't think it is, but let's say, for the sake of argument, that it is, and so you do it, because, well, because that's just what you would do. So, tick-tock for however long it takes, and then there you are . . . you're standing around somewhere, all by your lonesome, and you've finally got this thing figured out . . . you know exactly where it is that you end, and I begin."

She tilts her head a bit. "Now what?"

That playful look from her eyes.

"What would you do next?"

✧ ✧